"The traditional British cozy is alive and well. Delicious. I was hooked from the first paragraph."

—Rhys Bowen, award-winning author of *Her Royal Spyness*

"*Death of a Cozy Writer*, G. M. Malliet's hilarious first mystery, is a must-read for fans of Robert Barnard and P. G. Wodehouse. I'm looking forward eagerly to Inspector St. Just's next case!"

—Donna Andrews, award-winning author of *The Penguin Who Knew Too Much*

"A house party in a Cambridgeshire mansion with the usual suspects, er, guests—a sly patriarch, grasping relatives, a butler, and a victim named Ruthven (what else?)—I haven't had so much fun since Anderson's 'Affair of the Bloodstained Egg Cosy.' Pass the tea and scones, break out the sherry, settle down in the library by the fire and enjoy Malliet's delightful tribute to the time-honored tradition of the English country house mystery."

—Marcia Talley, Agatha and Anthony award-winning author of *Dead Man Dancing* and six previous mysteries

"*Death of a Cozy Writer* is a romp, a classic tale of family dysfunction in a moody and often humourous English country house setting. A worthy addition to the classic mystery tradition and the perfect companion to a cup of tea and a roaring fire, or a sunny deck chair. Relax and let G. M. Malliet introduce you to the redoubtable Detective Chief Inspector St. Just of the Cambridgeshire Constabulary. I'm sure we'll be hearing much more from him!"

—Louise Penny, author of the award-winning Armand Gamache series of murder mysteries

DEATH

of a

Cozy Writer

FORTHCOMING BY G. M. MALLIET

Death and the Lit Chick

A St. Just Mystery

DEATH

of a

Cozy Writer

G. M. Malliet

MIDNIGHT INK
WOODBURY, MINNESOTA

First Edition
First Printing, 2008

Book design and format by Donna Burch
Cover design by Gavin Dayton Duffy
Cover art © Polk Dot Images / Punch Stock
Gargoyle Cover Element © Jorge Mascarenhas
Editing by Connie Hill

Midnight Ink, an imprint of Llewellyn Publications

Library of Congress Cataloging-in-Publication Data

Malliet, G. M.
  Death of a cozy writer : a St. Just mystery. G.M. Malliet. — 1st ed.
    p. cm.
  ISBN 978-0-7387-1248-2
  1. Police—England—Cambridgeshire—Fiction. 2. Cambridgeshire
(England)—Fiction. 3. Murder—Investigation—Fiction. I. Title.
  PS3613.A4535D43   2008
  813'.6--dc22
                                                              2008013803

Midnight Ink
Llewellyn Publications
2143 Wooddale Drive, Dept. 978-0-7387-1248-2
Woodbury, MN 55125-2989 USA
www.midnightinkbooks.com

Printed in the United States of America

For my husband.

CONTENTS

ACKNOWLEDGMENTS

Many people helped this book into existence, but it might not have made it at all but for the early encouragement of playwright Terryl Paiste.

My sincerest thanks also to the tireless volunteers of the Malice Domestic conference, who further midwifed this novel via their generous award of the Malice Domestic Grant (now renamed in memory of the beloved William F. Deeck).

The members of Sisters in Crime, particularly those of the Chesapeake Chapter, were there when I needed them, which was often.

I would also like to offer heartfelt thanks to the staff of Midnight Ink, beginning with Barbara Moore.

Many thanks also to Muir Ainsley, who patiently and correctly answered all my questions about British arcana without once asking me to please leave him alone. Any mistakes in the novel are entirely mine.

And as always, thanks to my husband, for his patience, love, and support through what must have seemed to him an endless and everlasting process.

AUTHOR'S NOTE

While the city and University of Cambridge, England, are of course real, as are Scotland and Cornwall, I have entirely invented the characters in this book who act out their imagined lives against these beautiful backdrops.

Peterhouse likewise exists, but DCI Arthur St. Just is not a real-life alumnus of that hallowed seat of learning.

In some cases, I have invented a village or manor house, such as Newton Coombe and Waverley Court, and placed them somewhat randomly in Cambridgeshire.

And there is now a castle in Scotland that exists only in my imagination.

CAST OF CHARACTERS

Ruthven Beauclerk-Fisk—eldest son of Sir Adrian, ruthless Ruthven was heir-apparent to his father's vast fortune, until his father unexpectedly announced plans to remarry.

Lillian Beauclerk-Fisk—Ruthven's social-climbing wife, she mostly found murder frightfully inconvenient.

Sarah Beauclerk-Fisk—fuddled and unhappy, she inherited her father's gift for penning best-selling books. Did she inherit his mean streak, as well?

Albert Beauclerk-Fisk—Sir Adrian's youngest son. A failed actor and designated black sheep of the family, Albert's one remaining ambition was to protect sister Sarah from suspicion of murder.

Chloe, Lady Beauclerk-Fisk—Sir Adrian's former wife, and the mother of his unhappy brood. Did life with Sir Adrian drive her to drink—or to murder?

Sir Adrian Beauclerk-Fisk—a famous writer of mystery novels in the "cozy" genre, Sir Adrian had a devilish talent for making noirish mischief.

Jeffrey Spencer—Sir Adrian's secretary, an earnest American expat in search of his roots. His attentions to Sarah Beauclerk-Fisk enraged his employer.

Maria Romano—Sir Adrian's long-time cook, she was the only person at Waverley Court who seemed to have a soft spot for the cantankerous author.

William Watters—The elderly gardener of Waverley Court saw no evil—until someone tried to frame him for murder.

Jim Tanner—Proud proprietor of the local Thorn and Crown.

George Beauclerk-Fisk—Ne'er-do-well son, failed entrepreneur, and playboy, his sibling's death increased George's chances in the inheritance sweepstakes.

Natasha Wellings—George's latest girlfriend: slim, dark, and beautiful. People wondered: Whatever did she see in George?

Paulo Romano—Butler to Sir Adrian, Mrs. Romano's son spent little time butlering and vast amounts skulking about Waverley Court.

Violet Mildenhall—Notorious in her heyday, her marriage of convenience to Sir Adrian proved less than convenient when it thrust her into the middle of a murder investigation—again.

Martha—Mrs. Romano's daily help.

Constable Porter, Sergeant Garwin Fear, and **Dr. Malenfant**—Loyal aides-de-camp to Detective Chief Inspector St. Just of the Cambridgeshire Constabulary.

DCI Arthur St. Just—Crime halted his plans for a ski holiday when Sir Adrian's devious machinations snowballed into murder.

Mrs. Ketchen—Elderly maid to Chloe, Lady Beauclerk-Fisk.

Manda Croom—Ruthven's efficient business associate and once-besotted paramour, she viewed murder at Waverley Court as a career opportunity.

Quentin Coffield, Esq.—a supercilious solicitor who played along with Sir Adrian's dangerous propensity to change his will, at will.

Mrs. Butter—Sir Adrian's former secretary. Albert enlisted her help in learning what the secretive Adrian had been plotting.

Mrs. Mott—a nurse in Cornwall.

Agnes Grant—a cook who bore witness to a crime long, long ago in Scotland.

No one reigns innocently

—SAINT-JUST

INVITATION
TO A WEDDING

THE INVITATION, THOUGH EMBOSSED on the stiffest 100 percent rag-content paper Gribbley's, Stationers to Her Majesty, could produce, nonetheless had more than a whiff of the prepackaged Marks & Sparks sales offering about it. Ruthven could not remember ever having seen a missive so entirely festooned with angels, or, given his background, decorated with anything more festive than black engraving on woven cream.

Yet here, naked seraphim and cherubim peeked coyly from the pink lining of the envelope, and from every corner of the thick pink card itself, grinning lasciviously as they held aloft a lavender banner announcing what appeared to be an upcoming event, perhaps the end of the world. Their sly expressions duplicated that which normally appeared on Ruthven's own somewhat round features, which tended to hold a smirk, even in repose. He first scanned the card, then studied it more closely, then groaned aloud.

"The old fool's gone and done it. He's really gone and done it." He threw the invitation across the breakfast table in the general direction of his wife. It missed (for it was a very large table), ricocheted off the silver toast rack, and skidded off onto the highly polished wooden floor.

"Done what, dear?" Lillian, her gaze held by a large display advertisement for precious gemstones, and herself inured, by long years of marriage, to her husband's tantrums, ignored the card, which now lay face downward on the floor.

"He's actually marrying one of his little tarts, that's what."

Lowering the paper, she peered at him over the headlines relating the latest brawl in Parliament. Lillian, skimming the front page on her way to the advertisements, had noted it seemed to have something to do with child care. If they couldn't take care of the little brats, why did they keep having them, she wondered? The accompanying photo showed the Prime Minister emerging with a preoccupied scowl from 10 Downing Street, in conscious imitation of Churchill during the darkest days of the war.

She also had taken a glance in passing at the obituaries. She found it interesting that the unimportant people always seemed to die in alphabetical order. She was about to comment on this observable fact when the full import of Ruthven's words took hold.

"Marrying?" Her voice caught on the last syllable. "Which one? Not the one with the enormous—"

"Probably." Even with his wife, or especially with his wife, Ruthven could not bring himself to use the vulgarities that were the bedrock of his vocabulary in all-male company.

"—dachshund?" she finished faintly. "Has he lost his mind, do you think?" Her tone, although devoid of pity, suggested she thought it was a real possibility. On the last phrase, her voice rose on an ending squeak of hysteria.

"Far from it. Cunning and diabolical as ever, I'd say."

She roughly folded the paper into a heap on the table, the sale on emeralds forgotten. Lowering her voice conspiratorially, remembering Alice in the kitchen, she stage-whispered.

"What is he going to do, do you think? To you, I mean?"

Ruthven was not so blind to his wife's many faults as not to know what she really meant was, To Me.

"I haven't a clue," said Ruthven. "It could be his way of trying to cut me out of my inheritance entirely. But surely even he—"

"Try not to upset yourself, dear. Remember your heart . . ."

"Yes, yes."

Another thought struck her as she bent to retrieve the gaudy missive from the floor. She straightened.

"Your poor mother." This time the pity might have been sincere, a woman on the cusp of middle age viewing the fate of one many years past its vicissitudes. She looked at her balding, stout husband, so like his father (who looked more like a greengrocer than a famous author), and so unlike his mother, who was going to seed in a rather determined, yet fatalistic, way.

A fear seized Lillian, not for the first time in the twenty-odd years of her marriage. Although she had long ago rejected her religious upbringing as being inconveniently at odds with her avaricious nature, a prayer went through her mind: *Please* don't let it all have been for nothing.

"Yes, I had better ring her. Preferably before it gets too late in the day. You know how she—"

"Yes, I know. Good God, this is a disaster. Quite apart from it making the family the laughingstock of the world. A disaster. Ruthven, we must do something."

Meaning: Ruthven, you must do something. He sighed, stalling while he stacked the rest of the now-forgotten mail and put it to one side. One would have said his face held the expression of a man preparing to make a clean conscience of it, except that Ruthven had no conscience.

"My dear." He cleared his throat. "My dear, I think it's time we had a little chat."

———

There remain rental flats in the greater London area that, were estate agents given to truth in advertising, would be fairly listed as dark, grotty, unwholesome bedsits with living space too small in which to swing a cat. Maida Vale, although having enjoyed huge victories in the ever-escalating real estate price war that had driven the average population farther and farther afield in search of shelter, still at the time of this story retained unsavory pockets that the most visionary of entrepreneurs had rejected as not holding the remotest potential for renovation. These sagging Victorians, too run down after decades of neglect to be resurrected to desirable states of tweeness, had been divided up by landlords in the middle part of the twentieth century into mean little flats designed to extract the maximum rent from the minimum square footage.

It was in such a flat that Sarah Beauclerk-Fisk received her issue of the invitation to her father's wedding. Despite the hyphenated name, and despite the fact that the rent was far less than she could have afforded, Sarah had settled into her gloomy surroundings the way an animal will burrow into the smallest available space when it wants to hide from the world in general, and people in particular.

Everything in the place reflected darkly back on Sarah's personality: The carelessly chosen second-hand furniture included two overstuffed chairs covered in faded roses that clashed with faded wallpaper that might once have been green but was now an indecipherable muddish gray. While bookshelves lining the walls might have offset the gloom with brightly covered novels, instead the dozens of worn books on the shelves blended into the mud like rocks, their covers, mostly black or gray, announcing obscure religious tracts of long-dead martyrs and other assorted lunatics.

It was in one of the overstuffed chairs that an overstuffed Sarah, herself upholstered in brown, had subsided to contemplate the pink leers of the cherubs on the unwelcome invitation she clutched now in her pudgy hands. To her eye, there was something faintly sacrilegious about the ostensibly religious figures, apart from their evident delight in their flagrant nakedness. She wondered if her father or—that woman—had picked out the cards. Her father, Sarah recognized, could be a vulgarian at times but this particular choice was—she searched for the word—common. Common. Just, she imagined, like (she scanned the card again; what was the woman's name?)—Violet Mildenhall. So difficult keeping the names of her father's girlfriends straight. Violet. An old-fashioned, pretty name—

The telephone rang. That had to be Albert, if he'd received a card as well. And why wouldn't he? It wasn't like her father to play favorites; no, he treated all his children abominably. With an effort she hoisted herself to her feet; the telephone was in the kitchen, where Sarah spent most of her time.

"Sarah?"

"You've got one as well, then."

"Yes. Oh, God, yes. It's appalling, just appalling. He kept threatening to do it but I didn't believe him. You know how he just likes to create a fuss. I thought he was just playing with us, hoping for a fight. Bloody old tyrant."

"Well, letting him know we're unhappy about it will only feed his happiness," she said mechanically. At least he sounds sober, she thought, absentmindedly stirring the simmering pot on the cooker. Her love of food had after many years paid unexpected bonuses in the form of a book of baking recipes just out from her father's publishers, Gregson's. The book was called *What Jesus Ate*, ideas for which she had gleaned from a close reading of the scriptures; most of the instructions seemed to involve fish and olives and assorted desert plant life. Gregson's had told her they expected it to make pots of money in the New Age market, and indeed it had become one of the surprise best sellers of that season's list. She was currently working on *Cooking with the Magdalene*.

Albert sighed audibly, wondering, not for the first time, if his sister, although intelligent in her earnest, pedantic sort of way, was entirely *there*. He guessed she was just quoting from one of the idiot, platitudinous authors she read, although her apparent philosophical acceptance of the situation was grating. He didn't want any oil poured on troubled waters; he wanted it poured on the flames.

Albert knew no one in the world as—he searched for the word—nebulous as Sarah. After joining a convent while still in her late teens, she had left after one year ("The food was inedible," was her only explanation). She had next studied at one of the red brick universities to become a social worker, a trying period for the local poor on whom she had practiced. It was during this time she had gotten in touch with her true feelings and become self-actualized. Her enthusiasm for pop social and psychological theories now had morphed in some way with her brief flirtation with Catholicism into what Albert gathered was a garbled neo-pagan worship of Mother Earth, Father Sky. Where had she come by this stuff? Years of living with their father had made the rest of them tougher, cannier, albeit in different ways. It had also permanently obliterated whatever traces of the Judeo-Christian tradition he and his brothers had managed to have beaten into them in the medieval public schools to which they had been confined.

"It makes him happy, all right, knowing he's screwing his children out of any hope of a decent inheritance and embarrassing them to boot by marrying this silly trollop. Happy? I'm certain he is. I can just see him gloating now."

"What makes you say she's a trollop? Have you met her?"

"No, in actual fact. Just stands to reason. She appears out of nowhere and the next thing we know there's this pink horror in the mail. Clearly she wasted no time getting her talons into him."

"He's a grown man, Albert. I don't suppose we can have any say in it. Although one is tempted to try."

"There must be laws—"

"Waste of time, while he's alive," she said too quickly. So, her mind had already traveled down the same path as his. "Even if we had the legal right to challenge this, which I'm sure we don't. He'll have seen to that—or rather, his solicitors will. And he's not insane, at least by any standards that can be proven." She sighed heavily, adjusting the temperature under the yellowish mass thickening on the cooker. She was mixing ground sesame seeds, honey, and almonds. This, once stirred to the right consistency, was to be poured out into bars to make halvah. She was on her third try, and still the result was something you could use to build a house. But she was certain the Magdalene would have served this to all her friends, including Jesus. That and Chicken Provençal.

Sarah had reached this particular tortured conclusion after reading the legend that Mary Magdalene had done missionary work in the south of France following Jesus' death. This opening up all kinds of French/Middle Eastern gastronomic avenues for her book, Sarah had seized on the myth with all the fervor of the convert. Looking at the hardening glob in the pan, she wished the Magdalene could have indulged herself once in awhile with chocolate fudge, but, sadly, there was little evidence for this, in or out of the Bible.

"What difference does it make, anyway? I never had any great expectations of him," she said now, not entirely truthfully. Albert knew that, as with most of them, expectations there had been on countless occasions, but those expectations had been quickly, mercilessly dashed. Adrian liked to change his will as often as some women will change their hairstyles; it was part of the game he liked to play to keep them all on tenterhooks. "Although Ruthven and Lillian ..."

"Yes, the most recent beneficiaries. I wonder how himself and Lady Macbeth are taking this."

Sarah snorted.

"What do you think she sees in him?" Sarah asked.

"Lillian? I should think that would be obvious. His Visa card, his Barclay's account…"

"No, I mean—what is her name, I suppose now I've got to make an effort to remember if she's going to be my stepmother." There was a pause while the ludicrousness of the situation penetrated even Sarah's otherworldly brain.

"Violet. Same answer. Visa, et cetera. You can be taken by them anywhere." He paused as another thought struck him. "I suppose there's just a chance…"

Albert trailed off, calculating that since the marriage couldn't possibly last, there might be wisdom in simply holding one's tongue until Violet did simply take what she could carry and run with it. God knew there was enough money to go around. The old man's last book, *Miss Rampling Decides*, was still high on the best seller lists a year from its launch, and the old horror—his father—had been cranking them out like that every year for decades. The British public seemingly couldn't get enough of the wizened, serene old biddy who, by rights, should be well over 110 years old by now, living alone in the small village of Saint Edmund-Under-Stowe, its tiny population reduced to one by its mysteriously high crime rate.

Perhaps Adrian would finally write a book in which Miss Rampling was herself shown to be the killer of everyone in her village over the years, thought Albert. Wouldn't put it past the old bugger to play one last nasty trick on his reading public.

Although Albert had years ago given up reading his father's books, on principle, he had to admit his famous last name had helped him no end in his checkered theatrical career. Not without a painful self-knowledge, Albert recognized his career might have been even more checkered without the name to get and keep him in front of the footlights. The trouble was, he was fast reaching an age where even the rather wispy roles of pale yet interesting young supporting men suitable for Coward and Rattigan revivals were getting beyond his reach—or rather, he amended reluctantly, his age, despite nightly jaw-firming facial exercises. His brief flirtation with being a leading man had been just that—brief—for Albert, in spite of his looks, had always lacked the presence to command that sort of role. Becoming that dreaded thing—a character actor— was, he reminded himself firmly, at least five years in the future. But what to do in the meanwhile?

His sister's voice drew him back to the present.

"—although I don't think I want to go, I suppose there's really no choice."

"To the, er, nuptials, you mean?"

"What else? Not going isn't an option, of course; it would hurt his feelings—"

As if the old reprobate had feelings!

"—and it might look as if I cared"—that, at least, sounded nearer the truth—"but I'm on deadline for my next book, for one thing. And it might be awkward all 'round, don't you think? If George is there it will be unbearable." George was their elder brother, second in line behind Ruthven. Another thought gave an edge of panic to her voice. "And who—who is going to tell Mother?" There was a tentative pleading as she said that last that suggested she was hoping Albert might volunteer.

Not a chance, thought Albert. Let her favorite break it to her.

"I should imagine Ruthven is on the telephone to her right now, never you worry," said Albert.

Ruthven was in fact on the telephone to his mother, but it was she who had called him. The instrument rang just as he was getting ready to pick up and dial. Any distraction at all was welcome from the grilling he'd been receiving from his wife for the past half hour.

"Ruthven, is that you? It's your mother, dear. I've just had the most amazing, er, communication."

"He didn't."

"He did. Some cherub thing. The envelope looks like it was addressed by a twelve-year-old."

"That would be Violet. Not far off on the guess at age, I'd say. Oh, sorry, Mother, I didn't—"

"Never fear. The poor girl has my sympathy, not my envy. At my age, one is relieved to be past the attentions of men. But what can he—she—both of them—be thinking, to invite me? Surely he doesn't imagine I'll come, bearing gifts. Is he that far gone, do you think?"

"When I last saw him, which, admittedly, was several months ago, he seemed to be much as ever. Argumentative, repellent. Perhaps more reptilian than usual. Looking to pick a fight, as always. Fortunately, I didn't have time to give him one. This takeover bid with Grobbetter has been like perching in several rings of Hell simultaneously." Ruthven had made and lost several fortunes buying up small Midland newspapers, sacking most of their workers save the sales staff whilst sucking the places dry of every conceivable asset ("increasing productivity," was how his press releases put it), and selling the newly productive yet emaciated product to a competitor.

His take-no-hostages philosophy had made him a legend in the publishing world, certainly in his own mind. Thinking he would one day in all likelihood inherit his father's fortune made it easier for him to be fearless than other men.

"Funny. That might have been the last time I saw him, too. At any rate, it was several months ago."

"Really?" Ruthven was genuinely stunned. His parents had parted on chilly rather than acrimonious terms—his mother was too vague for the kind of knock-down, drag-out the circumstances almost certainly warranted—that seemed even more to guarantee a complete and final breaking of all ties between them. Even though her brood at the time had barely moved on from formula to solid food, she had never really looked back.

"Yes. He came down to London, on some pretext or other, I rather thought. Said he'd been for his annual in Harley Street. And something about his publishers ... Anyway, he showed up completely out of the blue, didn't telephone or write ahead. I thought I might faint, dear, when Mrs. Ketchen announced him. It was so unprecedented, I realized something must be up. Curiosity got the better of me. It has been a long time, you know. So many years I've lost count."

"I haven't. It was my sixth birthday."

"Yes, dear. Rather awful for you." She added, rather as if just remembering she had three other children, "For all of you, of course."

"What did he want?"

"He didn't say. That was the odd thing. I knew from the moment I saw him he was up to something—you know that gleam he gets in his eye when he's just about to turn the screws—but in the end he ended up just exchanging the most banal pleasantries and after about an hour he left. I'm still puzzled by it. And rather put out: I cancelled my bridge game to find out what it was he wanted—I thought it might have something to do with you, so I was determined to hear him out, however unpleasant—and yet he never got around to telling me. Talked about his stock portfolio, mostly, as if I cared. He said the gout was troubling him worse than ever, but he wouldn't take the painkillers the doctor had prescribed. He said he didn't want to end up looking like Elizabeth Taylor in rehab."

"Perhaps he wanted to hear your views on Violet."

"I'm sure he didn't have to ask to know my views," his mother shot back.

Oh, ho. So, she wasn't quite as indifferent as she sounded.

"I mean really, Ruthven. A girl like that, probably a Page Three girl." She was fairly hissing now. "What can he be thinking? People have always been most sympathetic, but the press will have a field day—a three-day's wonder, of course, it's not like royalty getting married or having its phone calls intercepted, after all, but still. The worst of it is, the real tragedy of it is, what it's going to mean to you. Has he given any hint? Have you heard from him?"

"You mean apart from this execrable invitation? Not a word."

"We'll have to put our heads together, Ruthven. There must be a way to make him see reason."

"Funny. Those are the exact words Lillian used."

THE LION IN HIS DEN

Sir Adrian Beauclerk-Fisk sat complacently surveying the luxurious study of his manor house, basking in the Rembrandtesque glow of its dark-paneled walls, the gleaming surfaces of which reflected light from the flames in the carved eighteenth-century fireplace—a real fireplace, thank you very much, none of the fake-coal contraptions so beloved by the common people. The light reflected as well off Sir Adrian's Toby-mug-like features, the silk of his smoking jacket, and the polished mahogany of the carefully chosen (by his hired London expert) antique furniture. Sir Adrian had shown the man a photo of the effect he wanted, torn from an article on Marlborough House in *British Heritage*.

He contrived to look, in fact, every inch the gentleman he was not. His expression as he surveyed the room through piggy eyes said as clearly as words, *Mine. All Mine.*

He picked up his twenty-four-carat-gold-nibbed pen and contemplated the scattered pages of manuscript before him. A Biro might have been less trouble than the pen, which constantly needed refilling from the antique inkwell, but the pen had seen him through thirty-nine best sellers and, writers being the superstitious creatures that they are, nothing could separate him from it—certainly not the lure of one of those infernal personal computers with their floppy disks. Besides, he had that poncy American secretary to do the drudge work of transcribing his mostly illegible writing and cleaning up his spelling.

Sir Adrian indulged himself in several superstitions related to his writing, in addition to the pen. He would write only on flimsy blue air-mail paper of a kind produced only by a certain manufacturer in Paris—the kind on which he had penned his first best seller. He now bought the paper in bulk, a hedge against the day its manufacturer might go bankrupt or change the content of the paper. His novels were always precisely twenty-six chapters long, often regardless of whether or not this served the needs of the narrative. His desk, although he had pointed it out to no one, especially the hapless reporters who liked to interview him on such things as when he worked and how he got his ideas, faced directly south, in imitation of the direction his desk had faced in the Parisian garret of his youth. Due south, which he had learned somewhere in his wide-ranging reading was the direction of good fortune in Asia. That this forced him away from the view of spacious gardens outside the French windows of the room was probably all to the good, the eternal Miss Rampling requiring more and more in the way of extremes of ingenious solutions to keep Sir Adrian's vast public entertained. He had tried to kill her off more than once; his agent had remonstrated and his publishers had refused to publish. He had tried another sleuth, but the public revolted, staying away in droves from his Cornish Chief Inspector. No, Miss

Rampling it must be, the reading public demanded it. He was wedded to the old bat as if by holy matrimony.

The reminder of matrimony brought a smile to his lips, a smile of the kind so accurately described by Ruthven as reptilian. Sir Adrian paused in his work, literally hugging his flabby girth with glee.

Sir Adrian felt he had a lot to smile about that day. The current book was going swimmingly—he was discovering that a *roman á clef* was much easier going than his usual fictional scampers down the too-familiar High Street and through the rectory of Saint Edmund-Under-Stowe with the sprightly Miss Rampling. He wondered if maybe he should adopt this method for future books. He sat tapping his pen, contemplating with serpentine relish the long list of his enemies, many long dead. At the age of seventy, Sir Adrian viewed with some regret the diminishing ranks of those he viewed as his opponents, most of them older mentors who had had their kindnesses to Sir Adrian repaid with his own peculiar brand of ruthless, childish spite.

Still, there was his family, he thought cheerfully. Yet he surveyed this field with some bafflement. Not one of them worth a tinker's damn. Only Ruthven even approached being worthy of the vast fortune Sir Adrian had amassed, for while George, if untalented, was certainly ruthless (which quality Sir Adrian admired above all others), only Ruthven possessed the perseverance necessary to turn the pitiless streak he had learned at Sir Adrian's knee into vast pots of gold. As for the younger two—not worth mentioning. That his youngest son had turned into a drunken, poncy, fourth-rate actor was a family disgrace—more so for the feebleness of his acting talent than for his ponciness or his drinking, vices Sir Adrian was willing to tolerate because of their upper-class overtones. Sarah he dismissed with two words—fat cow, then amended that in his mind to, stupid fat cow—unaware of any irony as he absentmindedly contemplated his own vast girth spilling over the rope of his smoking jacket.

They think all they've got to do is while away their time until I die, he thought. Cookbooks and revivals of deservedly neglected plays and art gallery openings. He made a snorting sound that cannot effectively be rendered into English, and was turning once again to his manuscript when he heard a tapping at the door of his study. Quickly, Sir Adrian gathered the scattered sheets and shoved them under the ink blotter on his desk.

"Come."

The door edged open to admit a blondish young man in the indeterminate middle years between thirty-five and forty-five. Slight of build, he still somehow exuded an American robustness that Sir Adrian found extremely tedious at the best of times. He was often to be observed prancing, as Sir Adrian put it, around the vast grounds of the estate, engaged in the pointless American pastime they called power walking. Sir Adrian predicted direly that the young man would not live to see his fiftieth birthday if he didn't learn to relax, take up smoking, and knock back a few ales at the local.

"What is it?" Sir Adrian demanded now. The secretary, for it was he, flashed him a blinding white smile, displaying the results of a lifetime of proper oral hygiene.

"Just popped in to give you the latest pages, and to ask if you've any more for me to be getting on with, what?"

Another of Jeffrey Spencer's many, many annoying mannerisms, to Sir Adrian's mind, was his adoption of what he hoped was a British accent complete with British slang and figures of speech. Sir Adrian, when in the mood, reacted to this by slinging back as much American speech as he could recall from his telly viewing.

"Nope, Jeff," he said now. "Reckon I'll hang on to these here pages a mite longer, pardner. But you can mosey on down t'store yonder and fetch me some of this here special ink fer the inkwell. I've done tuckered it all out."

Jeffrey—as he preferred to be called—blinked. There was something just that bit off in the phrasing of the last sentence. Sir Adrian wondered if he hadn't gone rather too far this time, laid it on a bit thick. But, no. He could see the American shrug inwardly at the request, delivered as it was in what was still, to his ear, unmistakably a British accent. *The old boy's just having one of his off days,* thought Jeffrey, wondering if he'd ever seen Sir Adrian having an on day.

"Rightee-o," he said. "I'll be back in two shakes of a lamb's tail." Again he flashed the fluoridated smile that could have launched a thousand ships, or at least, lighted them safely past the shoals, bouncing exuberantly on the balls of his feet.

"Okey dokey," came the rejoinder.

The door slammed. Sir Adrian sighed. The man was an idiot, but, partly because he knew how to wrestle a personal computer into submission, and partly because he was one of the few souls alive who could decipher Sir Adrian's handwriting, he had lasted longer than most of the secretaries, who, one by one, had been tested in the turbulent waters of Sir Adrian's charm and emerged, scalded and terrified.

Sir Adrian was faced with a dilemma, however. He was fast approaching the part of his narrative that he wanted to preserve from the world's scrutiny, at least until it was ready for publication. After all, the whole point of writing it was to ensure the world scrutinized it eventually. How far could he trust to Jeffrey's discretion, or at least to his naïveté? Everything Jeffrey knew about Sir Adrian's past and present he seemed to have gleaned from the pages of writers' magazines—largely fictional interviews with the Master of Detective Fiction: Sir Adrian made it a point to change his story with every new reporter who came along. Still, the public facts of his marriage to Chloe were indisputable, common knowledge. Would even Jeffrey be able to read between the lines?

Sir Adrian, reaching no decision, sighed again and heaved himself slowly and painfully to his feet. The activity resulted in a grunting, snuffling sound, like a sow approaching a trough. He suffered, like Henry VIII, from gout, which affected his disposition about as well as it did that of the jolly monarch, and was the result of a lifetime of much the same kind of overindulgence. While he hadn't left a trail of dead wives behind, the thought of beheading Chloe had more than once held temptation as being much pleasanter and more cost-effective than divorce. Grimacing, and with the aid of a cane, he hobbled toward the bell pull next to the fireplace to summon Mrs. Romano.

"He wants his tea, then," Mrs. Romano informed Watters, the gardener, both of them sitting over their cuppa at the vast refectory table in the even vaster expanse of the surprisingly modern, warm kitchen. Chrome and stainless steel shone from every corner while the scent of just-baked bread filled the air.

Waverley Court had been built in the early eighteenth century by a soldier of fortune who had been well rewarded for his efforts to preserve and defend the monarchy by whatever means necessary, no questions asked. The house seemed to reflect this rapacious gentleman's subsequent determination never more to roam: It squatted, a square, immovable mass, on many hundreds of landscaped acres, like an enormous pile of building blocks laid out by an obsessive-compulsive giant in the dead center of his green garden. Sir Adrian had acquired it all for a song of a million or so pounds from the improvident descendants of the nobleman, gleefully snatching it just in time from the jaws of the National Trust. Sir Adrian was not certain even now that he had ever visited all the rooms in his dearly bought stone pile.

It was a long walk to the study, for it was a ludicrously large house and Mrs. Romano was not given to doing anything in haste. Indeed, it took five minutes for her to undulate her way from the kitchen in the back to the study in the front, balancing Sir Adrian's tea tray the while. It was a ritual she had performed most of her working life for him and a task she would trust no one but herself to undertake, even on the days when her son, Paulo, who officiated as butler at the manor, was on duty. Best not to overtax Paulo, was her view: He's got his life yet to live. And, besides, Sir Adrian seemed to enjoy the ritual every bit as much as she did.

Reaching the library at last, she knocked at its massive double doors before entering. It had apparently also taken Sir Adrian five minutes to get back to his seat; he was just settling in as Mrs. Romano entered.

"Here's your tea, then. Repulsive English habit," she said, as she always did.

A genuine smile transformed Sir Adrian, a smile that would have astounded any member of his family or his few acquaintances had they ever been treated to it, which most assuredly they had not. It was a smile in which it was possible to see traces of the handsome man he had been, before corpulence, bad health, and worse temper had ballooned the features into a mask of petulance.

"Mrs. Romano. I do thank you so much." He pulled off his glasses. "Won't you join me?"

It was an inevitable invitation with an inevitable reply.

"None for me. You know it would spoil my supper."

Mrs. Romano had been Sir Adrian's cook for fifteen years, by far his most enduring employee. She was, in addition to being grounded by a bedrock of common sense, a marvelous cook, and Sir Adrian being known with some justification as a connoisseur of food and wine, she ruled not just the kitchen but the household as a result of her favored status. She and her husband had owned a *trattoria* in Cambridge that Sir Adrian had frequented on his trips to the bookstores. Mrs. Romano—Maria—had run the kitchen while her husband's contribution to their success had been largely to drink the proceeds with the customers. When her husband died and she discovered he had drunk even more from the till than she had realized, Sir Adrian had convinced her to sell out and work for him with promises of a fat paycheck, autonomy, and spacious living quarters for her and her son, Paulo. She had accepted with alacrity, sick, at her age—she was then fifty-two—of the hand-to-mouth existence of running a small restaurant, for her husband had, typically, left no insurance. She was touched then and now by Sir Adrian's kindness, and she had never looked back. As she told her mother back in Italy, "Sir Adrian is nothing like they say in the newspapers. Never to me." That Sir Adrian had gotten an excellent cook in the bargain was only fair, she felt, reveling in the chance daily to create new dishes to tempt Sir Adrian's jaded palate.

"Stay for a chat, then, Mrs. Romano," said Sir Adrian, motioning her to one of the chairs opposite his desk. She settled her generous form into the upholstered chair, mentally kicking her shoes off. This, too, was a frequent part of the ritual. More than most, she knew the solitariness of Sir Adrian's day; like no one else, she felt sorry for him.

"How are the wedding dinner preparations coming along?"

Mrs. Romano, who had been steadfastly avoiding the subject, sidestepped with a question of her own.

"I did wonder, Sir Adrian, if it wouldn't be better for me to speak with the bride about the preparations?"

"Whatever for?"

"Er. I mean, she is the bride, and traditionally..." She trailed off. Mrs. Romano was seldom without words or an opinion, but something, as the British say, was fishy here, and she wasn't going to venture too far without finding out first what it was.

"Tradition be damned," said Sir Adrian. "Violet wouldn't know a cauliflower from a pig's brain—always too busy worrying about her figure to actually eat anything. She wouldn't know what you were talking about."

Not for the first time, Mrs. Romano wondered at the oddity of this proposed May-December match. Clearly it was a case of Jack Spratt and his wife in reverse, for one thing. But there was something more that bothered her. She knew Sir Adrian better than most and there was something, she felt, *all wrong* about all this. Violet Winthrop had emerged as a name spoken by Sir Adrian only in the past few months, and now these sudden wedding plans, with only the family invited, no friends. Of course, Sir Adrian had no friends, she reflected sadly. The ceremony was to be performed here in the library by a multidenominational pastor Sir Adrian had apparently selected from the phone listings. Why, at his age? The obvious answer of post-midlife crisis seemed out of character for Sir Adrian. There were men and there were *men*, after all. There was nothing Mrs. Romano felt she didn't know about men. But she had never known Sir Adrian to face any crisis with other than blustering indifference.

And where was the blushing bride while all these preparations were going on?

"As for the refreshments after the ceremony," she said now, "Champagne, of course. And I thought maybe a nice—"

"Too soon to worry about that now," Sir Adrian said.

Too soon? With the wedding a few days away?

"Very well, Sir Adrian." Long experience had taught her that there were times to ignore Sir Adrian, and this was one of them. Privately, she began listing the provisions she would order from the greengrocer and butcher in town. Raised on Italian weddings in her small village where the drunken celebrations had gone on for days, with or without the happy couple, she was having trouble paring this celebration down to the hole-in-corner affair Sir Adrian seemed to want.

She left the library some ten minutes later, following a spirited discussion with Sir Adrian as to how to prepare a traditional British roast with garlic, no easier in her mind than when she entered. Something is wrong here, she thought, pulling the massive doors, thick enough to repel an army, closed behind her.

"Something is wrong here," she announced to Watters, having surged her way back to the kitchen more slowly than usual, lost in thought, looking more than ever like an older Sophia Loren in *Two Women*. She was not surprised to see Watters still sitting there at the oak refectory table, slowly sipping his highly sweetened tea. At eighty-two, his role as gardener at Waverley Court had largely been reduced to taking a few feeble swipes with the pruning sheers at the rosebushes in the formal gardens, and pulling whichever weeds yielded themselves to his ineffectual tugging. The real work of maintaining the grounds was done by a hired firm from nearby Newton Coombe, which came in twice a week and largely prevented Watters from doing more damage than he might otherwise have done.

Now he roused himself from contemplating the tea leaves in the bottom of his cup to peer enquiringly around the kitchen.

"No," said Mrs. Romano. "I mean here, at the house, in general. This wedding. Everything about it is not right. He is up to something, you mark my words."

"No fool like an old fool," intoned Watters, looking pleased, as if he'd newly minted the thought.

"Indeed," said Mrs. Romano, briskly gathering the tea things and traversing what looked, from a bird's-eye view, like miles of stone floor to reach the stainless steel double sink. "But that is not what I meant. I do not think he is serious about this at all. We are only days away from the wedding and—has he even mentioned flowers to you?"

Watters shook his head.

"He had me bring in a couple of Christmas trees and some of them poinsettia plants for the house."

"No, I mean *flowers*. You know, flower arrangements, for a wedding."

"Nah. I thought 'twere strange, that. Can't have a wedding without flowers, can you now?"

"Exactly. No, you can't."

Mrs. Romano folded her arms, strong as a ship builder's, under her impressive bosom. A crease appeared between her perfectly groomed eyebrows.

"I'll tell you what I think. What I think is I do not think there is going to be a wedding. This week or next week or any time in the future. I do not think that is what he has planned at all."

"Eh?" Watters' mind raced, trying to keep up with Mrs. Romano. "Don't be daft. The family will all be here, all invited, like."

"Yes," said Mrs. Romano. Absently, she flicked a dishcloth in the direction of a bread crumb. "Yes. The family will all be here. And I think that what Sir Adrian has planned is not a wedding, but the fireworks."

THE CLAN GATHERS

THE DAY BEFORE THE wedding dawned with a wintry brilliance that by midday had settled into a mind-numbing, cloak-defying chill only to be found in the unprotected surrounds of Cambridgeshire. Unshielded by barriers either natural or artificial, the area was pummeled throughout the winter months by an Arctic blast that from time immemorial had driven itself directly from the north across the sea, sweeping undeterred past shore, fen, farmland, and village, straight into the bones of rich and poor alike. It was hard to imagine a more unlikely time for a wedding.

Sir Adrian, surveying the wintry scene before him from the French doors of the drawing room as he sipped a pre-dinner sherry, was pleased. Yesterday he had traveled to Cambridge to sign his newest will in the presence of witnesses, and he had the sense of accomplishment that comes mainly to those who enjoy creating unholy mischief.

If he could have seen past the slightly rolling hills of the grounds as far as to the village of Newton Coombe, he would have observed a dilapidated red sports car approaching the village, veering danger-ously on the narrow road lined by stone walls that gapped unex-pectedly to reveal a loose sheep or a stray car attempting to cross the fray of the main thoroughfare. The driver of the car, reaching the outskirts of the village, indicated unofficially by a smattering of tiny worker's cottages tarted up to attract the highest bidder among fleeing suburbanites, gave a token tap on the brakes and slowed to within twenty kilometers of the speed limit before screeching to a halt in front of the Thorn and Crown. The car door opened, and the driver tumbled rather than slid out from the tiny opening thus cre-ated, just managing to escape the appearance of having landed on his hands and knees. He righted himself with elaborate dignity, and proceeded with careful steps toward the pub.

It was Albert, and Albert was very drunk.

The pub owner greeted him as a long-lost friend, as indeed he was. Albert, a generous tipper, generally well-behaved and with enormous drinking capacity, was always a welcome sight.

"As I live and breathe," he cried, already pulling a pint of Al-bert's usual.

Albert slumped onto a barstool, first checking carefully to make sure its four legs stood more or less evenly on the flagstones. More than once, he had found himself discarded on the floor when one of the rickety chairs seemed to vanish from beneath him.

"On your way to visit your father, is it, then?"

Albert laughed mirthlessly.

"'Home is the sailor, home...'" he trailed off, looking around him. "You've, er, fixed the place up, haven't you, Jim?"

Jim Tanner swelled with owner's pride. In response to sagging trade, for Newton Coombe was miles from the major motorways and only to be discovered by the most dogged American tourist, Jim had decided to give the customers what they wanted. What they wanted, apparently, were striped red velour seat coverings and antique farm implements suspended from the ceiling. The place now looked like a cross between a Victorian brothel and a cowshed.

"Nice," commented Albert, stifling an inward shudder. It was just what one of the major chains would have done to liven up trade.

"Didn't half cost the moon, let me tell you. Still, folk seem to like it."

The two of them sat in mutual friendly silence, both gazing raptly at the decor. In a chair nearest the fire, the orange tabby who had been alive since Albert could remember—could it possibly be the same cat?—roused herself, stretched, and began a fastidious cleansing of her paws, fixing Albert the while with a suspicious green-eyed glare. Disconcerted, Albert turned away. Apart from the cat, he and Jim were alone in the pub; it was both too late and too early in the day for his regulars.

"He must be getting on by now, your dad," said Jim, reverting to his earlier subject. It was unusual to find Albert down here at all; in fact, Jim was trying to calculate the last time he had seen him. Must have been well over a year or two ago, some family gathering. Sir Adrian's birthday, was it? If memory served, that had gone about as well as the other gatherings at the manor house. It was well known in the village that their most famous resident could be "difficult."

"He was seventy this year. Sometime in April, I think."

Jim registered the vagueness, rightly aligning it in his mind with indifference, pretended or otherwise. Straightening a few bar towels unnecessarily, for Jim ran a spotless establishment (his lady wife saw to that), he said casually, "Artists can be difficult, can't they?"

"I should know. I'm surrounded by them all the time."

"Oh, aye. Still in the theatre, are you?"

Albert winced. To have to be asked whether one was still in the theatre was a lethal blow to any actor's ego.

"I'm starting rehearsals for *Dinner at Eight* next month." He forbore to mention that the play was not only being produced by a repertory group, it was being produced by a repertory group in Sheffield. He felt sure even Jim would recognize this was about as far from the West End as any actor, respectable or otherwise, would care to be seen dead.

"Bit late for dinner, isn't it? Eight?" was Jim's only comment. "Generally we finish serving 'round here at seven, except for stragglers who've lost their way into Cambridge."

Albert grinned in spite of himself. He was still having a little trouble getting Jim's face entirely into focus.

"Quite sensible, too. My father certainly would agree with you. I suppose that's why this execrable family dinner of his is planned for seven tomorrow night. Did you know he was planning to get married?"

"Oh, aye, Watters was in here last week. He said he hadn't met the bride-to-be, although he had the idea she was likely younger than Sir Adrian. He didn't seem to know much else about what was going on. It all seemed to have come on sudden-like," said Jim, as if he were discussing a flu epidemic.

"Good old Watters. 'Younger.' There's an understatement for you. I'd say if you put her age around a third of my father's you wouldn't be far off."

Jim found from somewhere behind the bar a filthy rag that had escaped his wife's notice and proceeded to smear the highly polished surface of the bar with it. Outside, he could hear the wind kicking up to an unholy howl, the pub sign swinging madly on its hinges. Business would be slow tonight.

"It takes men like that sometimes, you know. Mind," and here he lowered his voice, glancing around as if there were someone other than the cat to overhear. "Mind, if the missus were to pop off I might be tempted to give a younger woman a try—who's there among us doesn't have our daydreams, eh?" He paused, remembering just in time that Albert's orientation was rumored to be in the other direction, and that his daydreams, presumably, were likewise directed the other way. Jim Tanner's mind, broad enough to encompass most of the variety of the human condition ("You see it all in my line of work," was his oft-repeated motto), still skittered away from wandering into any of the specifics of what might constitute Albert's daydreams. Recovering himself, he went on, "But I think on the whole a more mature woman's what a man my age needs. The missus when she were young were handful enough—a strong-minded lass, she were." He paused, paying mental tribute to the red-headed virago that was the Mrs. Tanner of forty years ago. "Not sure I could live through that twice, not at my age. You follow?"

"Oh, I follow all right. You mean he's set to make a gigantic fool of himself." For the first time, anger seeped through the alcoholic haze that had kept Albert barely tamped down all day. "And a fool of his family, while he's at it." He attempted to slam his fist on the bar and missed. The impetus from the swing nearly pulled him off the barstool.

Registering the change in climate, Jim decided that Albert's next beer would be one of those nonalcoholic pissbrews he kept on tap for just such occasions. When they were as drunk as young Albert here they didn't even notice the difference.

"You do realize what this does to us, his children?"

"Oh, aye, emotionally like—"

"Emotionally be buggered." Albert had known Jim most of his life and saw no need to pretend the Beauclerk-Fisk family laundry couldn't stand an airing like anyone else's, even had discretion ever been a part of his nature—which it had never been. Furthermore, a lifetime of theatre training, while rewarding him poorly in a financial sense, had encouraged a natural tendency to speak from the heart, regardless of the consequences.

"What I want to know is what he's going to do with the will this time," he continued now. "He's owned and disowned most of us several dozen times over the years—I don't think even Ruthven, the mercenary little shit, has any idea what Father is worth or how much, if anything, is liable to be Ruthven's cut. And with this wedding ... well, you do see, don't you? We don't any of us even know who this woman is."

Jim, who at his death would probably be worth no more than 5,000 pounds once the Inland Revenue got through raping his widow, still could appreciate the similarities. Where there was money at stake, even piddling amounts, the heirs were sure to behave badly. Why, when Mrs. Cottle up the way had died last year her two daughters had had a regular knock-down drag-out in her front garden over some trinket the old lady'd probably bought at Torquay for ten pence back in the 1930s. Jim, whose reading was largely confined to racing forms, had no idea what a famous writer like Sir

Adrian might have raked in over the years; he only knew the mansion itself was probably worth a few million. And if some stranger were to come along and grab the whole lot now that the old man was approaching his twilight years ... yes, Jim could see where this could lead to a right mess in any family. 'Specially this one.

"Sarah thinks—"

Just then, the wind caught the door, blowing it open with a crash. Its squat medieval frame was filled to capacity by a large form in black. Both Jim and the cat jumped; the cat was not seen again for many hours. As Jim told his regulars later, it looked like nothing so much as a witch blown in on the rising storm. Had he had either Albert's theatrical background or his level of alcohol, he would have thought the entire cast of the witches' scene in Macbeth had come crowding through the door at once.

"I recognized the car," announced the apparition, unwrapping itself from a dripping black anorak.

"Sarah!"

Albert stumbled off the barstool, again righting himself just in time. He threw his arms around his sister as far as they could reach. Jim thought he looked like a drowning man clutching a rubber dinghy.

"I see you had the same thought I did," said Sarah, gently disengaging herself. "No way am I going up to that madhouse without fortification. Jim!"

Sarah had two volumes, inaudible and bellowing. Her voice now rang out across the room, as if to be heard over a thronging crowd at the bar.

"How are you? Let's see the wine list."

Jim, who had two wines to his name, both plonk varietals in boxes from which he refilled the two bottles he kept behind the bar for appearances, was momentarily at a loss. Sarah, who shared her father's passion for only the finest when it came to drink, sensed the problem and sighed. "Just bring me a red, then."

She and Albert moved to a table in the corner near the fire.

"I decided I had to come," she announced, looking around as if she'd somehow found herself in the wrong pub by accident. An antique scythe hung from the rafters just over her head, she noticed, and shifted her position a foot or so to the right.

Jim brought their drinks to the table and then discreetly disappeared toward the back.

"I wouldn't give him the satisfaction of not being here," said Albert.

"More or less my thinking, too." Sarah was in a rare belligerent phase, thought Albert. She seemed all her life to have careened between knuckling under to their father and doing things designed to annoy him. Her weight—a bone, so to speak, of contention the whole time she was growing up—was one of those things. She was a pretty girl, Albert recognized, and had been heartbreakingly beautiful as a child, but by wearing no makeup and swathing herself in dark drapery she made sure no one would suspect. She gazed at him now out of blue eyes in a round face framed by a too-short brown fringe she clearly had cut herself, now plastered to her forehead in zigzag fashion by wind and rain.

"Has it occurred to you," she continued, "that he's done this deliberately? I mean, what else could get us out here in a howling gale like this?" She paused to wipe the fringe off her face, so that now it pointed skyward. "I've heard from Ruthven and George—

they're both coming, Ruthven with Lillian in tow, naturally. George is bringing a girlfriend."

Albert nodded noncommittally. He'd also heard from Ruthven, gaining the distinct impression in the course of the conversation that Ruthven was trying to discourage him from showing up. Fat ruddy chance, thought Albert. It had only put the seal on his decision to come.

"On the way down I was trying to remember the last time the whole clan was together like this. And I couldn't. Remember, I mean. It seems that even on one or another of his birthdays, one or another of us was out of favor."

"Out of the will, to be specific. Have you talked to him at all?"

"I rang to tell him I was on my way. Maria took a message."

"I thought it was regrets only. I have no regrets."

Sarah smiled. "What do you think the story is with—"

The pub door again swung open, fanning the fire into loud crackles of falling wood. This time, two lean black figures scurried in from the gloom.

George, shrugging out of a black leather jacket, glanced at the pair at the table, then looked around him, as if disappointed at the small audience. George never went anywhere he didn't expect or hope for a crush of frenzied females to come out of the woodwork. Sarah didn't recognize the girl who followed him in, flapping her arms and spraying water in all directions, surmising it was George's latest semi-permanent, and searching memory for her name. Natasha, that was it.

Sarah and Albert made room for them at the table. Albert noticed that, by creating some unnecessary disturbance for the rest of the party, George managed to seat himself where he had the best view into the gilt-edged mirror hanging on the wall opposite. Also, that his girlfriend was left to fend for herself in disentangling herself from her coat, George being engaged in arranging his long blonde hair back into the artfully tousled look he paid a London salon to maintain for him, at a cost of the average working man's weekly pay packet.

And they say actors are vain, thought Albert.

After exchanging the usual pleasantries ("If we'd traveled any farther, the wind would have sent us into a ditch," George explained), the three siblings quickly turned to the topic uppermost in all their minds. Natasha, unsurprisingly, as quickly looked bored—she had heard it all a million times on the drive down—and hoved off in search of drinks.

"Right," said George, clasping his manicured hands on the table in a without-further-ado manner. "I think we're all agreed that we've got to put a stop to this farce. The question is, how?"

"I had thought a confrontation might be in order. What they call an intervention," offered Sarah.

They both looked at her as if she were mad.

"He's not a drug user," said George, patiently, as to a child.

"I know that," she said, with some asperity. "But what's the alternative? I've never known reasoning with him one-on-one to produce the desired result. A show of force, on the other hand..."

"I think Sarah's right," said Albert.

"Should we include Ruthven?" she asked.

"No!" This from George and Albert simultaneously.

"He'll only try to grab a bigger share," said Albert, "and we'll be back where we started. Provided, of course, the whole thing isn't a joke to begin with."

"He's never gone this far before," said George. "This is different, I tell you. Playing around with the will practically every week is one thing. This marriage is another. I want to know—I demand to know from him—what the arrangements are."

"Demand, do you?" said Albert. "That will get you far. Besides, do you seriously believe he's going through with it? I don't. I think he's playing games with us, hoping to spark a reaction. I'd be willing to bet there is no bride, he's just making this up."

"Why?" asked Sarah, wanting to believe he was right.

"Because of the way he's gone about this. The invitation only last week. The fact that not one of us, so far as I know, has ever heard of or seen the bride before. It's almost like he's done the one thing he knew would send us all scurrying up here, as if he wanted us all on the spot, together, and this was the only way he could dream up that he was fairly certain would work."

"It's pathetic, isn't it?" said Sarah. "But the same thought occurred to me. Perhaps he's just … lonely … wanting to see us all together, knowing it would take something like this to bring us running, as you say."

"Fine family feeling at last? Decades too late for that. But … perhaps. He couldn't just ask us in the normal way, that's for certain," said Albert. "Knowing we'd all suspect a trap if he did." He took a long draught of his ale, wondering why it seemed to be sobering him up rather than having the desired, memory-obliterating effect. "God, for a normal father!" he added with feeling.

"Dysfunction breeds dysfunction," Sarah intoned. "We're all classic COA: Children of Alcoholics."

"Speak for yourself," said George, suppressing a glance at Albert. "I never once saw Adrian really drink to excess, come to think of it.

Nor Chloe, although it might have done her a world of good. She seems to be making up for lost time in more recent years, though."

Albert nodded drunken agreement. Whatever led him to drink, he felt, it wasn't his parents' example, just his father's continued existence.

Natasha had by this time returned to the table with drinks for herself and George (for which she had paid, Albert noted) and by mutual consent, or rather, bowing to the inevitable, the talk turned to George's latest tour of the European art galleries, which tour he pronounced to be a triumph. He next launched into his plans for a working vacation in America the next year. Albert took advantage of the moment to study George's companion. She was a stunner, and no question: coal black hair shimmered from a center part to frame high, delicate cheekbones on a heart-shaped face. She had strong dark brows and a high-bridged nose, features that would have over-powered most faces, but made hers that much more memorable. She wore the ubiquitous black sweater and slacks, but in an indefinably stylish way that recalled photos of Jackie O dodging photographers rather than the millions of young women who now wore that par-ticular New York uniform. How a vapid dumbshit like his brother reeled these women in, Albert couldn't imagine.

Seeing his eyes on her, she smiled and spoke for the first time, nearly reading his thoughts. It was a lovely smile.

"We're all wearing black," she pointed out. "You'd think we were headed to a funeral."

"No such bloody luck," said George.

THE HAPPY COUPLE

IT WAS SOME TIME later before the party of four was to be seen wending its reluctant way in the general direction of Waverley Court, a motley procession comprised of one red sports car, weaving somewhat less erratically than when it had arrived at the pub; one ancient Mini, this belonging to Sarah, that barely qualified as a passenger automobile apart from having the required number of wheels; and one roadster of timeless and well-preserved vintage containing George and Natasha. Having made the mistake of letting Albert take the lead, bobbing and weaving, they tooled faithfully behind him, not daring to risk overtaking in case he made one of his frequent and unexplained swings over into the oncoming lane. Fortunately, the wind had died and they were quite alone in this cortege, having earlier turned off the tarmac onto several miles of dirt road leading up to the manor house.

A final twist of the wheel—Sarah, following the red lights on the back of Albert's car, could not at first tell if he was inexplicably veering off the edge again or merely following course—and Waverley

Court hove into view. God, it was worse than she remembered. Although ablaze with light, there was nothing in its hulking mass as it rose from the surrounding mist that spoke to her of welcome. It only needed Mrs. Danvers running about the garden with matches and a can of petrol.

A silver Rolls Royce that could only belong to Ruthven was parked proprietarily at precise right angles to the steps leading up to the front door. She guessed, rightly, he and Lillian had arrived early in order to establish a beachhead.

The front door beneath an ill-proportioned pediment had an impressive coat of arms carved into its tympanum—lions and griffins rampant among towers and flowers. This door now flung open to reveal a Heathcliffe-type figure in butler's uniform: Brooding, dark, unfriendly, he observed them as they hauled their assorted belongings out of their assorted car boots. It was Paulo, needing only a knife clenched between his teeth to complete the image of menacing hostility. Sarah noticed he made no move to assist anyone but Natasha, who, à la Grace Kelly in *Rear Window*, seemed to be making do with a tiny makeup case, while Sarah herself struggled with an overpacked valise.

"Sir Adrian is waiting for you in the drawing room," Paulo announced, cutting short Albert's attempt at polite greeting. "If you'll leave your bags in the hall I'll see they're deposited in your rooms."

Freshening up from the long road trip was not going to be allowed, Sarah recognized, trooping in behind George, who was looking decidedly miffed, and Natasha, who was gaping in unabashed wonder at the baronial entry hall, the ceiling of which soared far overhead to disappear in darkness. The only thing lacking in here was a suit of armor, thought Sarah, but her father had had to make do thus far with an array of authentic and reproduction maces and battle-axes ranged along the walls. She had always itched to attach "Your Souvenir from Brighton" labels to their handles.

Meanwhile, Paulo had swung open the doors leading into the drawing room, then disappeared into the back reaches of the house, presumably on some errand more urgent than greeting unwanted guests. The four of them huddled in the entrance to the drawing room, taking in the scene.

Two chairs were ranged on either side of the fireplace, which flamed extravagantly in warmth and welcoming contrast to Paulo's greeting. In one chair sat the familiar form of their eldest brother, in the other the more elegant, less-familiar but more despised form of his wife, Lillian. She, interrupted in the act of inserting a cigarette into a black cloisonné holder, paused now to gaze at them each in turn from beneath painted-on eyebrows. Albert was reminded of the cat at the Thorn and Crown—the same unblinking green gaze, the same queenly contempt. Their brother similarly stared at them, but his eyes held a look neither George nor Albert could read. Sarah, frequent victim of his childhood cruelties, could. He was watching for their reaction, mentally rubbing his paws in anticipation.

Directly facing the fireplace was a large, high-backed sofa, above which could be seen the easily recognizable, balding top of their father's enormous round head. Having heard the visitors enter, he seemed to be engaged in a superhuman struggle to rise, judging by the snorts and snuffles emerging from his direction. A woman to his right was attempting to help him to his feet. They saw a strong back swathed in a tight-fitting white dress, sleek hair pulled back into a glossy chignon.

She turned to face the group, smiling as if for photographers. Blue eyes that the smile didn't quite touch grazed them in passing before returning their solicitous gaze back to the heaving bundle at her side. She was unquestionably beautiful, she was slender even beyond the stringent dictates of fashion, she was, in fact, pretty much everything they'd conceived in their worst May-December imaginings … except that she was also, unequivocally and unambiguously, a woman of a certain age. Fifty? Sixty? In the silence from the doorway, you could practically hear the separate brains performing their calculations, and arriving at a median estimate of late fifties.

Sir Adrian smiled at their discomfiture. If Violet noticed anything odd in the way they stood frozen in the doorway, she gave no sign.

"Violet, my dear," he said, patting her hand over his arm. "It's time to meet your new relatives."

———

Dinner that night was preceded by more than one hushed meeting behind closed doors.

They had spent an awkward half hour or so in the drawing room, clutching their drinks, pretending it was just a normal family gathering. As gatherings of the Beauclerk-Fisk family went, it was not, in fact, much stranger than the usual. Sir Adrian dominated the conversation by his presence, as always, but without saying much—it would be truer to say he steered the conversational boat, then sat back to watch them all flounder in his wake.

They had all gaped at Violet while trying desperately, in their different ways, to hide their gaping. They shook hands all around and then subsumed into chairs and uncomfortable silence. From long habit, and because of his advantage of being on the scene first, they all looked to Ruthven to rescue them. After an apparent struggle with himself, he decided to oblige.

"Violet was just telling us of her upbringing," he said smoothly. He was using his negotiator's face, the one that made it impossible to read his thoughts.

Violet waved her upbringing away with a red-taloned claw. Albert was reminded of photos he had seen of the Duchess of Windsor; unquestionably her worst feature, apart from her face, had been her big-boned hands dangling at the ends of her scrawny wrists.

She further managed to confound all expectations with the first words out of her mouth, delivered in an unmistakably upper-class drawl.

"And a very ordinary upbringing it was," said Violet, "until World War II intervened. I spent the time milking a group of un-cooperative cows on a farm in Wales." Mentally they revised their estimate of her age upward. She smiled, consigning war to the past with the recalcitrant cows. "My parents remained in London, of course, feeling somehow it was their duty—why *did* so many parents think they might survive the Blitz while their children certainly would not? Naturally, they did not survive, and I was left with my aunt and her husband. Frightfully nice people, of course. But they could not provide the kind of exciting life a young girl craves." She might still have been talking of the cows. "But, all of this is much too much in the past to do anything but bore you young people."

This last was delivered with the coquettish smile of a woman who knows she neither looks her age nor needs to fish for compliments.

Sir Adrian dutifully patted her hand, tut-tutting her age into oblivion. The young people, most of them hurtling through their forties, made the required deprecating motions with their hands. They were too busy wondering how they could have got it all so wrong.

George, who had been studying her in some perplexity, burst out, "I say, haven't I seen you somewhere before?" Even George blushed at having delivered such a cliché. But he felt he recognized her and was in that state of mental agony induced by trying to come up with the forgotten name of a person frequently met. Years of drug-induced intellectual fog weren't helping.

Again the stately, aristocratic smile. Like royalty visiting the contagion ward, thought Albert.

"I was blessed—or perhaps cursed—with a famous marriage. Perhaps you have seen my photograph here and there. When I was much younger, of course. Since my husband died I have been, and thankfully, more or less consigned to the shadows."

Again the tut-tutting from Sir Adrian, who seemed to feel that this was going modesty too far.

"Anyway, when I arrived back in London," she continued, "I knew almost no one, and where money was going to come from I did not know. In those days, even though the war had changed many things for women, it was expected that afterward one would simply go back to the house and bake bread for the returning menfolk. What had changed, of course, was that there were fewer menfolk returning. Fewer houses and less flour for bread, for that matter. I had a small income from my family—my aunt and uncle had died by this time. But it seemed the city was positively riddled with young women of a certain class, you know, not particularly skilled at anything except driving ambulances."

"And milking cows," put in Sarah helpfully.

"Quite." She focused her eyes toward the black hulking mass sunk into a brocaded armchair. It was clear that Violet, lost in her wartime memories, had forgotten for a moment Sarah was there, as people tended to do. Pausing to gauge Sarah's tone on her irony meter, and apparently finding nothing amiss, Violet went on. "Then one day I went to the British Museum—I was nearly in despair by this point, you understand—and there I ran into a photographer I had met at one of those dreary weekend parties in Scotland that people tended to have in those days—all grouse and beating bushes and smelly dogs and whatnot. I do not enjoy nature. We build houses to get away from nature, do we not? Anyway, this photographer shared my abhorrence for the sporting life and we passed the time at the party talking. I suppose when we met up again he could see my distress. He was very kind. Nothing like you might be thinking—he was merely a kind young man. He suggested I should create a portfolio—this is a word I had never heard before—a portfolio and he would take it 'round to some agencies he knew in London. This I did. They all said the same—I was a type that was 'in vogue.' It was true: Grace Kelly set the standard in those days—not that I was anywhere in her league. But it was a certain type they wanted. They told me they wanted to 'sign' me."

"Naturally," interjected Sir Adrian, reaching for a decanter. "They'd have been fools not to."

She rewarded him with a smile, her rather large, square teeth gleaming against lips outlined in a shade of red so dark it was nearly black. She looked the kind of woman who had found her style decades ago and saw no reason to change it. It was Lillian who noticed that her fine skin pulled rather too tautly against her cheekbones, exaggerating the wideness of her mouth and eyes, in a way that suggested the attentions of a plastic surgeon in the not-too-distant past.

Ruthven allowed his gaze to slide over to observe his father as he sat hanging on Violet's every word, the silly, universal grin of the lovelorn almost transforming his dewlapped, porcine face. He looked utterly content, precisely like a hog basking in cool mud on a warm day.

"What was so funny to me was that I was—am—tall and skinny," Violet continued. "Now this was somehow desirable, this thinness. I assure you, I was not like the others in my profession, who lived on coffee and cigarettes and nothing else. I went through all the adolescent agonies trying to gain weight but could not. And then suddenly it didn't matter." She shrugged at the absurdities of the fashion world.

She talked on in her high, cultivated voice, Sir Adrian beaming at her side like a proud curator unveiling a newly discovered Picasso. Sarah found herself mesmerized by Violet; this was a woman who tended to command, to dominate—qualities Sarah admired vicariously, knowing she would never possess them herself. The others were less smitten, reminding themselves they were in the presence of the enemy. Albert drank steadily, his usual response to novelty, boredom, or any condition in between; George, soon tiring of any conversation that did not revolve around himself, was surreptitiously studying his nails; Ruthven and Lillian exchanged meaningful glances across the Turkish carpet. Otherwise, the family avoided looking at one other. Natasha was wondering with admiration from what designer Violet had got her dress.

All this, in spite of his apparent state of blissful infatuation, Sir Adrian did not fail to notice.

Violet eventually subsiding, he clasped her strong, masculine hand in his pudgy, veined, wrinkled one. Sarah looked away, realizing she had never once seen her parents holding hands.

Sir Adrian raised his glass.

"To families." He beamed. It was all going pretty much as he had hoped. The only thing to make his happiness complete would be the appearance of Chloe, the mother of this despised brood. Sarah and Lillian each took a polite, submissive sip. George and Ruthven gave a half-hearted lift of their glasses but did not drink. Albert drained his glass.

Sir Adrian, having set the cat among the pigeons, was content.

———

Sarah was in the midst of unpacking in what had been her bedroom while she was growing up—growing up being a strange euphemism for the wrenching separation from everything her childhood represented to her: hostility, sarcasm, criticism, a general feeling of being the uninvited guest at her own party.

The room in fact bore no resemblance to the bedroom of her childhood. Sir Adrian had hardly waited for each of his children to be boarded off to school before bringing in a team of decorators to remove all vestiges of their occupancy. Sarah's was what was now called the Victoria room, festooned, quite unlike that stumpy, dark queen, in a glut of rose sateen and pink lace. Even Sarah, the most unworldly of people and the least aware of her surroundings, recognized that the room was hideous. The deep rose color reminded her of uncooked liver. The bathroom was even worse: Its ceiling, walls, and even its door were covered in red, flocked-velvet wallpaper. Shutting the door was like being sealed in a coffin. She gagged exaggeratedly as she looked about her, longing for the cramped but comforting darkness of her flat.

She was just folding one of the cavernous caftans she favored into a drawer when the knock sounded. It was Ruthven, accompanied by George and Albert. The loathsome Lillian was not in evidence, she saw with relief.

"Family council meeting? How nice," she said, trying and failing to remember them ever having banded together in the way they had today. A saying went through her mind: *The enemy of my enemy is my friend.* While their father had always been the common enemy, they had tended to deal with him before now—or rather, tried to—on their own, in their own ways.

It felt strange having her brothers in her room, grown men who through some miracle had become larger versions of the small boys she remembered: Ruthven, always the bully; George, always vain, but with no particular grounds for being so. Only Albert had changed, it seemed to her—he was diminished, smaller than she remembered, his striking good looks fast fading into the pale anonymity of middle age.

"I wanted a word before tomorrow," Ruthven said, naturally taking charge. Years of planning redundancies and squelching union organizers had given him the edge in any situation calling for hypocrisy or doublespeak. He smoothed a hand over the top of his head, as if it still held an unruly growth of hair that had constantly to be tamed into submission. "Although I certainly wish the old man well, I am sure we all arrived here with similar agendas of trying to dissuade him."

47

"You wish him well, do you?" said Albert, from his roost on Sarah's bed. "That's rich. And when did you first notice this altruistic side of your nature coming to the fore?" Sarah, watching him throughout dinner, had noted that his intake of food had been diluted by alcohol at the rate of about seven ounces to one morsel of food. He seemed to be looking around even now for more reinforcements. Something would have to be done about Albert.

"But it's obvious to me that for all the good we're doing, we may as well leave tonight," Ruthven went on, ignoring him. "There's no hope of influencing this ... course he's set himself on. He's clearly infatuated with the woman. Worst of all, I can even see why."

"She is rather charming, isn't she? Flirtatious in that rather old-fashioned way," said Sarah. "The kind who I imagine makes a man feel the center of the universe. Some women seem to have that sort of appeal all their lives."

George, who could seldom see the charm in any woman over thirty, grunted.

"On the way down here, we had talked of going to him *en masse* to see if we couldn't persuade him out of the idea," said Sarah, forgetting that Ruthven was to have been excluded from that course. George and Albert glared at her.

"And I gather I was to be left out," picked up Ruthven. "Not that I don't understand your reasoning," he said, "and not that I hold it against you"—although he made a mental note to hold it against them when it was more convenient—"but surely you see everything's changed now? Look, there is nothing we can say or do against this woman that would have any effect except to make him more pig-headed in his determination to go through with it. If I didn't know better, I'd say he was doing it for the publicity value. But he's not."

George, who was sure he understood all about publicity, perked up at this.

"What makes you say so?"

"Two reasons. He doesn't need the publicity to sell his books. He hasn't given an interview in years—at least not one where he wasn't pulling the interviewer's leg the whole time—and it's never stopped his books from spurting to the top of the best-sellers list. Everyone wants the newest Miss Rampling for Christmas—the irony, yes, yes, we all know that better than anyone, but that's how it is. In the season of good will, his murderous little books sell themselves."

"The other reason?" asked Sarah.

"The other reason seems nearly impossible, but as Miss Rampling would say, in her muddled way: 'What isn't impossible, once all the real impossibilities are excluded, must be the truth.'"

"You've actually read his tosh, then?" said Albert.

"Since it's one day going to be my tosh, you can bet I have."

George, Sarah, and Albert exchanged glances. *Not any more, it's not.*

"Anyway," Ruthven went on. "I think the real reason is the old fool is in love—or in such a state of extreme infatuation as makes no difference. Because the kind of publicity he will receive from this is of the kind even he would blanch at—and, as I've said, of a kind he doesn't need, anyway. But it's an occupational hazard, I'd guess, in his case."

"You're talking riddles," said Albert. He wanted to go in search of the nearest liquor cabinet, but the whirling room when he attempted standing defeated him.

"You do realize who she is, don't you? Her maiden name was Mildenhall but her married name was Winthrop."

He looked around him, to be met by blank stares.

"The Winthrop murder. Surely you remember? She was accused, and people think, rightly so, of murdering her husband."

A STORY FROM THE PAST

"My God," said Sarah. "It can't be."

"I already have someone in my office checking the files, but you can be sure I'm right. It was sometime in the mid-1950s. We were unborn, then, of course, and even later you might have been too young to care about such things, but I, before long, was reading every newspaper I could lay my hands on. The coverage and speculation about the case went on for years."

Interested in what he was saying, they all nodded encouragingly, suppressing irritation at Ruthven's image of himself as child prodigy, tackling at a tender age the baroque yet subtle nuances of the *Daily Mirror*.

"Oh, yes, it's she, all right," Ruthven went on. "I recognized her face before the name dropped into place. Her photograph was everywhere at one time, and photographers simply hounded her for decades."

"What a pretty, sanitized version we heard of her past this evening," said George. "What was it she said about having made a famous marriage? Well put, that. I thought I'd seen her some-where. But it was more recent."

"No doubt," said Ruthven. "Every so often the papers dig up the story for a rehash of the mystery."

"They never caught who did it, did they?" said Sarah.

"They never tried," said Ruthven. "They already *had* who did it. But money talks, then as now. There was even some question of evidence being removed, tampered with, although it was prob-ably a matter of incompetence more than outright corruption. By the time the police got through trampling all over the clues and losing the evidence, there was no question of ever bringing her to trial. A complete farce. The old man had no family to speak of so there wasn't even much of a stink raised from that end. And there was, indeed, a certain camp among the reading public that tended to plump for her innocence. Even then, it was felt a woman couldn't have committed any crime that didn't involve a little gen-teel poisoning."

"He was bludgeoned to death, wasn't he?" said Sarah.

"Something along those lines, I believe. I'll have the details by tomorrow."

"It is hard to picture her doing that, having met her," said Sarah doubtfully.

"No doubt the police felt the same. Lizzie Borden, always the model for this kind of thing, was a big bear of a girl, and people had trouble believing her capable of wielding an axe to such stun-ning effect."

He clapped his hands on his knees and rose to leave.

"So you see, it's a thornier problem than we thought. I would suggest we all sleep on what to do about it."

"We have to tell him," said Sarah. "Warn him."

"Don't be daft," said Albert. "He must know. In fact, knowing him, it's part of the attraction."

Sarah frowned, doubtful.

'Marrying a known killer?" George considered. "I suppose I wouldn't put it past him, but still, it does rather give one the creeps. I can't say I like the idea of sleeping under the same roof with her, myself, come to that."

Ruthven soon left, and after some further discussion of the "Can you believe this?" variety the rest wandered off to their assorted rooms.

Sarah took the precaution of locking the door behind them, before preparing for bed and settling down to a disturbed rest. Her last waking thought before drifting off was, "I don't care what Ruthven says. I must warn him."

———

Breakfast at Waverley Court was always an informal affair. Guests staggered down from upstairs as hunger moved them, to where vast quantities of food sat keeping warm under covered dishes on the sideboard. Sir Adrian always had a tray in his dressing room while he savored his latest fan mail, too voluminous to answer personally, even had he been inclined to do so. It was one of Jeffrey's duties to keep from him any letter containing even a hint of criticism of him or his books, and to forge his signature on a standard form reply to his admirers.

Sarah was first down, looking decidedly the worse for wear, clumping into the room in giant Birkenstocks that made her look as if she had strapped cow pats to the soles of her feet. Today she was draped in a brown serge fabric gathered at the waist with something resembling hemp rope, making comparison with a sack of potatoes unavoidable.

She stumped over to the sideboard and investigated the contents of the warming pans—eggs, bacon, ham, kidneys, haddock, and cold pheasant—then began heaping large selections from each onto a Wedgwood plate. Paulo, who was supposed to be standing by at breakfast time, was nowhere to be seen. Sarah helped herself to a coffee that was mostly cream and castor sugar.

Her resolve during the night had flickered like a dying candle, becoming fully extinguished as the first streaks of dawn appeared. What had decided her, for the moment, against going to her father about Violet was the same fear that keeps honest citizens from going to the police: the fear of not being believed; the fear of being held up to ridicule and scorn. There was also, of course, the risk of retaliation from the offended party. In her muddled way, however, Sarah realized she feared retaliation from her father, not from Violet. It would be too much like telling the emperor he was wearing no clothes.

"Another early riser, I see."

She turned from the sideboard to see Natasha, pencil-slim in black, gliding in on a waft of what Sarah imagined was insanely expensive French perfume.

"Yes, good morning. I find I never sleep well when I'm at home. When I'm away from home, I should say."

"I have rather the same problem. A hotel bed, no matter how comfortable, is never the same as having all one's familiar things around, especially when one awakens in the night. Once in Paris

I nearly plunged off the balcony, thinking I was on my way to the loo."

"Have you stayed at many hotels?" asked Sarah, anxious for something to say, then flushed, realizing how peculiar that might sound.

Natasha laughed. "Only about a hundred nights a year. My job, you know."

At Sarah's even more stricken look, Natasha hastily added, "I'm an interior architect. I design art galleries, mostly. The occasional boutique or restaurant. I—well, my firm, actually—we gut and renovate old buildings, smarten up new ones. That's how George and I met."

"At a boutique?"

Natasha blinked. Was Sarah really as dim as she seemed? Kindly, she smiled. "No, we met at his art gallery."

"Oh! Yes, I'd rather forgotten he'd gone in for all that. He and I don't really stay in touch. And he's had several careers, you know. George always had a bit of trouble … settling."

With this she herself settled at the table and began digging into breakfast, wondering whether or not she should expand on this theme of George's restlessness on such short acquaintance with Natasha. Really, Natasha seemed like quite a nice girl. Most of George's girlfriends that she had met had been nice, although perhaps a bit more brittle upon leaving the relationship than upon entering it. Was she morally obligated to warn Natasha? The thought brought her back to her other moral dilemma of the day regarding her father and Violet. The dual quandary made her head start to pound.

"Really?" Natasha carried her toast and coffee to a seat across the table. Sarah watched as she dabbed the thinnest possible shaving of butter on the toast, then proceeded to cut the slice into dainty quarters. Her hair as it fell on either side of her face in the winter's light was as black as a bruise, the slight upward tilt to her eyes even more pronounced as she bent her head to her task. Sarah wondered if there weren't Russian blood somewhere in her background.

In the best tradition of the Girl Guides, Sarah believed that a hearty breakfast was the preventative for any ill ranging from dropsy to bubonic plague. Natasha couldn't live another fortnight on the little she appeared to eat.

"Well, it looks as if he may have found his niche at last, then," Natasha was saying. "The gallery is getting quite a reputation already, and in London, that is definitely saying something. George has a sharp eye for—" she stopped. Sarah was almost certain she had been going to say "the main chance." Instead she continued, "—the up-and-coming young artist."

"You amaze me. He never showed much interest as a child. My father has quite a good collection of paintings here, you know. Ancestors. Also horses and dogs from the tally ho! period. Quite rare, I understand. You should look around, if you're interested in art."

Natasha, who had already done a mental inventory of the contents of the house on public display, smiled. Sir Adrian might be a canny old fox when it came to his mystery plots, but someone had certainly sold him a bill of goods on some of the furniture and paintings.

She glanced at the crackle-glazed horror hanging over the fireplace to her left. Surely she'd seen the original somewhere in

Wiltshire? But there, the Duke or whatever he was hadn't appeared quite so wall-eyed and deranged, whatever his famed eccentricities, as he appeared in this appalling copy.

The George II sideboard at least was real, standing on leaf-carved cabriole legs ending in big hairy paw feet—a style she fervently hoped would never come back in favor. But as for ancestors: my grandmother's arse, she thought. And the hunting scenes you couldn't sell to a purblind rich American.

"Perhaps later," she said. She hesitated, clearly wondering whether to broach a delicate subject. "I hope it's all right, my being here."

"Being here?"

"On such a family occasion. I feel rather like I'm intruding, but George insisted."

"George never could stand to be alone for a single minute." Then, fearing she had been rude, she hastily added, "You're no more a stranger here than the rest of us. And it helps, somehow, having...an outsider. If you know what I mean. Not that you're really—I mean..."

"I do," said Natasha hastily, to stem the flow of unneeded apology. There was something rather touching, and at the same time alarming, about Sarah's goucheness. A painful honesty that kept the truth just gushing out of her mouth. "I am completely an outsider, having known George—or Scorpio, as he prefers to be called these days; it's the name of the gallery—such a short time. I gather there was quite a family powwow last night. He was livid when he came back to our room. Also worried, I'd say. Not the kind of fine emotion I'd often connect with George."

Sarah heaved something that might have been a sigh of relief. Natasha seemed already to have taken George's measure fairly well, relieving Sarah of the responsibility for any dire warnings.

"The marriage, you see. It changes things."

"I don't see why."

"Don't you?"

Sarah had allowed a touch of asperity to creep into her voice unbidden. She chased a bit of sausage around her plate, then rose for a refill. While in London she tried to adhere to the dietary prescriptions of her books, here at "home" no hold appeared to be barred. She felt ravenous; hummus was all very well, but there was nothing like a good fry-up on occasion, with eggs swimming in a fine film of bacon grease.

Turning back to Natasha, she said, "It's the will, of course. They're wondering what he'll do, now that there's another potential heir in the picture. Heiress, in this case."

"If you don't mind my mentioning it, it appears to me there's more than enough to go around," said Natasha. "You can't enter a bookstore anywhere in this country without tripping over a display of Miss Rampling, peering accusingly at one through her pince-nez."

Which, on the face of it, was true, Sarah reflected. Or would be true, if her father weren't the kind of man he was: more than capable of cutting any or all of his children out as it suited him, to the full extent allowed by law. Oh, there would probably be something left to all of them, an amount nicely judged to prevent any of them from going to the bother and expense of a lawsuit. The sad thing, to Sarah, was that Albert was the only one of them who really needed the money. George just *wanted* the money, almost as if he needed the reassurance his father still remembered who he was. Ruthven wanted the money, also, but because he felt it was his by right, as the eldest.

As for Sarah, she was already making more money than she could spend: the kind of wealth in royalties and advances guaranteed to bring on the unwanted scrutiny of the Inland Revenue. Most of it just sat in her bank account, earning more interest for her to pay more taxes on. People who claim to have simple tastes are generally the first to run out and buy a Jaguar as soon as they win the pools. Sarah really did have simple tastes, and no particular interest in cars. (She had accidentally run over a squirrel using her provisional license; it was years before the guilt receded enough to allow her to attempt driving again.)

She returned to the table with her refilled plate.

"I don't think it's the money—not entirely, or not in all cases. It's that my father has made money into a substitute for love, if you want to know what I think. And the boys have bought into that. After years of neglect they're all looking for some sign that he acknowledged their existence, even if it did come too late, after he was dead."

Love. She blurted out the word in her earnest, wide-eyed way. Natasha felt she was speaking for herself rather than her brothers. Certainly, Natasha believed George when he said his father could drop dead any time, for all George cared, whether or not there were money involved.

Natasha studied Sarah thoughtfully, mentally rearranging her first impressions. Not as stupid as she appeared. Naïve and lacking in confidence, certainly, but not stupid.

"Of course, it doesn't help Ruthven that he has Lilith whispering in his ear all the time," Sarah was saying, warming to her subject. She found she was quite enjoying this all-girl's chit-chat. She had so few acquaintances, male or female.

"Lilith? Surely you mean?—"

"Oh, sorry." Sarah erupted in schoolgirlish giggles. "It just slipped out. That's my private name for Lillian. Lilith means "Night Demon" in Arabic. Much more fitting, don't you think?"

"Do you think so?"

The voice from the doorway held all the warmth of the Queen's in some of her later private conversations with the then-Princess Fergie.

"Lillian! I didn't—"

"Yes, the old demon seed herself." With the poise born of complete indifference to such as Sarah, Lillian swept into the room. She began to select from among the several newspapers arranged on a tray near the sideboard before helping herself to coffee.

"Night Demon," corrected Sarah automatically. "I'm sorry, Lillian, it's just something I came across in my research. Lilith was supposed to be Adam's first wife. Somehow, the name just stuck in my mind. I didn't mean …" She trailed off slowly, her unnatural honesty preventing her from finishing the sentence.

"Lillian means 'lily flower' in Latin, did you know that?" she finished brightly.

"What a bore this must be for you, Natasha," said Lillian. "You'll find our little family has its ups and downs, just like all families, although most of my acquaintance are far too well-bred to air their differences beyond the confines of the family group." Complacently, she shook out her copy of *The Guardian* and, flipping noisily to its version of the society pages, began reading.

Natasha admired the woman's self-possession. It was an excellent impersonation of aristocracy putting the revolting masses back in their place. Natasha, who had done her own research, found the act nearly pitch-perfect—for an act it was, she was certain. She wouldn't have put it past Lillian to have arrived at breakfast dressed in jodhpurs, cracking a whip against her highly polished boots, despite the absence of a stables for forty miles or more. Instead, Lillian had opted for the simple wool sheath bedecked with a king's ransom in pearls at neck and wrist: the uniform of the bored society matron. But not, Natasha recognized, quite the done thing for breakfast in a country manor house.

"Well," said Natasha, dabbing at invisible crumbs before putting her napkin by her plate, "I'm off. Time to mobilize George. We're going into Cambridge today to have a look in the Fitzwilliam, perhaps visit some of his old haunts."

Ignoring the pleading look in Sarah's eyes that said more plainly than words, *Don't leave me here alone with her!*, Natasha took herself off. High time Sarah learned to stand up to bullies and snobs, she told herself.

Lillian aimed an insincere but well-bred "Enjoy your day" at Natasha's back. Natasha turned at the door, smiling, and said, "Oh, never fear." Lillian's newspaper shielded her from the chilly smile, which was just as well. With a kindly wink at Sarah, Natasha was gone.

SECOND SEATING

"I CAN SEE WHAT he sees in Mrs. Romano," Albert was complaining, "but why the deuce does he put up with Paulo?"

"Deuce?" drawled Ruthven, from behind his paper. "Do you know, I can't recall the last time I heard anyone use that expression."

"Occupational hazard," muttered Albert. "Too many drawing-room dramas."

"I thought you were excellent in *Noises Off*," said Lillian.

Albert looked at her. For one thing, he had never actually been in *Noises Off*.

"Thank you," he said at last. Lillian, he decided, was probably always so fashionably late to the theatre it was doubtful she'd ever actually seen a play.

"To answer your question: 'Package Deal,'" Ruthven went on, turning a page of the *Times*. "The price for having a dream of a cook who happens to make the old sod think he's starring in a remake of *La Dolce Vita* seems to be that he gets saddled with her son, a butler/chauffeur who drives like a maniac, when he can be induced to work at all."

"I rang for coffee ten minutes ago. Where in hell is he? My head is splitting."

Indeed, all the excesses of the day before were written large on Albert's prematurely aged face. Ruthven began calculating, not for the first time, when Albert might drink himself out of the running in the contest for heir apparent. The old man was in bad shape but his youngest son was in demonstrably worse.

Complacently, Ruthven surveyed his own solid paunch, giving his biceps an unobtrusive flex. Sound mind in a healthy body, that's the ticket, he thought. If Albert drank himself to death, Sarah ate herself to death, and George orgied himself to death, it would nicely clear the field without his having to lift a finger. The appearance of Violet had put something of a damper on this happy prospect, but that, he was convinced, was a temporary inconvenience, soon disposed of. The flood of faxes into his laptop, starting at nine this morning, had only buoyed his hopes in that regard.

At the thought, he turned to his wife.

"Lillian, my dear. Would you be so kind as to see if you can persuade Mrs. Romano to replenish the sideboard, if her worthless son cannot be found?"

"I?" The raising of one of Lillian's painted eyebrows would have quelled a lesser man, but Ruthven was this morning determined to have a private word with his brother before Albert's habitual cycle of drunkenness began for the day. He estimated that he had less than an hour before Albert began his "hair of the dog" regimen.

With the perception born of long years in marital harness, Lillian read the significance of Ruthven's nod in Albert's direction.

Stifling further protest, she set off in search of the kitchen, rather like Magellan seeking a new passage to the Spice Islands.

She could be gone for days, thought Ruthven, not without a frisson of pleasure. He took the precaution of shutting the double-paneled doors after her. He knew Sir Adrian always took a breakfast tray in bed, but God knew if his inamorata was with him or if she might appear downstairs at any moment. He'd seen George leave with the delectable Natasha. Sarah, Lillian had told him, had rushed from the room without explanation shortly before his own appearance.

Albert, meanwhile, had laid his head on the table, displaying to full effect the tonsure that had started to form in the center of his hair. He was emitting periodic mewling noises.

"Buck up, old sport. This is important," said Ruthven.

This was greeted with a weak moan. "Not so loud," Albert whispered.

"Here, drink mine, I haven't touched it yet. Come on, man, pull yourself together."

Albert accepted the proffered coffee with trembling hands. He doubted it would help his heaving stomach but his pounding head was winning, for the moment, the pain war.

"My office came through this morning with everything you could want to know, and more, about the Winthrop murder. Here—" he removed several folded sheets from his inner jacket pocket—"is just a sample. It's Violet, all right. And the story's even more sensational than I recalled."

Albert took the pages and unfolded them, fumbling for his glasses. The fax machine had rendered the small newsprint almost unintelligible. The top sheet was dominated by a photo of a woman sitting sidesaddle in full hunting regalia atop a horse awash in a sea of beagles. Even allowing for the bleary quality of the reproduction, he could see she was strikingly beautiful, with the widely spaced eyes, high cheekbones, and chiseled jawline bestowed by the gods on only a blessed few. She even seemed to have a tiny cleft in her chin, which was rather gilding the lily, thought Albert. The only thing marring the impression of exquisite porcelain fragility were the hands holding the reins, Violet's hands—not as pronouncedly veined and bony as they were today but still unmistakably large and out of proportion.

"How old was she then?" asked Albert.

"Early twenties. Twenty-one, I think one of the papers said."

"'Was this the face that launch'd a thousand ships?'" The headline over the photo was at complete odds with this image of heavenly near-perfection. The headline asked, simply, "Lady Murderess?"

Albert squinted at the page, holding it up to the light from the mullioned windows behind him, able to make out only the words in bold in the caption and the dateline: November 15—Edinburgh. The caption read, unhelpfully: "Lady Winthrop last fall, on Dundee Prince near the Winthrop estate in Gloucester."

"There's more, loads more," Ruthven was saying, "photos and the lot, but on the next page is a summary from shortly after the inquest adjourned."

"I can't make it out," said Albert.

"Here." Ruthven took back the pages. Adjusting his glasses lower on his nose, he scanned the type until he found the section he wanted.

"It begins by announcing the verdict of 'Murder by person or persons unknown,' and the adjournment of the hearing. There never was an official finding beyond that, apparently. The coroner concluded that the police were stumped—reading between the lines, you understand. There was the usual jargon about pursuing various lines of enquiry—and pretty much it was left at that. Lady Winthrop herself was never called to give testimony; she got her physician to stipulate she was prostrate with grief. All nonsense, of course. If she'd been a charwoman they'd have brought her to the inquest on a litter. I haven't been in Fleet Street all these years without knowing how these things go."

Albert, now holding his temples, made a "speed-it-up" gesture with his index fingers.

"Very well," said Ruthven. "On the night of November 10, the Winthrop household—it was Sir Winthrop's estate near Edinburgh—was awakened by a crash of glass and furniture from the direction of the old man's study. This according to the testimony of one Mrs. Grant—Agnes, the head cook. Much of what she actually said was summarized—the reporter, I gather, having trouble rendering her brogue into received English. But the substance was that she herself was already awake, having been unable to sleep and having taken herself to the kitchen for a cuppa, probably laced with Scotch, again reading between the lines. But she testified plainly enough that she heard scuffling sounds and shouts. When asked if she went to investigate she replied"—and here Ruthven adopted a passable Scottish accent—"'It ware jest th' ghostie so no a reason fare me to stir.' This produced some laughter, according to the reporter, at which Agnes took umbrage. 'I seen him meself many a time, I have. Headless, he is. 'Tis the fairst Laird Botwin, we think, him as were kilt by the Catlicks. He main us no harm so I let him gae on aboot his business, like mare folk should do.'"

"Anyway," Ruthven went on in a normal voice, "more in this vein, but then she testified she heard a loud crash, followed by the sound of someone running."

"'He ne'er doon that afore,' she said. 'It scairt me, like, so I thought I'd best go have a look, me in me robe an' all, but I dinna like the soond of it.'"

"The ghost didn't scare her but a ghost acting out of character did. Good for Agnes," said Albert.

"Wait for it. Apparently the coroner also was caught up in the ghost-as-suspect possibility." Ruthven read again from the newspaper account: "Asked what it was the ghost had never done before—caused a loud crash or run away—Mrs. Grant replied, 'A ghost dunna run in high heels.'"

"A headless Lord in high heels," mused Albert. "Not impossible, granted a public school education. Still, I don't see where Lady Winthrop comes into it. Unless she was the only woman in the house who owned a pair of heels. Not likely."

"Agnes gets to that. All the women visiting the house—it was one of those 'play cards and shoot whatever moves' weekend parties such as Violet described yesterday—were lodged in the West wing that night. Agnes Grant was adamant she heard the high heels clicking their way toward the family quarters on the East side of the house, where Lord and Lady Winthrop resided in solitary splendor. Agnes gives it as her further opinion that only Violet of all those present would caper about at three AM in high-heeled slippers, 'her bein' a real clues-hearse as she is,' but the coroner ignored that, of course, and rightly so."

"What makes me think Agnes would soon find herself out of a job?" said Albert.

"She gave her opinion on that, as well: 'I'll not stay another night 'neath that roof to be mairdered in me sleep, even by her ladyship, who has always traited me fair.'"

"So much for the fealty—not to say the discretion—of old retainers. Well, if that's all the coroner had to go on I'm not surprised at the hazy verdict."

"Oh, there was more. What is evident from the testimony, wrenched as it had to be from the guests, who had clearly decided it was an occasion for all titled hands to the pumps, was that Lord and Lady Winthrop were not getting along."

"Well, how very rare an occurrence amongst married couples. I'm surprised they didn't clap her in irons on the spot."

"Wait for it, will you? Agnes wasn't the most sensational witness, not by a long shot. That came later, a witness who testified that Violet Winthrop was with him—*him*—at the time Agnes heard the crashing and banging coming from the study."

Albert perked up at this. At least, his eyebrows did, until he realized even that small movement made his head throb. Carefully, he narrowed his eyes again against the light, and said:

"At three AM?"

"Precisely. In high heels or no high heels, she was with him, so he said. Precisely what the gentleman was doing with Violet is not spelled out, but the implications were—and are—obvious. That must have sent the press in a virtual stampede out of the room to telephone in their stories. It's the classic tale—older man, younger woman. All anyone had to do was fill in the blanks. Winthrop was"—and here Ruthven flipped back through the pages—"about forty years her senior."

"Hmm," said Albert. "A fact she failed to mention on first meeting, although one would hardly expect her to. Who was this Lothario of the wee hours, anyway?"

"One John Davies, who, having provided Violet with an alibi, seems promptly and handily to have disappeared without a trace. He may be long dead by now, of course, but I have my men on it. If he's around, they'll find him."

"You sound like the head of Scotland Yard, with all the resources of Interpol at your fingertips."

"Not too far from the truth," said Ruthven complacently. "As I say, they'll find him if he's out there. Doesn't help, of course, his having a common name like Davies. But if not him, someone else staying at the house that weekend, whose tongue may have been loosened by the passage of time."

He set aside his glasses and folded his hands on top of the pile of faxed clippings in a "getting down to business" manner.

Uh oh, thought Albert.

"Now the question is, what do we do with this information?" asked Ruthven.

"Surely you mean, what do *you* do? I haven't a clue."

"Really? I should think you'd have several."

"Go to Father with these clippings, you mean? Perhaps shove them under the door of his study and then scarper like hell? Do you seriously think that wily fat fox is unaware of all this—hasn't, perhaps, done his own digging, himself? You forget the man's stock in trade is murder—fictionalized, with preposterous plots and methods and motives, granted, but murder, just the same. He probably has a rehashing of the case in one of those collections of unsolved crimes he has sitting on his bookshelves. We agreed, I thought, that part of the attraction he feels toward Violet may in fact be her bullet-riddled past."

"She bludgeoned her elderly husband to death; she didn't shoot him."

"According to the coroner, she did neither. Also, according to her lover."

"If he was telling the truth. You're forgetting the times in which this happened: the mid-fifties. This wasn't a case of *White Mischief* in the peat bogs, you know. It wasn't even Brits misbehaving on holiday in Majorca. Casual affairs among the upper crust weren't quite as winked at—even expected or encouraged—as they might have been even fifteen years earlier. They aren't entirely winked at today. This was the same era in which Princess Margaret was forced to end her relationship with Townsend because he was divorced, for heaven's sake. In other words, one wouldn't cheerfully own up to an affair while under oath unless the alternative were much worse. And the far worse alternative might have been *not* to produce an alibi for Violet—even a phony one."

"You mean that a real gentleman of the Empire would have lied under oath to protect Violet with a phony alibi, while only a scoundrel would have kissed and told the truth, even to save Violet from hanging?"

His headache, he noticed now, was blessedly beginning to recede as he focused on the implications of Ruthven's tale. He thought he might just manage some toast, if he were careful.

"Something like that. Either way, she was in disgrace, especially for the times. Being a murderess was probably considered not much worse than sleeping around. The two things may have tied in a dead heat in the minds of the reading public. Certainly, had it come to a trial, a jury might not have made the distinction. Luckily for her, it never came to that. But that's where we come in."

Again, Albert raised an eyebrow at the "we" but held his tongue.

"As you say, all this may not come as news to Father, although I'd be willing to bet any version he's heard from Violet has been highly sanitized." Ruthven, recalling the look of besotted infatuation he'd seen on his father's face the day before, added, "I doubt he cares what the truth of it is. It's obvious he's mad about her."

"Yes, so I think you've mentioned before. Sickening, isn't it?" Struck by a new thought, he said: "I wonder where they met?"

"At one of his book signings, according to George. Apparently he got that information out of her last night at dinner. Love at first sight, it was, so she says."

"That I don't believe. I can see what Adrian sees in her—even given her age, she's quite lovely—but what in God's name does she want with a bad-tempered monster like Adrian?"

"Perhaps the same thing we want with him."

"Money? Surely not. To all appearances—"

"I know what you're going to say. Certainly, she looks like she's led a pampered life. Still, appearances mean nothing—as an actor, you know that better than I do. She's had plenty of time to run through her husband's fortune. Besides, his scattered family may have kicked up a fuss over the will, given the circumstances. My men—"

"Yes, I know, your men are on it."

Ignoring him, Ruthven returned to his earlier theme.

"We have to do something to stop this marriage in any event, agreed? And if it's money she's after…"

"What?" said Albert. "I should go offer her my stamp collection if she'll promise never to darken our doorway again? I have no money, you know that. At least, not the sort needed to buy someone off. I doubt I could buy off a poodle."

"Between the three of us—me, George, and Sarah—I think we could come up with a goodly sum. Goodly enough to turn the trick. That leaves you to make the actual offer."

"Me?" Albert had begun turning a table knife over and over, as if considering the best angle with which to stab Ruthven through the heart.

"Yes, you. It's only fair. If we put up the money, you—"

"I do the dirty work. And if she refuses? Is insulted? Goes running to Father in high dudgeon with the tale that his no-good sot of a son tried to buy her off? Then I'm the one neatly out of the running, even if I happen to mention who put me up to it."

Anger, whether at Ruthven's clumsy attempt to set him up as a patsy or at the stupidity of the plan itself, had a salutary cleansing effect. He rose from his chair like a member of parliament during a Q-and-A session, riding the crest of a surge of intense dislike for his brother.

"Wait, I haven't told you—"

"Told me what? Why I was chosen? Oh, I know why. Sarah hasn't the guts to do it. George can't be trusted any more than your average addict can be. You thought my own—fondness for drink—might make me malleable. Well, surprise. If you think this is such a hot idea, do your own dirty work. Or get one of your 'men' to do it for you."

"Albert, wait—"

When Albert had been four and Ruthven about six, he'd locked Albert in the cellar overnight, threatening to do worse if Albert told on him. Interestingly, none of the adults in the house had noticed Albert's absence—his mother had been long gone by then, but where, Albert wondered now, had been the nanny? The cook? Someone? But Albert eventually did tell—his father—who had only laughed. And Ruthven had kept his promise to do worse.

Whenever Albert was tempted to think in terms of cause and effect—their mother's leaving in relation to Ruthven's general shittiness—he remembered that Ruthven had always been like this. From the cradle, so far as Albert knew. The loss of their mother had perhaps just accelerated the effect, like throwing manure on a weed patch.

Now Albert slapped his napkin down on the table, disarranging the tableware and startling Paulo, who was just making his belated appearance with a second coffee urn. Albert thought it might be time for something a little stronger than coffee. A reward for having stood up to Ruthven—this time.

Albert paused on his way out only long enough to wonder how long Paulo had been standing behind the door, listening.

TOO MANY COOKS

SARAH WAS AT A loss. After getting herself out from under Lillian's wheels, she had wandered into the library (as distinct from her father's study, which she would not have dared enter at any hour). Opening off the great hall with its macabre display of weaponry, the book-lined room always had an enormous fire crackling in the fireplace, and she often had it to herself. Only Albert shared her passion for books, one reason her bond to him was stronger than it was to the others. But Sarah's magpie penchant for collecting esoteric tidbits of knowledge was something she felt she alone had inherited from Sir Adrian.

There was a second entry to the library via the smoking room, seldom used now. The layout of the house was a leftover from the days of clearly defined male and female territories: Across from the smoking room was the billiards room, where men at the turn of the nineteenth century often would repair after the ladies had gone to bed. Her father's study was just next to that all-male bastion, but playing billiards was of course forbidden while Sir Adrian worked. The stairs to what had been called the "bachelor bedrooms" ran along the other side of the study, allowing easier access to the upper floors of the house.

Sarah now stood surveying the content of the shelves. Her father's collection ranged widely among the classics, from Plato through Shakespeare, but then leapt the centuries to Fitzgerald and Hemingway, stopping somewhere in the 1950s. Few outpourings from the great minds of the last half or so of the twentieth century were in evidence, and only the Hemingway novels and Golden Age mysteries looked well-thumbed.

But Hemingway's macho style held little comfort for Sarah today, and having Violet in the house, she felt, provided enough real-life mystery. She was turning away when she heard the door behind her opening from the hall.

"Oh! I'm so sorry; I didn't mean to disturb you."

The American accent was unmistakable, sounding rough to her ears, like the blat of a car horn. But the smile was friendly, the face open and guileless.

"Not at all. I was just leaving. I can't seem to settle to anything this morning."

"Yes, I know how that can be." He came forward, hand outstretched. "It's Miss Beauclerk-Fisk, of course. I'm Jeffrey Spencer. Your father's assistant. Well, secretary, officially. Although in the States 'male secretary' is freighted with so many connotations I try to avoid the term."

She smiled. "It's Sarah. Pleased to meet you. How do you do?"

Having gotten through the conventions, she was at a loss to know what to say next. Fortunately, Jeffrey seemed anxious to talk. He sat down in one of the leather chairs by the fireplace and leaned forward on his elbows, his expression indicating he couldn't wait to hear what she had to say for herself. He so clearly wanted company, she sat down across from him.

"Sarah, then," he said. "Thank you. Wonderful name. It means 'princess,' you know."

A man after her own pedantic heart. Sarah blushed to the roots of her hair.

"In Hebrew. Yes, I know. How extraordinary of you to know that. Doesn't suit me, though."

"Oh, I don't know about that. I would have said it suited you wonderfully."

"Only in the sense that my father is rather like a king, or thinks he is. I suppose that's where it came from. I never bothered to ask him."

"No, it's just … I don't know. Perhaps it's your way of carrying yourself. 'Queenly' might be a better word."

Sarah, completely unaccustomed to flattery, was dumbfounded. Her thoughts suddenly filtered through white noise, all she could register was the transparent grayish-blue of Jeffrey's wide, candid eyes; everything else ceased to exist. She attempted to smooth back her hair, which as usual made the fringe stand on end. To her dismay, her lips emitted a little squeak of nervous laughter.

Shut up! she commanded herself. He'll think you a fool.

Lips pressed firmly together, she glared at him, eyes wide with the effort of self-control.

Jeffrey was alarmed. "I say. I'm so sorry. I didn't mean to give offense."

"No!" she croaked. He jumped, startled. *Damn!* Clearing her throat, she tried again. "I mean, what I meant to say was, erm, thank you."

After a long moment when Jeffrey, afraid to say anything more, did not speak, she mumbled again, "Thank you," wondering if the little skip in her heart was happiness or an impending seizure. She turned away in confusion, stammering:

"I should go and help Mrs. Romano. Luncheon. Or dinner. She'll—she'll need me." She jumped from her chair and scuttled crab-like out of the room, unfortunately clearing only part of the open, carved double doors leading into the library. One of them crashed loudly against the inner wall on her exit.

Jeffrey, feeling he had once again somehow stepped into a bottomless puddle of British reserve, called after her.

"I say! I am sorry. I didn't mean ..."

She didn't, couldn't, turn back to look at him.

"Damn it all," he said, under his breath.

———

"Sod it all," said George. "Parking in Cambridge always was impossible."

Natasha braced herself, neck whiplashing, as George again attempted to jackknife his car into a too-small space on St. Andrew's Street.

"Ouch! Park in the garage, for God's sake."

"What's wrong with you?"

George, as Natasha knew by now, had a high tolerance for pain—other people's pain.

"Oh, forget it. Look, where shall we meet up? And when?" While she could usually trick George into giving his plans away, he had been maddeningly close-lipped about his reasons for this trip into town.

"The Eagle. In about an hour. Maybe two."

Which meant closer to three.

"George, I really don't fancy hanging around a pub by myself."

"I'll be there when I get there. Cheer up. Who knows? You might get lucky and meet another rich bloke."

With an unpleasant laugh, he retrieved a Gucci backpack from the back seat, got out of the car, and slammed the door. A small avalanche of snow fell from the bonnet.

It took all her considerable control not to tell him to sod off. Something like prudence won out as she decided the better course of dealing with George—usually—was to ignore him. It was a long taxi ride back to Waverley Court and he was more than capable of leaving her stranded.

Not looking back, she started down Sidney Street, headed toward Market Square and the shops, preparatory to doubling back to see which way George was headed. A half-dozen awestruck undergraduates watched her silken progress. One of them wrote a highly derivative sonnet about her that night, something about women lovely in their bones.

She ignored them. She ignored traffic, with near-fatal consequences. One day, she thought, George would go too far. With the wrong person.

———

Violet was bored. Bored, bored, bored, and wondering how soon she could decently make an escape.

Redecorating Waverley Court, top to bottom, to which she had initially looked forward as the ultimate challenge, could wait, although as she looked around her sitting room now, she knew it couldn't wait forever. With a delicate shudder—purple velvet draperies with gold tassels. Really!—she returned her gaze to the *Vogue* through which she had been flapping in a desultory way for the past half hour. That was boring, too, as she already owned nearly everything pictured in the issue worth owning, thanks to Adrian.

She stood up and stretched her lithe dancer's frame. Smoothed her hair. Checked her makeup. Perfect, as always. Simple perfection. But … what, she wondered, peering closer, had happened to the girl who had set all of London on end? Where most people saw only the taut, transparent skin, Violet saw crow's feet, the nap of loosening flesh at the jaw, and lines etching the brow and upper lip, despite the best efforts of the creams advertised on every other page of her magazines.

A phrase from a poem she had once read drifted into her thoughts. Something about "thy mother's glass."

When Violet had been young and aspiring to join the Aristocracy, as she thought of it, she had read straight through an anthology of famous poetry, trying to make up for her lack of formal education. But once she had breached the portals of the upper classes and realized most of them were far stupider than she was, she had given it up, specializing instead in the small talk that greased the wheels of cocktail and weekend parties, along with copious amounts of alcohol. Not that she really drank—bad for the complexion—but she had perfected the art of carrying around the same half-full highball glass for hours, flitting from group to group, laughing maniacally at jokes she only half understood. For some reason, this had gained her a reputation for wit.

What a long time ago it all seemed now. Looking back on the path her life had taken, she could only say now that she wouldn't have changed a thing. Not really. Not even Winnie...

Perhaps a cruise...

———

Sir Adrian was stumped. He had scribbled away happily in his study for hours, rewriting the pages of the day before and adding a page or two more, but when it came time to write about the Chloe of his youth, he ran straight into a wall. It was not as though he had drained the well of his malice—far from it—but when it came to remembering Chloe as she once had been, he found only the haziest ghost could be summoned, like an out-of-focus photograph faded even more by time.

Chloe as she became, he could recall with clarity. Frequent child-bearing had inflated her, rounding her moon face like—yes, he thought: like a pink balloon. Sir Adrian laboriously scribbled the words in a margin of the page, stared at them a moment, and angrily crossed them out.

Let's see. Tap tap tap went his sausage fingers on the desk.

The young Chloe had been tiny, with slim legs tapering down into narrow, elegant feet. A gust of wind could have blown her over. That had changed, too, the straight piano legs swelling into something like those umbrella stands made from elephant feet.

But apart from balloons, pianos, and umbrella stands, Sir Adrian had made little progress in the past hour, and the writer's block remained cemented in place, impeding the normally smooth flow of vitriol onto the page.

He threw down his pen—that same special pen that had helped him so much in Paris. These were the times he most resented the aspic of writerly isolation. Maybe a talk with Mrs. Romano would help. Strangely enough, he did not think of going to see what Violet was doing. He was slightly afraid of Violet: Having captured his long-sought prize, he feared too much familiarity might breed contempt—on her part.

Sir Adrian reached for the tasseled bell pull to summon Mrs. Romano, then decided he would visit her in the kitchen instead.

Slowly, painfully, he raised himself onto elephantine legs and began his long progress to the back of the house.

———

Sarah was again at large in the rambling house, and without the book with which she had hoped to while away the hours. Having told Jeffrey she was needed in the kitchen, she felt morally obligated to be as good as her word, in keeping with her general inability to separate the white from the black lie, and her footsteps led her in the direction of Mrs. Romano's domain, where she knew she was neither needed nor, probably, welcome.

The smell of something delightful on the cooker greeted her as she walked in.

"Oh, what's this then?" she said, lifting the lid on a large saucepan.

"Sauce. For the cappelletti."

"Alpine hats? Wonderful. I've published a cookbook, you know. It's been quite well received. Perhaps I could help …"

Sarah rummaged in a drawer and produced a teaspoon. She again lifted the lid of the saucepan. Mrs. Romano, ruler of all she surveyed, watched her with growing annoyance. She had flipped through one of Sarah's books one day at W. H. Smith's in Cambridge. All lentils and dried grass and barley, from what she could tell. She wouldn't have fed such food to a donkey.

"It needs some mace," pronounced Sarah.

"Mace? *Mace*? Most definitely it does not need some mace."

"I assure you—"

"This is a traditional dish. I make it always the same way. For years. Always. The. Same. No. Mace."

"You'll see. Mace is just like nutmeg, only slightly more robust. It's actually made from the nutmeg shell. Few people realize that." Sarah was now innocently rummaging among the spices over the cooker. She found the mace jar and, turning, held it aloft, beaming, triumphant, and blissfully unaware of the gathering storm.

"And you shouldn't keep these spices right over the cooker, you know," she went on. "They get overheated. Spoils the flavor."

Mrs. Romano, ire thoroughly aroused, appeared to be the only thing in the kitchen in danger of overheating. Stepping smartly (for her) across the kitchen, she snapped shut the door of the cupboard over the cooker, nearly onto Sarah's fingers.

"If I want to use nutmeg, I use the nutmeg," Mrs. Romano said flatly. "No mace. No nutmeg. The sauce, it is perfect, just as it is." She made a grab for the mace jar in Sarah's hand, which Sarah held aloft, just out of reach.

"Give it to me," demanded Mrs. Romano.

"No!"

"*Testa di cavolo!*"

"How dare you call me a cabbage head!"

Just then, the colossal form of Sir Adrian dropped anchor in the doorway.

"Hello, hello, what's all this?"

"I'm just trying to help Mrs. Romano."

"Mrs. Romano, if she needed help from the likes of you, would not be employed here."

Stung, Sarah said, "I have written a best seller about cooking, and my publishers think the next one—"

"My books are also best sellers. That doesn't mean I'm an expert on killing people, any more than it means you're an expert at cooking. Stay out of this kitchen."

"They even want me to do a cooking show on the telly," Sarah persisted.

"Really? Then I have a title for them. *One Fat Lady.*" Deciding this was rather a good one, he laughed uproariously; then, seeing the injured look on her face—her sadness always infuriated him, especially when he was the cause—reverted to his former cold manner. "I'm not saying it again. You are to stay out of this kitchen and leave Mrs. Romano alone."

"It's my kitchen, too, isn't it?" she said.

This he didn't bother to answer. Mrs. Romano, a person quick to anger and quicker to forget, felt sorry for the girl. Woman, she corrected herself. Sarah so clearly wanted her father to admire her intellect and achievements, while these were the last things Sir Adrian cared about in a female. Like all fathers, he wanted Sarah to make a good marriage and produce basketfuls of chubby grandchildren, to Mrs. Romano's way of thinking.

Funny, how all of Sir Adrian's children had let him down in that regard. It was, in her opinion, the real reason behind all this messing about with the will, like Henry VIII fiddling with papal bulls. A grandchild, especially a male, would have put an end to all that nonsense. His posterity assured, Sir Adrian might have been a happy man.

———

Albert had found the liquor cabinet, but he had found it locked, perhaps in anticipation of his visit. Mrs. Romano, he felt, and not for the first time, took a bit more upon herself than met her official job description. But Albert knew where the cellars were, and moreover, he had long ago taken the precaution of having an extra key made.

Getting to the cellar itself posed no problem, as it opened off the main hall, with entry through a narrow door, designed for tiny medieval priests, built into the paneling under the stairs. Looking exaggeratedly to left and right like a burglar in a silent film, Albert painfully opened the creaking door, exposing the stone stairway to the bottom. Good thing, he thought, he was usually sober on his way down. Coming up was another story.

The cellar, the inspiration for which might have been *Tales from the Crypt*, was original to the house, and Sir Adrian's pride. Collected in temperature-controlled rooms and cabinets fitted snugly against the cold stone walls were vintage bottles—some, Albert reflected, worth more than his annual income in a bad year. Most years, he amended.

The small keys to the cabinets containing the most expensive bottles remained firmly in the care of Mrs. Romano. Albert suspected they nestled all day somewhere in the vicinity of her redoubtable cleavage. For all Albert knew she slept with them dangling from a chain around her neck. She did not appear to have a man in her life to object to that—odd, when he thought about it, because she exuded such an earthy appeal. Maybe giving birth to a shit like Paulo had put her off sex forever.

But for Albert's purposes, the keys to the actual cabinets didn't matter. There were plenty of good-quality spirits lying about that were not deemed worth locking up. They would do just fine. With any luck he'd be awake and sober in time for the cocktail hour.

It was a little early for whiskey, even for Albert, but he spied several cases of Guinness stout tucked against the wall. He reached up to drag a case off the top of the stack. As he did, he dislodged the case underneath, tumbling it to the floor. Bracing himself for the inevitable crash of broken glass, Albert was surprised when the box fell with a delicate *thud* on the stone tiles. Setting aside the top crate of beer, he bent down and pulled back the cardboard flaps of the fallen box.

Paper. A small stack of thin blue paper, slightly disarranged by the fall. The top page carried only a few words. A title page, laboriously printed in capital letters. Albert held it up to the light from one of the crenellated windows high in the wall.

"*A Death in Scotland*," he read aloud. "By Adrian Beauclerk-Fisk." It bore a recent date across the bottom of the page.

His latest manuscript, presumably. He flipped through the pages. Page after page of scrawl. Perhaps the light would be better in his room. Albert tucked the pages in his pockets, hoisted a case of the beer, and headed back upstairs.

HELLO MOTHER

As ALBERT CARTED AWAY his treasure, Jeffrey was writing to his mother back home.

In coming to Waverley Court, Jeffrey had found himself in an Anglophile's heaven. Having completed his B.A. in English back in the United States, he had found himself in the same position as all newly minted English majors—that is, unemployed and unemployable. He had mooned around his mother's house in Minnesota for a while—Jeffrey's father, who had emigrated from Britain, had died when Jeffrey was a toddler—implementing various of her DIY projects with decidedly mixed results. Then one day, bored and broke, he had joined the Air Force, beguiled by a recruiting poster showing hard-jawed men and women at the controls of F-15s. The Air Force had taught him Russian and transported him and his duffel bag to England, where he spent the next four years with headphones clamped to his head, translating risqué jokes swapped by Russian pilots cruising over the Baltics.

Not surprisingly, four years of this experience also left him unfit for gainful employment. But his first May week in England—one of those flawless, golden weeks only England could produce—had made him decide he must remain in the country forever—somehow. He responded to every promising advertisement in the *Times* without result until one day he saw an ad posted by the recruitment agency employed by Sir Adrian. That had led, by some miracle of good fortune, to his current position in the Beauclerk-Fisk household.

The woman at the agency had done her best to quell Jeffrey's enthusiasm for the post.

"You're the fifth one this year, you know." It was then July.

"Then I'll be the last," Jeffrey had replied, with all of the optimism and determination imbued in his blood by pioneer ancestors.

The woman, Mrs. Crumpsall—middle-aged, tired, and ready for her afternoon tea—had removed her glasses, regarding him with basset-hound eyes. She felt it must be something in the American diet—all that corn, perhaps—that made them this way. But then—Sir Adrian had flattened every British specimen she'd sent his way. Perhaps Jeffrey's unbounded, puppyish enthusiasm would see him through.

The building provided Jeffrey for his lodging predated the main house by many decades. It was a wattle-and-daub, timber-framed building that may once have housed people before being turned over to livestock in a later century. His rooms had only recently been nicely modernized into a self-contained unit over what were now the Waverley Court garages. The little flat came complete with kitchen, washing machine, and the snarl of cables required for television and Internet communication. Apart from the fact he still drove an American-model car the size of a UFO, Jeffrey had adapted admirably to his new environment.

He stared now at his laptop screen, rereading what he had written, not quite satisfied that he had conveyed in full the adventure of his new life in England:

> *Dear Mother:*
> *How are you? I am fine. I just received your letter…*

(This was not quite true, but she would blame the delay in his response on the overseas mail service, which she seemed to believe was still being conducted via whaling ship.)

> *… and was, as always, glad to hear you are feeling well…*

(This was also not quite true, as Mrs. Spencer's letters tended to be one long and tedious recitation of her various imagined ailments. Jeffrey had found that sympathizing with these ailments only made the recitations in her toilsomely penned replies longer.)

> *… You asked what kind of 'boss' Sir Adrian was. Liege Lord is more like it, with myself in the role of vassal. Let's just say Sir Adrian is quite a challenging employer. He cannot write a line without rewriting it a dozen times, which makes him cross. I must be the only living person who can decipher the resulting mess of a manuscript, which does at least offer me some form of job security. Yes, he writes everything by hand, unbelievable in the era of the PC…*

(Here Jeffrey backspaced, realizing that she probably wouldn't know what PC meant, substituting the word "computer" instead.)

... and passes along the resulting chicken scratch to me. I think sometimes I will go blind from trying to decipher what it is he means to say, but whatever he's been working on lately he's been keeping awfully close to his vest, which gives me some free time.

His family are all at Waverley Court at the moment—quite interesting for me, of course, to see them all together at last. They arrived last night.

Ruthven, Sir Adrian's eldest son, arrived first, with his wife, Lillian. She looks a bit standoffish ...

(Jeffrey didn't feel he could tell his mother Lillian looked like a prize-winning Rottweiler.)

... but Sir Adrian's daughter, Sarah, is quite a jolly girl.

(Well, Jeffrey felt she had the potential to be jolly, although rather skittish at the moment.)

There is George, who is the second son, and Albert, the youngest. Both are quite well-known in London circles. George brought a young friend with him. She's extraordinarily beautiful, perhaps in her early-to-mid thirties, sensible-looking, yet graceful as a swan.

Satisfied with what he had so far written, he resumed typing:

But the person here who is causing the most speculation is Sir Adrian's 'intended.' I wrote you about her earlier. Her appearance, at long last, has been an occasion for rampant speculation among the staff. She arrived just hours before the others, which is odd in itself—that I hadn't seen her before. I caught just a glimpse, but there is no question she is a strikingly attractive woman, for her age, slim and dark-haired...

He paused. Something had raised a flag in his mind, but he couldn't think what the matter was—what elusive thought or memory had surfaced as he tapped away unselfconsciously. It had submerged itself again so quickly he couldn't spear it now, whatever it was. Then he remembered his mother was probably the same age as the bride and backspaced diplomatically over the potentially offending phrase referring to her age.

Jeffrey paused, rereading, hoping he had failed to convey the toxic atmosphere he felt brewing within the house. Mrs. Romano had told him at length about her own trepidations. She had taken a liking to Jeffrey ever since she'd learned he'd been in the service. In her mind, Jeffrey was one with the World War II American servicemen who had marched through her native Italy, dispensing food, chewing gum, and hope.

"I never," she had told Jeffrey "saw anything like this family. I suppose Sir Adrian can marry who he wants, but ... She cannot possibly love him—do you think?"

They had sat in the kitchen late the night before over a brandy and coffee, a ritual they occasionally shared when there was gossip to go around.

He found himself wondering if there weren't a little jealousy behind her words. She and Sir Adrian had been together a long time.

"How did they meet?" he asked.

"He says in London, at a dinner party given by his publisher."

"He says?"

"You know Sir Adrian. It may or may not be true. But however they met, it is clear this is what they call a whirlpool romance."

"Whirlwind. I rather think the word you want is whirlwind."

"I think I had it right the first time."

Jeffrey laughed.

"Well, you know, Mrs. R, at his age, it's not right he should be alone."

"He's not alone. He has his work. He has people he can trust around to take care of him."

"You mean his family? Yes, of course, that's a blessing—"

"No," she said simply. "I mean me. And Paulo, of course. This family of his, it is no blessing."

Jeffrey, who had yet to speak with most of the key players in this drama, wasn't quite sure what she meant. But he trusted Mrs. Romano's instincts, and some of her anxiety had rubbed off on him as well.

"I'm sure it's not as bad as all that," he'd said.

But now, having seen them all and gained some definite first impressions, he wondered. George, he felt sure, was no prize. And he rather had the idea Albert drank.

Omitting these impressions, he was concluding his letter with a reiterated promise to return home at Easter for a visit, a promise he had only vague intentions of keeping. He liked being just where he was, more so than before. As he reached across his desk for an envelope, his eye caught a movement beyond the sheltering evergreen trees outside his window. It was Paulo, carrying a plastic bag of rubbish out to the gardening shed.

He didn't pause to wonder why Paulo would be carrying rubbish to, not from, the shed: There was a dumpster affair hidden near the kitchen wall. But he did pause to think that Paulo, despite his mother, was a man he wouldn't trust an inch.

LAST MEAL *EN FAMILLE*

DINNER THAT NIGHT WAS the kind of extravaganza at which Mrs. Romano excelled. Where one entrée would do, she offered three. Where two savories would have sufficed, she produced four.

But as Paulo cleared course after course, bringing down the plates for washing by the local girl brought in for the occasion (her name was Martha, and she seemed to suffer from adenoids), he thought only Sir Adrian might entirely be enjoying the repast.

Jeffrey, who sat in chummy silence watching Mrs. Romano and Martha work, occasionally offering a helping hand with the heavier dishes, listened to Paulo's bulletins with increasing interest. Really, it was like one of those nighttime soap operas.

Sir Adrian had emerged from his bedroom at seven PM, a cumberbund stretched like a rubber band to breaking point around his colossal perimeter. Trotting into the drawing room, he found his family already amassed, and stretched his rosebud lips into a semblance of a welcoming smile. He skipped over to Violet—it would seem in his present good mood his gout wasn't troubling him as much—and made too big a fuss of noisily kissing her cheek. Or so it seemed to Sarah, who, with Albert, warily watched the pantomime from near the fireplace.

George sat snaked across one of the Queen Anne sofas, which Natasha stood behind, both of them managing to look disheveled, but in an interesting, expensive way, like an advertisement for Ralph Lauren bed linens. Natasha wore a silk poet's blouse with long sleeves ending in ruffles at her wrists; George, a velvet coat that recalled Lord Byron about the time England was asking him never again to darken its shores.

Ruthven and Lillian stood apart, looking like the same advertisement aimed at a somewhat older demographic.

Violet, rising to the occasion, was sheathed in gray silk falling to mid-calf, flapper style, with a long string of pearls knotted at her navel. (Lillian spent part of the evening trying to tell if the pearls were real, decided that they were, and the rest of the evening calculating their retail value.) She stood alone beneath the traceried ceiling-high windows, her graceful form framed by French doors. It seemed a deliberate choice; the discreetly lighted formal garden outside provided a dramatic backdrop that drew the eye to her slender, solitary silhouette.

Only Albert and Sarah had been latish in arriving. Albert to all appearances was sober, to the surprise of his family. Albert sober was a rare event, somewhat like a comet sighting. He also appeared to be feeling rather chipper, a slight smile playing at the corners of his mouth. Both George and Ruthven eyed him with suspicion.

"Won't Jeffrey be joining us?" Sarah asked, her voice so studiedly casual it immediately raised eyebrows among the women in the group, with their special radar for love in bloom. For the occasion

Sarah wore an embroidered caftan of African origin, unaware that the design included fertility symbols of a particularly explicit and ribald nature.

Her father raked her with a wintry stare, all traces of good humor vanished.

"No. Nor will Watters nor any of the other servants. Good heaven, what an idea."

Sarah, still smarting from her earlier adventure in the kitchen, said: "I don't see why not. After all, according to the Bible we are all brothers."

"Surely that didn't include Americans," said George.

Ruthven smiled appreciatively at this witticism over the top of his sherry glass.

"Nor the French," he said. "Really, Sarah. Lighten, as they say, up. You really can be such a prat."

"I think you're just being horrid," said Sarah sulkily. "He's quite nice, actually."

George seemed to twig the situation for the first time.

"Oh, I see." He chanted the sing-song of the playground: "*Sarah fancies Jeffrey.*"

"Stop it. I feel sorry for him, that's all. Being so far from home and—"

Sir Adrian cut in: "You can all stop it. I get enough of the man during the day. All that perkiness: it's like having Meg Ryan scampering about the house." He cast eyes upward, beseeching an indifferent heaven, then glared at each of his offspring in turn. "Whatever did I do to deserve this quarrelsome family?"

"It rather begs the nature versus nurture question, doesn't—" began Albert.

"That's enough!" Sir Adrian could bellow, when he wanted to, loud enough to shatter glass. "This is a joyous family gathering and you are all, for once, going to behave yourselves. What must Violet be thinking of us?" He gave her a little hug; her narrow form seemed to disappear somewhere into the folds of the cummerbund.

"It's just that it's nearly the holidays, and he's far from home, that's all," repeated Sarah.

Now even Sir Adrian began to twig. He turned on her—or rather, maneuvered twenty degrees more in her direction, like a submarine.

"Don't even think it," he said. "No daughter of mine is going to get involved with an *American secretary*." From his tone, he might have been contemplating her elopement with a Bedouin tribesman.

For perhaps the first time in her life, real defiance welled up in Sarah. She drew herself up in what she hoped Jeffrey would think of as a queenly posture.

"You think to tell *me* with whom I may or may not get involved? Under these circumstances?" She cocked her head in Violet's direction. "Are you forgetting why we're all here?"

It was the first time any of them had referred even indirectly to the happy occasion which had brought them together. Her siblings stirred uneasily.

"At least he's not a mur—"

"Not a what?" Violet could match Sir Adrian's frosty tone, icicle for icicle, thought Lillian. *Bravo.*

Having come to the edge of the cliff, Sarah found she couldn't leap.

"Under these circumstances?" Sir Adrian repeated slowly. "Yes. Under these or any other circumstances I will tell you exactly what to do. You're my daughter and if you expect to ever see a penny from me you'll drop the whole subject right now."

"I don't want—"

Ruthven, seeing an opportunity to ingratiate himself with his father at Sarah's expense, cut in. "He's only after your money, Sarah. Don't be such an ass."

The fear that what Ruthven said might be true made her lash out. With a nod in Lillian's direction, she said:

"You should know all about that."

Albert, who had only been half-listening to the conversation up to this point, said,

"I say. That is rather rich, coming from you, Ruthven. I doubt you've ever done a deed in your life that wasn't motivated by money. Same goes for you, George. Just leave Sarah alone for once."

"Coming from me? *Me*?" said George. "As if *you* hadn't spent all your life sucking up to Father over money."

"*I?*"

Sir Adrian roared: "*I said that's enough.*"

He looked at each member of his rancorous brood in turn with steely eyed displeasure, his face contorted like a gargoyle's on a Gothic cathedral. It had the hoped-for, withering effect.

"Not another word or I'll see you all regret it."

To Violet's amazement, they all—including Natasha—exchanged quicksilver glances, as if relaying some pre-arranged signal. In unison, they clapped their mouths shut, like a perfectly orchestrated firing squad having used up its round.

Paulo, who had been lurking in the hall outside, admiring his long, dark hair in the Louis Quinze mirror while eavesdropping on the conversation, judged it a good moment to step inside and announce, in perfect imitation of the perfect servant, "Dinner is served."

Sir Adrian offered his arm to Violet and without a word began heaving his slow way in the direction of their meal.

———

"I don't know what you mean," shouted Sarah to Albert.

They sat across from one another in the *trompe l'oeil* dining salon reserved for formal occasions. Reminiscent of the wedding invitations, and probably serving as the inspiration for same, the decorative panels lining the walls featured cherubs, scantily diapered in clouds, sitting atop Roman columns, the whole in a style that somehow managed to marry the worst of Gothic and Renaissance excesses.

Paulo had by this point brought in the fish with its accompanying wine. The volume of conversation seemed to have increased exponentially with each course.

"What are you saying? You'll soon have the *real* story?"

Albert noticed for the first time that Lillian, to his right, had torn her attention away from Violet to tune into his conversation.

"We'll talk later," he shouted back. By this time, he had had more than his share of wine, although his eyelids hadn't yet started dropping to half-mast as they normally would have done by this point. Instead, he seemed animated by whatever news he was hugging to himself.

That sleepy look of his could sometimes be deceptive, Sarah knew. Albert was becoming well-known for giving entire stage performances—some of his best performances, at that—whilst completely intoxicated. Often, it wasn't until he collapsed back-stage after the final curtain call that his fellow actors realized he had been in the bag the whole time.

Somehow they got through the meal, making inconsequential replies to each other's small talk and surreptitiously watching Sir Adrian and Violet the while. She sat at the opposite head of the table from Sir Adrian—a blatant indicator of her elevated status, which Lillian, demoted to her left hand, had not failed to notice.

George, on Violet's right, pointedly refused to engage her in conversation, and, most unusually, made small talk with Sarah about her book. Never retiring on this subject, Sarah warbled forth, relieving George of the task of doing anything more than feigning interest as he shoveled in food.

When Paulo began serving the port and Stilton, Lillian quickly rose to lead the ladies away for coffee in the drawing room, pre-cisely as if she owned the place. Sir Adrian waved her back to her seat. He tapped a spoon against his glass and a hush descended. Turning to Violet, he said, "I think it's time we broke the news, don't you, my dear?"

"I think it is well past time, as I've told you previously, darling," she said.

Sir Adrian stood and, raising his glass, beamed at them in turn.

"My happy little family, once they hear the news, will under-stand all and forgive all. Isn't that right?"

In unison, they folded their hands politely, no one but George making a move to prepare to raise a glass in toast.

"You've all journeyed far to be here and to share my happiness on this day. Do not think your joy in the occasion has gone unnoticed. To have my own flesh and blood in my home to share this moment is … well, it is a happiness beyond description. Without further ado, I ask you all to drink a toast to my wife, Violet, the woman who has made me the happiest man in England."

"Father, you mean, future wife, don't you?" said Sarah.

"Trust Sarah to nail it on the head. No, my dear, I do not mean 'future.' I mean 'wife.' Violet and I were married in Scotland last week, in a small private ceremony at Gretna Green."

There was a silence in which, suddenly, no glass clinked, no spoon rattled against saucer, no foot shuffled. Even Paulo stood stock still, except for his ears, which Sarah imagined she could see flapping. They all—with the exception of Violet, who looked down at her plate—stared back at him, their mouths rounded into small circles. It was Ruthven who spoke first.

"You don't mean it," he said flatly.

"Oh, but I do. We are lawfully man and wife. Violet is your stepmother. It is what I believe Jeff would call a 'done deal.'"

"Yes, all right, fine, but—Why? Why not tell us?"

"Why not tell you before?" Sir Adrian looked at him. There was a cold glint in her father's eyes which Sarah, usually perfectly attuned, could not read. "Oh, my dear boy, I think you know perfectly well why not. You would have tried to talk me out of it. Tried to talk me out of marrying the most wonderful woman I've ever met in my life. Not that it would have done a bit of good. But I simply did not want to listen to you on this subject." The "you" was perhaps just that bit too nicely shaded to be polite.

"I did want to tell you all," said Violet, looking beseechingly around the table. "It's quite awkward, I realize—"

"And I forbade it," said Sir Adrian. "Much better this way, I said. And I was right."

Lillian, meanwhile, whispered furiously to Albert.

"It's just a stunt, I tell you. He's pulling a stunt. Like Agatha Christie, when she disappeared."

"Except that people could actually be bothered to look for Agatha."

"No, my dear, it's no stunt," said Sir Adrian, whose hearing, as Lillian unfortunately had forgotten, was excellent, particularly for the higher ranges at which Lillian excelled.

Sarah and Albert, meanwhile, were telegraphing frenetic glances across the table. Only George looked unperturbed. He's planning something of his own, thought Ruthven, who caught and accurately read the cat-in-cream expression on his brother's face.

"I say, Father," said George. "This is excellent news. Congratulations. Congratulations are due all around. Paulo—" and here he waggled his fingers as if to signal a *maitre d'*—"more champagne. For Natasha and I have news of our own."

Ignoring the frantic appeal in Natasha's eyes, he stood.

"It gives me great pleasure to announce that Natasha and I are expecting the first addition to the next generation of the Beauclerk-Fisk line. Sometime in July. A boy." He lifted his glass to his father. "A boy who shall naturally be named Adrian, in honor of his grandsire."

He looked around his audience to gauge the reaction, and was not disappointed by the pole-axed stares of his siblings. Violet seemed uncertain what to do with her expression, then, remembering perhaps that babies were supposed to be good news, she beamed a smile down the table at Sir Adrian.

"I say," George continued. "Isn't this truly the family occasion we've all so longed for? Paulo, I said to fetch some champagne. What's the matter with you, man?"

Paulo turned to Sir Adrian for direction in this unprecedented situation. There was a silence now that went deeper, if possible, than before.

But Sir Adrian, having like Violet tried on several poses, seemed finally to settle on that of avuncular squire. At least, he pulled back his lips in a fearsome smile and said,

"Well, well—well! Another wedding in the works. I must say, George, I am pleased. Well done."

It may have been the first time George had ever done anything right in his father's eyes. As he was basking in the unaccustomed glow, a voice shot coolly across the table.

"Oh, no," said Natasha. "I don't think so." She tucked her silken dark hair behind her ears, the better to hear any objections.

Sir Adrian, giving the waiting Paulo the high sign for champagne, said, "You don't think so what?"

"A wedding is not in the offing. Baby, yes. Wedding, no."

George, to whom this clearly was news, and whose thoughts had been miles from the altar in any event, flushed an ever-deepening red. He was not used to being rejected before he had even thought of proposing. He especially didn't like the public style of her rebuff. What woman in her right mind would turn down marriage with George Beauclerk-Fisk?

"Nonsense," said Sir Adrian gruffly. "A child needs a name. A quiet ceremony is in order to be sure. Perhaps right here, in the conservatory? I'll have to ask Mrs. Romano. Now, the invitations—"

"I really don't think—"

"I've told you my views. The subject is closed. Now, you could take a leaf from my book, but as Violet can tell you, Scotland doesn't have a lot to offer this time of year."

"Far too cold," agreed Violet.

"Perhaps the Round Church in Cambridge. Quite romantic, but intimate. Do you have a large family, m'dear? I do think a small—"

For his part, Albert could only seem to take in one bad piece of news at a time, and decided to tackle the bad pieces in order of appearance.

"You got us up here on a wild goose chase over this wedding of yours," he began. "Even for this family, it's a new low."

"A wild goose chase?" Sir Adrian's jowls quivered in mock, hurt outrage. "Surely your joy must be twice as much, to hear the happy event has already transpired. This way you don't have to come up with a suitable present."

Albert managed to focus his eyes into a glower. Only by firmly clenching his jaws together could he still the trembling that had set in around his features. Unfortunately, this pressure started off a tic in his right eye. Decades of his father's indifference had not made betrayal, as he saw this, any less painful.

"I gave up an important meeting for this weekend. With—" (and here he invented wildly)—"with Agnus McGee, the producer.

Just to be here for this momentous non-event. This non-wedding. At the very least you might not have wasted all our time."

"Agnus McGee? Really?"

"Yes. It's about his new play. That he wants me to be in."

"Spear-carriers being thin on the ground in the West End?" said Sir Adrian.

"Not as a spear-carrier, goddammit." His fist hit the table and a fork careened into a glass. Red wine spread slowly across the immaculate white tablecloth. Already, he hated himself, but he could not seem to stop. "I was *never* a spear-carrier."

"Agnus owes me a favor. I could put in a word." This from Ruthven.

Albert swung on him, unleashing the hounds of fury he could not quite bring himself to set loose upon his father.

"Shut. Up. I don't need any favors from *you*."

Anger pushed him further, desperately, to extremes. As he turned again to his father, he said, with elaborate insouciance:

"As it happens, Agnus wants me for the role of Clarence in his new play. A pivotal part, he says. He came to me"—and at this point, Albert stepped into role, completely forgetting he was inventing—"to my flat. Last Monday night." He nodded and set down his drink, as if having just settled a difficult point about the earth's being round. "For a meal, he came. We had an Alsatian stew he'd told me was his favorite."

"Oh!" cut in Sarah, knowing he was making it all up, and trying to shovel him out before he got in too deeply. "*Bacheofe*. Is that difficult to make?"

"Not at all. You know me, not much of a cook, but I just managed."

Lillian and Ruthven exchanged glances.

"How very odd," said Ruthven. "Lillian and I dined with Agnus Monday night." Ruthven, busy dissecting the Stilton as he punched a new hole in his brother's ego, did not even bother to look up.

"Then it must have been Tuesday night," Albert snapped.

"Besides," Ruthven went on inexorably, "isn't Agnus a vegetarian? Rather tiresome of him, I think. It took us forever to agree on a restaurant."

Sarah glanced from brother to brother in alarm, wondering if Albert's eyeballs might actually detach from his head as he wound himself into an apoplectic froth. She didn't need to look at her father to know what his expression would be.

For she could easily trace the thread of the conversation back to its source. Anyone without experience of Sir Adrian might have thought he had played a passive role in the conflict, with Ruthven the aggressor and Albert the easily aggrieved. An outsider might have been forgiven for thinking her father's look of bafflement genuine: the hapless parent, mystified by the cutthroat, murderous dislike among his children, in spite of his own best efforts as peacemaker.

How, she wondered, did Father always so easily ignite the spark that led to a full-fledged conflagration?

"You have no right to say anything to me," Albert was saying now.

"Oh, really. And you have rights?" Once again, Ruthven couldn't be bothered to look up from his meal, which only pushed Albert nearer the edge.

"As a matter of fact, I do. Yes, I do have rights, dammit to hell." But Albert, catching the plea in Sarah's eyes at that moment, with a monumental effort held his tongue.

"Don't be tedious," said Ruthven. "I was only trying to help."

"I've had enough of this—this Happy Meal," said Albert. For the second time that day, he stood and stormed with great dignity out of the room, only slightly spoiling the effect by tripping over the carpet fringe and nearly landing on his head.

Into the deadly silence that ensued Sir Adrian, having turned Cain against Abel once again, said:

"My book is going well. Quite well indeed. My publisher, that slave driver, will be very pleased. Would you like to hear a brief synopsis?"

"No." This from several voices in unison. Only Violet said, "That would be lovely, dear. I confess I am rather curious."

Only Natasha noticed when Sarah crept away from the table, missing her favorite pudding, in search of Albert.

———

She found him in the bottom of the garden, in the boxwood maze, sitting on the cold stone bench in the center. This bitterly cold night the plants wore a dusting of ice that sparkled under the moonlight like broken glass. The back of the house rose in the distance, a thin, undisturbed coat of snow resting like sifted sugar atop its crenellated towers and across its vast formal lawns. The wind that had shredded the sky earlier in the day had dropped, allowing thick, snow-laden clouds to lour overhead; a light powder fell in a steady perpendicular curtain. It all looked more than ever like the enchanted garden that had been part of their make-believe games as children.

Albert wore a heavy coat against the cold, along with padded mittens like boxer's gloves. She was surprised he'd had the presence of mind to protect himself from the weather. He clenched and unclenched his fists in the outsized gloves, whether in anger or in an attempt to keep warm, she couldn't tell. His face in the moonlight was planed in shadow and light, more like marble than flesh.

"I'll kill that shit some day," was all he said.

"Which one?"

Albert emitted a harsh laugh, shaking his head.

"You could always make me laugh, Sarah. Sometimes even intentionally. My God, I am afraid for you sometimes. The world will tear you to pieces."

"Don't worry about me, Albert. I may be tougher than you think."

He eyed her doubtfully.

"Which one, you ask? Such a wide field to choose from, isn't there? But at the moment, Ruthven. The world would be such a better place without him."

"Yes," she said. "I've often thought so myself. Him *or* George. At least, the universe would register that an irritant had been removed, somewhat like getting a cinder out of one's eye." She tapped an index finger against her upper lip meditatively, like a housewife trying to decide whether to paint or wallpaper the sitting room. Ruthven or George? George or Ruthven?

"I really didn't mean George, at the moment," said Albert.

"One of the great romances, there," said Sarah.

"George and Natasha? You must be joking. And now, baby makes three. Great God. A little niece or nephew for us all. I don't suppose Father will waste any time changing the will again, now there's a Beauclerk-Fisk dynasty in the offing."

"I actually was speaking of George's love for himself. Now, *there* is a love that will last 'til the end of time."

"Ha! Quite right. Still, Natasha seems to have got a leash on him, for the moment. At least, she seems to know how to play against his ego."

"It won't last," said Sarah sadly. She traced a heart in the snow on top of the stone bench, then roughly obliterated it. "George is too unstable. The child will only make things worse, and I think Natasha knows it. But—it's Father who is the center of the storm, as usual. Playing us off against each other, playing with us. It's so silly, this whole charade about the marriage. Why does he play these stupid games?"

Albert tore his gaze away from the house, which seemed to have held him spellbound.

"I'll kill that shit some day," he said again.

"Albert, you mustn't even think such a thing, much less say it. About any of them."

"Why not? What difference does it make?"

"I don't know. I suppose because—because people may believe you mean it."

"I do mean it."

"No! Whether you mean it or not, you mustn't say it aloud. People mustn't know, don't you see? I mean, if anything were to happen to Ruthven, or George, or Father, you'd be blamed. Don't you see the danger?"

Albert looked at her closely, at the lines of anxiety furrowing her brow. She was frightened, he could see that. But why? Did she seriously think he was going to kill someone? Or was it simply frightening to hear him vocalize her own wishes and desires?

"Sarah," he said gently. "The thought doesn't necessarily become the deed, you know. But I agree, it doesn't pay to let people into one's mind too much. Look, anything said between you and me goes no further, right? Like when we were kids?"

Sarah nodded, putting on a brave smile.

"Like when we were kids. You tried to protect me, Albert. From Ruthven and Father both, and from George. Whenever they remembered I existed, that is. All in all, I was happiest when they forgot I did exist. I haven't forgotten what you did." Her voice rose in intensity. "I've forgotten nothing." She wrapped her arms tighter against the cold. "Maybe, some day, I can repay you."

A faint alarm sounded in the farther reaches of Albert's brain.

"Sarah, exactly what is it you have in mind?"

ONE HEIR LESS

ALBERT SAT AT THE desk in his room in the small hours of the next morning, a frown of concentration distorting his handsome features. He'd slept only a few fitful hours, disturbed by a recurring dream in which he stood frozen onstage, in full costume and makeup, staring blankly at a hostile, hooting audience, lines forgotten. His fellow actors hissed at him from the wings. Suddenly he would realize he was in the wrong play altogether, but he couldn't move off the stage: Someone had nailed his shoes to the boards.

Around four o'clock he'd given up hope of getting back to sleep. Remembering the manuscript, he put on a dressing gown against the chilly room and stoked the fireplace back to life, thinking he may as well spend the long hours until breakfast attempting to find out what the old man was up to.

"'As soon none hive owl,'" he read aloud. "No, that can't be it. This is worse than Chaucer. What the devil is he trying to say? 'Nearly damaged bug loot, he went—' No, wait, it's 'Nearly deranged by lust, he went—' Went where?"

That American chap Jeffrey must be the only man alive who could read this scrawl. Albert doubted even his father could read these days what he had written, between his poor eyesight and fading health. The lines ran up and down the page like a print-out from an EKG. Albert threw down the papers in disgust, then carefully gathered them again. He had a feeling whatever they were about, they were important. And he hesitated to ask Jeffrey for help.

No, he felt altogether it was not safe to ask Jeffrey.

But this was ridiculous; he'd never be able to sort the mess out himself. And he was beginning to worry that his father would sooner or later discover the manuscript was gone. For the first time, he wondered how his father had ever managed the cellar stairs to hide it in the first place. In any event, Albert felt he'd better put it back for now where he'd found it.

Then he had an idea, slapping his knees at the thought. Maybe he could enlist the aid of—what was her name? Mrs. Pepper? Mrs. Muffin? Something like that—a former secretary who was among the droves who had quit the job as fast as their legs could carry them. One had resigned, from a safe distance, by mail. But his father had often declared regretfully, for him, that Mrs. What's-her-name had had a genius for being able to transcribe his handwriting (while never admitting he'd had anything to do with her abrupt departure).

Albert crept to his door and peeked out, knotting his silk gown more tightly about him. His room was one of four ranged along the corridor, at the end of which was a servant's staircase leading to the attic and down to the kitchen. He thought for a moment he saw the door to the staircase closing—just the merest sliver of light that disappeared before he could be sure it had been there at all. He listened, straining, but could only hear the wind in the trees outside his own window, the eaves of the old building seeming to creak in response.

It is a truism that the more one tries to move stealthily, the more noise one seems to make. Every stair tread leading down from the first floor squeaked almost musically, each tread hitting a different register. In the darkness of the landing, he had a nearly fatal collision with a statue of Aphrodite, making a grab for her marble hips just before she could plunge from her pedestal. He inched along the downstairs hall: almost there now. He felt for the handle to the cellar door and braced himself for the whine of the old hinges.

The cellar stairs were worse; after groping for the light, he made his way down with aching slowness, pausing now and again to listen for sounds from overhead. Nothing.

As he approached the stack of crates from which he'd earlier retrieved the manuscript, he experienced a sudden, inexplicable tremble of apprehension: Something about the room was just that bit askew. Something was here or something had been taken away since his earlier visit.

He turned around, searching the shadows for whatever it was that was set to pounce. Maybe Agnes and her friendly ghost were starting to get to him.

So it was that he didn't see Ruthven so much as sense that there was a shape huddled inside one of the glass-walled, walk-in cabinets. A dark round shape among the square boxes that hadn't been there before, and that had no business being there now. Albert walked closer, cautiously, straining to see. A pile of laundry. No, not unless the laundry happened to be wearing bedroom slippers.

It was Ruthven and Ruthven was as dead as Dickens' Marley. There was no doubt whatever about that. If the dark circle staining the floor around his head were not sign enough, there was also the odd angle at which his slippered feet were splayed in impossible directions.

Something splattered like dark paint across one side of the cabinet, something cascading down the glass in drying rivulets. Something that could only be blood, no matter how Albert's mind scrambled for a different explanation.

Then there were the eyes. Most of all, the dark eyes—staring, accusatory, and quite, quite devoid of light, death having dried them of tears.

Albert, who had nearly tripped over many a seemingly life-less corpse, but only on the stage, told himself that this was the real thing. Since it wasn't in the script, he had no idea what to do. Fleetingly, he wondered if he should check for a pulse, before he realized he had not the least idea how to do so correctly, and no desire whatsoever to touch … it … him. He was shaking so much, anyway, he doubted he could have felt anything but his own heart, thudding madly against his ribs.

Worse, the sight of Ruthven, the thing that used to be Ruthven, was pathetic as much as frightening. He longed to at least straighten out the legs—Ruthven looked so uncomfortable there, against the cold stone floor in his climate-controlled cage.

Albert ran, the now-forgotten manuscript still in his pocket.

ST. JUST IS DELAYED

THE 999 CALL, MADE by an incoherent Albert, came into the Cambridgeshire Constabulary minutes later, which enterprise gauged Albert as a probable nuisance drunk and reacted accordingly. Nonetheless, minutes later the Parkside Police Station dispatched one Constable Porter of Newton Coombe, a member of the Special Constabulary whose day job was pastry chef for the St. Germaine restaurant on Silver Street.

As Porter drove up to the imposing Gothic gate and saw the brass plaque announcing Waverley Court, he began to think he might be out of his depth. Wanting a break from the monotony of *petits fours*, Porter had been finding police work met the bill. Until now. There was such a thing as too much excitement. Careening up the long drive to the house, he had time to think that if some nob really had got himself killed, he, Porter, didn't want to be the first and only man on the scene.

A surly, olive-complexioned man admitted him at the front door. As Porter reluctantly entered the armored hall, gazing about him in wonder, a blonde man tumbled out of a nearby door, collapsing into his arms as he gasped, "Murder! Cellar! *Murder!*"

Albert, grabbing the constable by the lapels, nearly dragged him to the top of the cellar stairs. Porter hesitated, reluctant to go down and muck up a crime scene, and instead tried to calm Albert, who reached ever more hysterical pitches with each passing minute. Eventually wrenching himself free, Porter called for backup. A higher layer of law-and-order appeared twenty minutes later in the form of Detective Chief Inspector St. Just and Detective Sergeant Fear of the Cambridgeshire Constabulary.

"What's all this then?" the larger detective asked as he stomped in, brushing past Paulo, precisely as if he were there to break up a pub fight. A barrel-chested man with legs like tree trunks, St. Just was the same height as his subordinate but gave the appearance of being twice the size.

Constable Porter made sure Albert was safely propped against the wall before leaving him to come forward.

"Bloke says it's a murder. In the cellar, he says. Says it's his brother. That's about all I can get out of him."

"You've not gone down to look?"

"I did not want to disturb a crime scene. No, Sir."

"Let's hope the poor bugger really is dead, then."

The poor bugger really was dead, and he'd been dead awhile. St. Just thought it was little wonder the man who said he was his brother was in such sad shape. The body in the wine refrigerator or whatever it was called was a mess, the skull thoroughly crushed in. The face itself, however, was intact: In profile, it retained the aristocratic, pampered visage of what the coroner would undoubtedly describe as a well-nourished, middle-aged man. The corpse wore a satin dressing gown, the legs of striped pajamas visible beneath.

"Look at that, Sir," said Fear.

St. Just looked where Fear pointed, following the trail of splattered blood, to a dark, round, spiked object, apparently thrown into the nearest corner of the enclosed cabinet, with no attempt made at concealment. What in hell was it?

"Get forensics out here."

Fear was already punching numbers into his mobile, but finding he could get no reception through the two-foot-thick walls. He started to run back up the stairs.

"Tell Porter or whatever his name is to keep everyone out of this cellar," St. Just called after him. "Let's leave it to forensics. Then tell him to round up the rest of the inmates for a chat. Come on. I want a look around this palace."

———

The snow, while pockmarked by sleet, lay otherwise undisturbed, except for their own prints and a set of rabbit tracks leading away from the house. St. Just thought with a sigh of his long-planned ski vacation in the Pyrenees, scheduled to begin the next day.

The pair circled the manor carefully, eventually arriving back at their departure point at the front door. The wind by this time had died down, the sun making its first reluctant appearance over the treetops.

"No one's been out here, then," said St. Just.

"Looks like. Perhaps whoever it was used a snow-blower to cover up the tracks."

St. Just was never certain when his Sergeant was serious.

"Without waking the house? I think that highly unlikely."

"Maybe the rabbit did it, then," said Fear. "But it wasn't someone casually wandering by."

"It wasn't an intruder, that's for certain. The area had a light, steady snow and it stopped well before midnight. No one's been on this grass, no one except the rabbit. Ah, here's Malenfant now."

They watched as a tall man with slicked-back dark hair approached, his face wrapped to the eyes in a gaily striped college scarf of blue and orange.

"Good morning, Dr. Malenfant," said St. Just. "What do you have for us?"

"The victim was in fairly good health, until he died, that is. He'd recently had surgery, within the past few months. Judging by the scars: clogged arteries, poor circulation, your basic white-collar executive's disease. Still, no reason to think he wouldn't live forever, the poor bugger. That kind of procedure is routine these days. The weapon is interesting."

"Yes, what is that thing?"

"It's called a morning star. Medieval, of course. It's like a mace but with the enhancement of the spiked ball being attached to its handle by a length of heavy chain. The weapon was apparently taken from that ghoulish display in the hall. At a guess, someone waited in one of the many little alcoves of the cellar for the victim, then jumped out at him, and *whoosh*. Would take no strength at all, really."

"So, male or female…"

"Certainly, not a problem either way. You finding anything out here?"

"Rabbits," said Fear. "Whoever did this, it looks like they came from inside the house."

"Let's go and see which one of our rabbits looks most wide awake," said St. Just.

———

Sir Adrian looked wide awake—excited by the novelty of police in the house, if anything—when St. Just and Fear found him and his wife in the study.

St. Just thought it a handsome room, although insistently upper class in a way that rendered it not quite authentic: The real thing was often worn to the nub by centuries of use or neglect. He looked more closely now about Sir Adrian's study and thought it all had just that bit too much a whiff of the new about it, apart from the linenfold paneling, which he imagined had been there since the year aught. That beautiful piece of workmanship was interspersed with floor-to-ceiling bookshelves weighted down by reference works of all kinds—glossaries, atlases, dictionaries—as well as brightly colored hard-bound copies of Sir Adrian's books translated into what looked like several dozen languages.

Sir Adrian himself was resplendent in a ruby dressing gown tied with a gold cord and with a white cravat at the neck. His wife wore a velvet robe, but, unlike her husband, seemed thrown off balance by the rude awakening to the day. St. Just saw her stealing a glance in one of the room's mirrors and surreptitiously attempting to smooth her hair.

Sir Adrian grunted his way to his desk and picked up an old-fashioned pocket watch, staring at the time as if he couldn't believe his eyes, before turning the full force of his gaze on St. Just. Violet perched on the edge of a sofa next to the fireplace.

"I hope you're not going to drag out this interview the way Constable Stool would do," Sir Adrian said.

"I beg your pardon?"

"Constable Stool. My fictional detective. The plodding village bobby of Saint Edmund-Under-Stowe, my counterpoint to the razor-sharp Miss Rampling."

"I'm afraid I'm not familiar with your books, Sir Adrian."

Sir Adrian looked at him, displeased. What kind of idiot had the Superintendent sent out here?

"Then you are in the minority, Sir. Now, you'll need a complete inventory of what's missing, won't you?"

"I wasn't aware anything was."

"Stands to reason. Whoever broke in here and did this, they were thieves after money and goods. Ruthven was in their way."

"In the cellar, Sir?"

"The perfect spot to break into the house."

"Possibly. But there's no sign of forced entry, and no indication anyone was on the grounds last night." Nor any earthly reason for Ruthven to be in the cellar in the middle of the night, he added to himself.

"Nonsense. You simply haven't looked carefully enough. Do you have any idea who I am, man? This was no random crime. They'll be back, you see if they aren't. I shall telephone the Superintendent myself and demand that Scotland Yard be brought in."

St. Just had somehow been expecting this; he was quite used to people demanding Scotland Yard be brought in, for every case ranging from a housebreaking to a missing cat. What struck him was that Sir Adrian seemed more upset by the invasion of his property by an interloper than by the loss of his son. St. Just had had more than his share of delivering bad news to parents, and felt he had seen every possible reaction to grief. The death of a child was the only occasion he knew likely to make grown men weep openly, unashamed. Here there were only bluster and anger—another, not uncommon, reaction. But the bulbous blue eyes were dry. Surely the violent loss of one's son rated at least a token show of unbridled grief?

"It doesn't appear to be what you would call an 'outside job,' Sir Adrian," he repeated calmly.

"Nonsense. Of course it was. What else could it be?"

"There's not a trace of disturbance in the snow outside that can't be accounted for by my own men. No one broke into this house last night."

"Nonsense, he—"

Then Sir Adrian paused thoughtfully, in mid-flow, as though St. Just had just set him an interesting puzzle. Folding his pudgy fingers across the expanse of his gown, he said:

"Perhaps they formed a pact to do him in, what do you think?"

"Who?"

"The entire household, of course. That was in fact one of my more innovative plots in *12:40 from Manchester*, which came out—oh, about ten years ago."

St. Just was taken aback. Even he, who seldom read mystery novels, had heard of the plot of *Murder on the Orient Express*.

"But, Sir Adrian ... Surely Dame Agatha thought of that one first."

"Of course she did. But my book was better."

No blushing violet here, thought St. Just. And what a strange, detached way to discuss anyone's death, let alone that of a family member who happened to be a son, let alone one who so violently had been killed.

The thought of violets, however, turned him to Violet as—with any luck—a more useful source of answers to his questions.

"Now, Mrs…"

"Lady Beauclerk-Fisk. As of last week," interjected Sir Adrian.

"I see. Well, er, congratulations. How sad this unhappy event should impinge on that happy one. But Lady Beauclerk-Fisk, perhaps you can give me some background on the situation here at the house. For example: What about the staff? How many are there?"

Sir Adrian may have thought it strange he was not asked—after all, he would know better than Violet—but she spoke right up, and Sir Adrian sat beaming as she got nearly all the answers right.

"There is Mrs. Romano, her son Paulo Romano, and Watters, the gardener. What is his Christian name, Adrian?"

"I'm not sure. William, I think. We've always simply called him Watters. Been with me for yonks."

"That is the entire staff?

"Yes," answered Violet. "Mrs. Romano gets in help from the village, of course, and a professional team to take care of the grounds."

Violet looked apologetic. Possibly she was thinking of the days when grand houses could lay claim to throngs of servants scurrying about the backstairs like mice.

"Would you describe for me what went on in this house yesterday evening, and during last night?"

As she gave a somewhat edited account of last night's dinner, Violet studied him, sizing him up. He was a handsome man with a full head of thick, dark-brown hair just turning white at the temples. Cornish, judging by the name: Celtic, at any rate, judging by his broad, open face and muscular build, but he was unusually tall for someone of that stock. The slight beak of his nose might owe something to the French pirates and smugglers who had long terrorized the villagers at the farthest Western reaches of England's coastline. His hazel eyes seemed to survey the world calmly from under an overhanging thatch of untamed eyebrows, but those eyes gleamed in a way that suggested they didn't miss very much.

"And after dinner?"

"Drinks. Conversation. We had an early night, given all the excitement."

"You stayed upstairs all night, then?"

"Yes. I read for a while before ... No, wait: I'd lost a diamond earring during or after dinner. I went downstairs to look for it."

"What time was this?"

"Midnight or so. I couldn't really say."

"You saw nothing out of the ordinary?"

"Nothing."

"My men will need to interview everyone in the household. If you can provide us with a room to work in for the time being?"

"I think the—"

Sir Adrian answered for her.

"The conservatory would be best. It's not as much used in the wintertime as the rest of the house."

St. Just looked at him doubtfully.

"I imagine that will be all right, Sir. If not, we'll let you know. Sir Adrian, can you add anything? Did you hear anything, see anything out of the ordinary?"

"Not at all. But let me think about it. What luck for you, eh? Having a professional detective writer, right here on the spot?"

"Yes, how lucky. I would warn you, Sir Adrian, to take extraordinary care until this case is resolved."

"I?" He appeared genuinely baffled. "Whyever should I take care?"

Because you're an appalling, mean-spirited jackass, thought St. Just, who felt he had seldom come across a more likely candidate for murder, especially murder done by his nearest and dearest. In her narration, Violet had mentioned the means by which the family had been collected here, while somehow avoiding laying the blame for the scheme in her husband's lap, where it clearly belonged.

"No reason in particular," St. Just responded blandly. "But it stands to reason: There is a murderer in this house. Every inmate of this house should be on his or her guard."

"Just like in one of my stories. Oh, I say, that's jolly good."

———

So it was that St. Just, Fear, and Lillian came to be sitting, framed by elephant's ears, drooping ferns, and African violets, in the humid confines of Sir Adrian's conservatory. It was perhaps a half hour later, by which time Mrs. Romano had shifted into high gear to cope with the unexpected situation, providing coffee and a minimum of hand-wringing, for both of which St. Just was grateful.

"You and your husband—you had children?" St. Just asked Lillian now.

He was sitting opposite her in a surprisingly comfortable chair upholstered in a zebra-striped fabric. The room as a whole might have been plucked from the sound stage for *Out of Africa*. Sergeant Fear peered out on the proceedings from beside a potted palm tree. St. Just wondered if Sir Adrian had chosen the room for its inappropriateness, but decided the old boy might be disappointed in that. The setting was so relaxed and calming, it was ideal for an interrogation of suspects. At this preliminary stage, at any rate. St. Just wondered if he should bring up the idea of themed interrogation rooms with the Chief Constable. Perhaps not.

Lillian was dressed for the day in impeccable black with a Peter Pan collar, so right for those occasions when one's husband has just been found bludgeoned to death. Altogether, St. Just was having a hard time getting a handle on her. She seemed no more put out over the situation than had been her father-in-law.

"No. No children. Most unfortunate." But she did not look particularly regretful; she might have been talking about her rose garden doing poorly that year. "Ruthven couldn't—"

Instinctively, St. Just held up a hand to forestall any too-intimate revelations.

"That's quite all right, Mrs.—"

"Oh! Oh, I didn't mean that," she said. "No, no, I mean he was quite *capable*." She gave a strained little laugh, as if to assure the Inspector that her husband was quite as good as anyone else's, thank you very much. "Good heavens. No, no, everything quite all right in that department. It's just that he couldn't abide children."

"I see. You had been married—how long?"

"Oh, twenty years or so."

St. Just reminded himself again that the reaction to the sudden death of one's nearest and dearest can take many forms. Her demeanor was just odd, since indifference was not generally one of those reactions.

"Can you think of anyone who would want to harm your husband?"

"No one." Now she began straightening what he supposed was her engagement ring, which rode high atop a plain wedding band— the diamond, the size of a small almond, had not surprisingly shifted heavily on her finger like a capsized boat. "Well everyone, I suppose, really. But no one *really*."

"Everyone?"

"Everyone who did business with him, I mean. Ruthven was a brilliant businessman. Well, everyone's heard of him—everyone who reads the financial news." She seemed to pause here to consider whether he and Sergeant Fear were the types to peruse the daily financial news, looking for stock tips. Uncertainly, she went on, "He and I sometimes appear together in the society pages, as well. *Used* to appear, I suppose I must say now." As it occurred to her these two stalwart policemen were even more unlikely to scan the Royal Doulton ads, she said, "Well, in any event, when one is enormously successful, one tends to make, well, enemies. Among the small-minded or jealous."

"Disgruntled employees? Wronged partners? Unhappy stockholders? That sort of thing?"

"Yes. Quite. In fact, I remember there was one man—oh, wait, he committed suicide, that's right." Metaphorically snapping her fingers at the memory lapse regarding this unfortunate, she went on, "But you do see what I mean. There are the weak and there are the strong. I've always felt the weak to be far the more dangerous, when aroused. Don't you agree?"

Marie Antoinette couldn't have said it better, thought St. Just.

"It's a possible theory, of course. But the fact is there is no sign of a break-in from outside. The man—or woman—who murdered"—and he used the brutal world here calculatedly, looking for a reaction, but still there was no one at home—"who murdered your husband almost certainly came from within the house."

This made her sit back in her chair, nearly upsetting her cup of coffee from its saucer. Her hand shook as she set the drink on a rattan side table.

"One of us? Here?" She looked around her, as if an axe-wielding in-law might jump out from behind the curtains at any minute. "But that's quite impossible. There's been some mistake."

"I don't think so. Now,"—and here Sergeant Fear took his cue, opening his black policeman's notebook to a fresh page, smartly snapping back the used pages with the attached black elastic—"about last night. How did you spend the evening?"

"How did I?"

"You. You and your husband. The family. Whatever you can tell me may be of help."

"Oh. Well. We had dinner together *en famille*, you know, except for this young friend George brought with him. Natasha. From outside. He brought her in from outside."

St. Just hid a smile. Apparently, having found the outsider in their midst, she was preparing to hand her over, hog-tied, to the police at the first opportunity.

"And how did this dinner go? Was it pleasant? Tense?"

"Oh, I suppose you'd say rather tense. You see, it was at the dinner Sir Adrian broke his news about his wedding."

"You had none of you known about it before?"

She shook her head. "Hard to believe, I know, but the fact of his remarriage came as a total shock to us all. We only knew when we arrived here he was engaged to be married, not actually married. He'd even sent an invitation to his former wife, Chloe. An extraordinary show of spite, even for him."

Just then, an electronic noise erupted from behind St. Just. He turned to see Fear scrambling to retrieve his mobile from his inner pocket. Incredulously, St. Just recognized the tune as the first notes of "Jingle Bells."

"Sorry, Sir." Fear blushed, punching madly at the buttons of the machine. "Emma."

With a sigh, St. Just turned back to Lillian.

"How was the news about Sir Adrian's wedding received, exactly—other than being a source of shock?"

"We were, well, surprised, Detective Chief Inspector. In his fifties, Sir Adrian had had the typical midlife crisis. Undesirable types of women friends, very young women—you know the kind of thing I mean. We had survived all of that somehow. Violet came as a surprise. Not a welcome surprise exactly, but—oh, I'm saying this so badly..."

"But it could have been worse?"

"Yes," she said, nodding gratefully. "That's it exactly, Detective Chief Inspector. It could have been far worse, I suppose."

Sergeant Fear noted that she used St. Just's full title at every opportunity. Probably a question of status; she seemed the type to like titles.

"Did your husband express any particular worries? Apart from this wedding news?"

"Not really. Except … my husband was not in excellent health, but I wouldn't call that a great worry. He'd had surgery recently for his heart, but the doctors assured him he'd live to see 100 if he took proper care. He took the warning frightfully seriously. Oat bran and vitamins. Started going to the gym again, that sort of thing. Quite tiresome, really, arranging the menus around oat bran. And now, it's all for nothing." She sighed. "Anyway, Sir Adrian came to see him in hospital. Quite nice of him, really, given that his own health is poor."

"The visit was out of character?"

She considered.

"Rather. But Ruthven is—was—his favorite. Really, Sir Adrian seemed quite agitated, until he'd talked with the doctors himself."

"I see. Well, just to prepare you: We'll have a team looking through your husband's things, and taking some of his belongings away for analysis, I would imagine. Did he happen to travel with a computer?"

She nodded, already appearing to lose interest in the conversation.

"It would be best if you made arrangements to stay in another part of the house for now. We will need you to remain nearby in case there are further questions that arise."

This didn't please her. The green eyes narrowed beneath the penciled brows.

"That's quite out of the question. I have obligations in London."

Involving menu arrangements, no doubt, thought St. Just.

"You're to go nowhere without my permission, Mrs. Beauclerk-Fisk. I hope I am making my position clear."

"Well, I don't know … and I suppose now there's the funeral to think of, too."

Either the woman was innocent or completely stupid. He found himself inclined toward the latter view.

"The remains won't be released for some time. I am requiring that you stay available to us. We are likely to have additional questions once I've had the chance to speak with the rest of the family. Good day to you."

She wasn't used to being dismissed, either.

More gently, he added, "Again, I am sorry for your loss."

He would have sworn she was going to ask, "What loss?"

Once she had carried herself off, he turned to Sergeant Fear.

"Make sure the I.T. people have a go at downloading the contents of the victim's computer, and right away. When you get back, we'll have a look at the rest of the family. By the way, what was that infernal noise just now?"

"Emma got hold of my mobile and reprogrammed the ring, Sir. I can't figure out how to change it back."

Emma was Fear's four-year-old.

"She's jealous of the new one on the way," Fear went on, again madly pushing buttons, which seemed only to stir the instrument to new musical heights. "Says she 'don't want no stinkin' sibling.'"

"Then get the I.T. department to look at it, too, for God's sake. Now, hop to it. We've got to make damn sure, Sergeant, they're not all out there trading alibis."

MY BROTHER'S KEEPER

"HE HAS NOT DIED. He is, at this moment, struggling to slip the bounds into another state of being."

Sarah, George, Albert and Natasha had all gathered by unspoken agreement in the library, where Sarah sat stoking the fire to dangerous reaches as she expounded her theories on Ruthven's whereabouts.

Paulo had been the one to bring them the news, waking them from their beds—and not without a certain satisfaction at seeing them all up and about at his own usual hour.

"I wonder if they organize redundancies in the afterlife? That would be Ruthven's idea of heaven, I imagine," said George. "Frankly, I prefer to think of him as dead and gone, Sarah. If you would mind not prattling on right now I'd be grateful."

"He hasn't yet passed; I feel that strongly," she said. "The chains that bound him to earth were too strong. He has issues."

Albert fought to suppress a smile, in spite of the appalling situation in which they found themselves. Sarah must have gleaned the "issues" word from her reading of self-help books, which always seemed to be American in origin, the British not having yet gotten around to writing *Keeping a Stiff Upper Lip on Your Inner Child*.

"Whatever," said George, patiently, for him. "Sarah, please, I beg of you. My head is throbbing."

"I know just the thing for headache," said Sarah. "You make a paste of ground cloves and almonds and then apply it to your forehead."

"Really? And you walk around all day like that, do you?" said George. "I think plain aspirin would be fine."

Albert was starting to marvel at George's self-control. Normally, that kind of remark from Sarah would have rated at least a sneer. He suddenly realized that for the first time in memory, he himself was without a hangover and not in need of aspirin. It was disconcerting, like walking from a dark room into daylight, and he wasn't sure whether he liked it.

Natasha rose.

"I'll go and fetch some for you."

They made sure she was gone before they resumed speaking.

"I suppose I should offer belated congratulations," said Albert. "She seems an extraordinary woman."

"Like you would know. What do you think happens to the will now? With Ruthven gone?"

Albert shrugged. The question didn't surprise him, considering the source. "Father will have to write another. Nothing's changed, has it, really? He'll just start to play the old shell game again, only with fewer peas."

"Except my slice of the pie just got bigger, didn't it?" said George.

"Did it? Well, if you want to pursue food metaphors, it's not as if the pie were ever evenly divided. And we still don't know what provisions he's made for Herself."

"Violet, you mean. Yes, of course. Still…"

But Albert was no more in the mood for speculation about money and inheritance than George was prepared to discuss Natasha and the impending, suspiciously convenient, birth.

"You do realize, George, don't you, that Ruthven was murdered. Here, in this house. Possibly by one of us here, in this house?"

He couldn't quite bring himself to say, "in this room," but that was certainly what had him preoccupied.

"One of us? Don't be silly. An intruder—"

"An intruder wouldn't be much of an improvement on the situation, would he? What if this intruder comes back?"

"Do you really think so, Albert?" said Sarah. "That he might come back?" She shivered, rubbing her hands before the fire. "It's awful, isn't it? Poor Ruthven. He must have been terrified."

"I refuse to feel sorry for him," said George. "When did he ever feel sorry for me?"

Albert felt the "for me" was rather typical. Ruthven had been dreadful to all of them.

Sarah might have been thinking along similar lines.

"It's not always all about you, George."

George seemed honestly baffled by this comment.

"Who else would it be about?"

Sarah sighed.

"Really, George. I must say, your self-absorption is quite … complete at times."

"Self-absorption? That's a nice way of putting it," said Albert. In a portentous voice, he said: "Send not to ask for whom the world turns: It turns for thee, George."

"And just look who's talking."

"Not now," said Sarah. "I won't be able to stand it if we all start fighting now. If ever there were a time to close ranks—"

She was interrupted by the arrival of law and order, in the person of Sergeant Fear. Having been listening outside the door in an attitude reminiscent of Paulo the night before, Fear had been trying to decide which of them sounded sufficiently strung out to be ripe for questioning. None of them sounded serene. But if Fear understood the situation correctly, this George person was now the eldest and next in line for the throne, his brother having conveniently been painted out of the picture.

One thing St. Just had drilled into him was first to ask, "Who profits?" Judging from the look of George (once he had settled on which of the two men he was—there was not much choice between the handsome blonde one and the handsome dark-blonde one), they might be able to wrap this one up by lunchtime.

Snotty little upper-class twit, was Sergeant Fear's summing up—the kind he used to revel in pulling over for speeding before he'd been elevated to the detective ranks. Not that he didn't still enjoy doing that from time to time, but he had less time in his schedule for it now. Priorities.

"Mr. George Beauclerk-Fisk," he said, with elaborate, and deceptive, politeness. "If you would be so kind, DCI St. Just of the Cambridgeshire Constabulary would like a word."

George looked as though he might like to claim a prior engagement, but could think of none. Languidly, he unfolded himself from the sofa and followed Fear out of the room.

Albert leaned over to say something to Sarah, but just then his eye caught a movement in the doorway. No sooner had Fear left his listening post than he had been replaced by a young constable, who stood fidgeting there uncertainly, trying and failing to become invisible. Clearly he had his marching orders: Keep an eye on this lot.

St. Just found George, as he slouched into the conservatory in his male-model way, no more inspiring than Sergeant Fear had done. As much as he tried to quell the natural tendency, St. Just's own experience was that fleeting first impressions—positive or negative—were often perfectly correct. While outwardly George was the image of the hip young man about town beloved of sports car manufacturers, St. Just was more strongly reminded of the lads he'd had to pull in for questioning when he first joined the force. That haunted look around the eyes meant drugs, in those cases, nearly always. Drugs in this case, also?

He motioned George to the cheetah-patterned chair opposite and quickly ran through the preliminaries—name, address, occupation. The beginning of an investigation seldom allowed time for in-depth questioning, although St. Just had a feeling George would have a lot more to contribute as the inquiry progressed. For the moment, St. Just was simply flying without instruments, using visual cues as his guide. Frequently, it was not what people told him that was of value—so often people took forever to get to the kernel of what they knew—but how they behaved during the telling. At times, he found just asking questions to which he knew the answers perfectly well to be a useful technique.

"Now, Mr. Beauclerk-Fisk: What was your relationship with your brother?"

"Quite civil," George replied evenly. "Of course, we saw little of each other, which helped."

"No sibling rivalry to speak of?"

"Not beyond the usual." George began to study his manicure with riveted interest.

"Ruthven was the eldest?"

"Yes. I was second eldest, followed by Albert and Sarah. We came along at quite regular intervals; in fact, we all have nearly the same birthday, in April. We concluded from this that the mating season for my father was every August, when my parents took their annual holiday in Torquay. They never seemed to get along the rest of the year. These were all in the line of miracle births, Inspector."

"Your parents are divorced, I take it?"

"Yes," George said flatly.

"I see. Now, about your movements last night…"

"You would have to ask Natasha. My, er, fiancée. I would have said my movements were quite spectacular—even better than usual."

It took a moment for what he was saying to sink in.

"I take it from that you claim to have been in bed. Together."

"You take it correctly. And, not asleep, either. Well, at least, not until the small hours." He smiled complacently, his pale eyes unfathomable, ice on a winter lake.

Sergeant Fear wrote down George's alibi, putting a little star by it, meaning "Check out this statement." He had developed his own five-star system over the years, much like a travel guide or a restaurant critic. One star meant: Probably True, for Sergeant Fear trusted no one completely. Five stars meant: Certainly a Lie. After some hesitation, he gave George three stars—somewhat the benefit of the doubt, for Fear, who struggled to be fair with suspects, did not like George. He hadn't cared for the comment about the mating season; the delivery had shown disrespect, in his view. Moreover, Sergeant Fear, who wore his blue collar on—well, on his neck, rather than his sleeve—could see that George was the kind of blue blood born to be Fear's natural enemy.

———

Sarah sat down in a swirl of billowing fabric, looking like an unsorted pile of hemp atop the cheetah chair. Her large eyes in her pretty, round face regarded St. Just anxiously.

"Your brother George tells me you are all quite close in age," said the detective.

"Yes. All of us are Taureans, too. My father, as well. That didn't half cause some friction among the five of us."

"I don't follow you."

"Taurus," she explained, taken aback by his ignorance. "The Bull. Stubborn, you know. Oh, our external personalities are quite different, but at basic core we are similar. Very. I, Inspector, write cookbooks. If you don't think that requires a stubborn, bulldog nature ... Just because the cake falls doesn't mean you give up. No, it's try, try again. Now, Capricorns, on the other hand—"

St. Just felt it was time to divert the astrology lecture into more useful channels.

"And your brother, Ruthven? Stubborn, would you say?"

"Ha! I would indeed. But, again, our personalities revealed themselves in different ways, shaded by our experiences." She began worrying at one of the folds of her tent-like garment as she talked. "Ruthven as the eldest was the hyper-achiever—the responsible one, if you like. Made lists, set goals, achieved them—quite, quite driven. The rest of us—George and Albert and I—well, no. Not to that degree. No."

"You say he was responsible. He looked after all of you?"

"He looked after himself."

There seemed to be no rancor behind her words. She was simply stating a fact. Quietly, Sergeant Fear gave her comment one star.

"But, who would want to kill Ruthven?" she said. Then, realizing that the answer to her question, as with Lillian, might be, "Everyone," she added, "I mean, *really* kill him?"

"Not just think about killing him, you mean?"

"I suppose that is what I do mean. He was horrid, my brother. Anyone who ever worked for him or with him, I suppose, would wish him ill. But to actually—oh, you must know what I mean! It's … it's horrible, what's happened."

St. Just nodded. As conversant as he was with murder and all the motives for murder, it was never less than horrible. Seeing her agitation, he changed his approach slightly.

"Were you surprised at George's news?"

"About the baby, you mean? I was gobsmacked, as Watters would say. We all were."

"A baby on the way is not that rare an event, in the grand scheme of things, though, is it?"

"It is if you knew George's track record. I think his longest relationship lasted three months. I doubt Natasha's been around that long, in fact. And…"

"And?"

"It's hard to put into words, but she is entirely the wrong type for George. I mean, the right type, but not the type he'd ever had the sense to become involved with before. Completely different from his usual run of girl. Not a girl, for a start, but a young woman. Bright, well-educated. A classy brunette rather than a trashy blonde. No, not at all George's usual sort."

"I see," said St. Just. "Perhaps he's just maturing, your brother."

"I doubt it."

As the point didn't seem worth debating, St. Just changed tack again. "Now, your mother left Sir Adrian when all of you were quite small, I gather."

"Yes." Her mouth closed shut like a gate on the word. No need to ask how she felt about that.

"Must have been hard on you," St. Just said mildly. "On all of you."

"I don't suppose we noticed, really. I was two."

"Did she never explain why she left?"

"You'd have to ask her yourself."

St. Just said nothing. Fear shifted restlessly, feeling the entire line of conversation was irrelevant. He never understood St. Just's patience in drawing out witnesses, although he had to admit it paid dividends more often than not.

St. Just continued to wait, apparently absorbed in watching a spider knit her web across a nearby jade plant. Sarah struck him as the anxiously polite type of woman who would rush to fill a void of silence. He hadn't long to wait.

"I understood her leaving," Sarah said then, softly. "If I'd been old enough to walk I would have been right behind her. But I didn't understand her leaving *all* of us. She never gave an explanation for that that made sense to me. Maybe you can get it out of her. I'd love to know."

St. Just imagined this was a conversation she had held inside her own head many times, for having started on it, it seemed now she couldn't resist the opportunity to run it by an audience, brought here especially for the occasion by her brother's murder.

"Ruthven was her favorite—he kept in touch with her more than the rest of us. Because he was the eldest, I suppose. I always heard that the baby of the family was supposed to be the favorite, the spoiled one. That's what all the experts say."

How old was she? Forty-two? Older? Far too old to be thinking of herself as the baby, in any event. St. Just felt irritation rising, but in the next moment, a rush of compassion, remembering the many troubled, abandoned children he'd come across in his years on the force. He didn't imagine that money filled the void, any more than reaching adulthood automatically effected a cure for that unique brand of loneliness. Part of the problem seemed to be that if at too young an age you lost the voice that taught right from wrong, danger from safety, you never learned to internalize the necessary restrictions.

"Last night—" he began.

"I went to my bedroom straight after that ghastly dinner," she said quickly. "I came down after a bit to get a book out of the library. But I heard nothing, saw nothing. All night."

"I see," said St. Just. "Did you ever wish him dead, your brother—the favorite?"

"'If wishes were horses,' Inspector?" She studied her hands. "Honestly, no. No, I don't think I ever did."

———

By bad chance or design, St. Just's interview with Natasha Wellings followed hard on that with Sarah. The contrast between the two women was painful. St. Just felt he had never seen any human being so extraordinarily flawless. Just managing to keep from staring, seeking out the flaw—there must be one, he reasoned—he began to ask about her background.

"Oh, the usual," she shrugged, pushing a shiny lock of hair back into line. "I worked as a chalet girl in Switzerland and later as a nanny. Hardly career-builders, so once I caught on to the fact I needed a real job, I returned to England and started a course in interior architecture. Turned out to be the thing I most enjoyed, much to my surprise. I met George when he was looking around for someone to redesign his gallery."

"I had no idea. Isn't the whole point of galleries that they just have walls on which to hang paintings?"

"Oh, my, you are behind the times, Inspector. No, the whole idea is to create an 'experience' for the viewer, beyond just looking at things hanging on walls. There's a science to it, as well as a lot of smoke and mirrors. You'd be amazed."

"I imagine I would. Now, you came down here this weekend with George. How did that come about?"

"I called him, just to chat. He mentioned this … situation … with his father. He seemed to feel he would need moral support. I gather

I was also brought along to prove that little Georgie was becoming a grown-up with responsibilities, at last. I was curious to meet the famous author, Sir Adrian. So naturally I said I'd come along. Rather wish I hadn't, now, of course. I say, are we going to be held here long? George and I were planning to leave Monday."

"I'd change my plans if I were you."

"Would you really?"

"Tell me a bit about what's gone on in this house since you arrived."

"Until now, nothing. A bit of argy-bargy last night at dinner—George had warned me the family was quarrelsome but I had no idea. Of course, they all had nearly as much to drink as Albert, which didn't help. I couldn't get away fast enough and went upstairs as soon as I could."

"With George?"

"He came up about an hour later."

"And you were together all night?"

"As far as I know, yes. Excepting the parts where I was asleep, of course."

"Hear or see anything unusual?"

"Not a thing. Sorry. Wait ... wait—I'd nearly forgotten. Ruthven made a telephone call. Or someone rang him. I overheard part of it, on my way toward the stairs—there's a phone in the hall there. He didn't sound happy, whoever it was."

"Did you overhear a name?"

"As a matter of fact, I did. An unusual name ... Manda. I don't recall the exact words, but it was clear he was trying to—extricate himself from something unpleasant. When he saw me walking toward him, he rang off."

"I see. We'll need you to stay around, indefinitely, of course." He held up a hand, fending off her look of dismay. "No, I can't tell you for how long. When you're free to go my sergeant or I will be in touch. Thank you in advance for your cooperation."

Natasha looked about to say something but decided against it. With a shrug, she rose and glided out. The woman seemed to move on wheels.

"Crikey," said Fear. "Whatever is a woman like that doing with a prat like George?"

"It's a mystery, Sergeant. Well, is that it—the whole lot?"

"Well bred, well spoken. One of these modern women, but less annoying than most."

"Yes, thank you, Sergeant. My impression, generally speaking, as well. Your other thoughts? For example, is she telling the truth?"

"They're all more or less telling the truth. It's what they're not saying that's important. George didn't just dislike his brother, he hated him."

"Right you are. So, who's left?"

"One more. The other son, Albert. Oh, and the secretary. Jeffrey Spencer."

"Let's first see what this Jeffrey person will or will not share with us. At least he may have a more objective view than the others."

———

Barely awake, Jeffrey appeared in the conservatory in due course, sleepy eyed and wearing the standard-issue uniform of jeans and sweatshirt.

"I see you played for the Vikings, Sir," said St. Just. He shook Jeffrey's proffered hand and then waved him to a seat.

"What? No, no, just showing my support. Paulo told me the news. Jeepers, I can't believe this has happened." His blue eyes opened wider, as if that would somehow help him process the news.

Beneath what appeared to be Jeffrey's genuine shock, St. Just felt he could detect that frisson of excitement so many people seemed to experience at being in the thick of a murder scene. Often, the one who turned out to be the killer seemed just as excited as everyone else.

Just wait until they've seen a hundred scenes of crimes, he thought wearily.

"What time was he killed?" Jeffrey was asking.

St. Just saw no reason not to answer, since they had only the vaguest time frame to go on at the moment, anyway.

"At a guess, between ten and two AM. The medical examiner is the only one who can be more specific."

"I think I can help with that. I ran into—the victim—in the library around midnight, it must have been. He said he was looking for a book."

"What book was that, sir?"

"*Crime and Punishment.* Awful coincidence, what? Then Sarah came in. We spent some time chatting. Well, a long time, actually. A long, long time. Very long."

Sergeant Fear peered at him skeptically from beneath raised eyebrows. Jeffrey had just earned several stars for his insistence on the time. Fear's experience was that the more people repeated themselves, the more doubtful it was they were repeating the

143

truth. It was a bit too obvious this bloke was trying to give Sarah an alibi.

———

"You won't have to look far for a motive. *Cherchez la femme*. Like father, like son."

Albert had to some degree composed himself by this point, although he still looked like a man emerging from a sleep-deprivation experiment. Still, St. Just could see the resemblance to his siblings, who all had that undefined, eerie likeness of brothers and sisters.

"Ruthven tended to philander, like his father, do you mean to say, Sir?"

"Dear God, yes. They once chucked Father out of Yaddo—hardly known as a monastery—years ago. He dined out on that story for ages. Ruthven was worse, if anything."

"And how did Lillian, his wife, react to this behavior?"

"She didn't care."

"Surely, Sir—"

"No need for the 'Sir' and no need for the disbelief, either. I tell you, she didn't give a tinker's damn. Lillian's attitude seemed to be, let someone else bonk him—just don't let it interfere with my shopping."

"All right. About your brother's movements before he was killed. Did you see him during the day?"

"At breakfast, yes. And at dinner."

"What did you talk about at breakfast?"

"He'd dug up the old dirt on Violet. Quite a bit of it, in fact. In brotherly fashion, he shared this news with me. I wish I had done what he wanted, now."

"And what was that?"

"He wanted me to—what is it they say in the gangster films?— grass her out? Spill the beans on her past. I refused. I doubt it would have made any difference. Oh, I don't really know if it would. But if you're looking for a killer, we are reputed to have quite a catch right here. Violet Winthrop. You must have heard of her."

St. Just barely managed to hide his shock. Fear was drawing a blank, but carefully wrote down the name.

"Yes, I've heard of Dr. Crippen, as well. Thank you. Do you know, the others didn't actually mention anything about that."

"Not surprising. They know it would antagonize the old man. Lillian especially will be wondering if she's even in the picture any more, but she won't want to scuttle her chances."

"I see. We'll certainly be following up on that train of thought. But what possible motive could Violet have to kill Ruthven?"

"Do deranged killers need a motive?"

"She struck me as anything but deranged," said St. Just mildly. "However, to answer your question, they do, without exception, have a motive, these deranged killers. It's just that it's not a motive that makes sense to normal people."

"I can understand why you would look to Ruthven's near and dear for a motive," said Albert. "But I can tell you this much: My sister is incapable of this. Absolutely. So am I. My father—I can't see him having the physical strength. And George doesn't have the gumption. You'll need to look elsewhere than the immediate family."

"Thank you, Sir. We'll certainly keep that in mind. How did you come to be the one to find the body?"

"I went down to the cellar in the small hours to get a drink."

"There must have been an easier way to get a drink in this house."

"Not without provoking comment on how much I drink in general, Inspector. Besides, I wanted a particular kind of brandy. *Bourgogne*. Father has everything you can name stashed away down there."

"I see. You saw no one there, or on your way there?"

"Not a soul. Except … I did think I saw a door closing into the servant's stairs. I can't be sure …"

They talked for some minutes more, but Albert did little more than reiterate that no one could possibly have killed Ruthven, while it was patently obvious someone had. At last, St. Just gave Albert the usual warnings of staying within easy reach, to which Albert acquiesced with surprising ease—enthusiasm, even.

"Well, Sergeant, what have we got?"

"Part of the truth, as usual."

"Yes, as usual. They're all scared, that's obvious. But of what?"

"I would venture to say, Sir, that it's a case of 'all hands to the pumps' in the current crisis. That Albert doesn't want us looking too closely at his sister as a suspect, that's for certain. He would prefer that we take a close look at Violet. Or one of these supposed mistresses of Ruthven's."

"We'll do both—all."

Sergeant Fear looked encouragingly at his superior. The sheer physicality of the man should have had witnesses quailing, so Fear had always thought. Instead, it was comforting—walking reassurance that the great British public was safe in his large, capable hands. While St. Just kept some arrows in his quiver for special occasions, overall his demeanor was genial, disarming, and entirely effective in getting witnesses to say more than they intended.

Fear had never known him to fail. Still, it seemed to him the more questions they had asked, the more the motives became blurred. And all of them, especially that actor fellow, he was sure, were keeping something back.

He was about to ask about Violet when his mobile erupted again. Maybe, thought Fear, his wife could talk Emma into reprogramming it back to the way it was. Or at least talk her into helping him find the volume control.

——

Albert had once been in a play where he carried the part of a drunken polo-playing prat who lied to the police about his involvement in a hit-and-run accident. That had not ended well for the prat, as he recalled. But in many another play, Albert's character had gotten away with all kinds of things, up to and including murder.

Albert wondered if his moral compass were being constantly reset by the last part he had played, the last movie he had seen. It was a sobering thought that made him reach for the glass of whiskey at his elbow. He sat back, looking at the faded tapestry hanging on his bedroom wall, a depiction of Cain bashing in Abel's head as a naked Adam and Eve watched, wringing their hands, from a distance. Surely they had learned to clothe themselves by the time the children came along? Albert wasn't sure if the wall-hanging were yet another example of his father's macabre sense of humor or his poor taste in decorators. Probably a bit of both. Given the circumstances, something about the portrayal struck him as prophetic. Albert looked away.

He drained his glass and thought some more about his find in the cellar—not Ruthven's body, but his father's manuscript. Instinctively, he wanted to know what was in that manuscript—the manuscript he had carefully avoided mentioning to St. Just—before he handed it over to the police and unleashed heaven-knew-what furies on himself, Sarah—on all of them, for that matter. One thing was certain: With Adrian as the author of whatever secrets it might contain, the manuscript could only be a ticking time bomb.

TO LONDON, TO LONDON

THE NEXT AFTERNOON ST. Just found himself in Chelsea, his car penned in by Mercedeses, BMWs, limousines, and other necessities of the wealthy. Why did the French call it *circulation* when nothing moved?

The house he was seeking—its address yielded by Ruthven's laptop—was tucked discreetly away in an enclave overlooking houseboats docked along the Thames. The eighteenth-century structure had at some point been converted into three flats. St. Just didn't dare estimate what they cost their owners; he would probably be off in his guess by half.

The flat of Chloe Beauclerk-Fisk, as he saw when he had shown his warrant card and been admitted by a diminutive maid with a pronounced dowager's hump and a flesh-colored hearing aid in each ear, was decorated in a spare, minimalist style with a strong Asian influence. Looking around him as he minced behind the woman leading him through the foyer, shortening his long steps to keep from running her down, St. Just felt that Chloe Beauclerk-

Fisk, Ruthven's mother, might be a devotee of—what was it called? Dung Shoe or something like that. Sung Fu? The latest craze where yuppies who had spent their lives acquiring rubbish now couldn't wait to pay someone to get rid of it.

He decided on short acquaintance with Chloe herself that overall, this minimalist décor might be a good thing, perhaps even prolonging her life, for he gained the strong impression within five minutes in her company that she was half in the bag most of the time. The lack of clutter probably helped prevent her falling on her face all day long.

Seeing him and the maid hovering at the entry to the drawing room, Chloe waved away the old woman with one hand while signaling him to enter with the other, like someone guiding a plane in for landing. A Pekinese teetered over to inspect him—one of those dogs he always felt looked like it came with batteries—and apparently finding nothing amiss, disappeared on unknown canine business.

Still without a word, she indicated that St. Just should sit in an unyielding wooden structure that resembled nothing so much as the executioner's chairs he had seen in American documentaries on the telly. The chair proved to be lower than he had calculated and he fell into it hard, like a collapsing bridge.

She herself chose to remain standing—rather, weaving, though ramrod-straight—by the fireplace. She was a stout woman, her figure sheathed in unyielding foundation garments, her bosom a shelf-like, impenetrable Latex fortress. Two round earrings the size of walnuts eclipsed the lobes of her ears. Pouches of fat padded her chin and cheeks—perhaps she was hoarding the rest of the nuts. But her face in profile as she turned to gaze out the window was flat, the nose nearly bridgeless. She wore a coral shade of lipstick, carelessly applied—a difficult color for any woman to wear, an impossible one in her case.

He looked around. There was little else in the room on which to rest the eye, excepting a large Japanese screen hung over the fireplace in place of the traditional painting. Beneath it sat a glass of what probably was vodka, and a waterless vase holding one stark, dried tree branch.

Her voice when she spoke was deep, seductive, whiskey-soaked, like Lauren Bacall doing voiceovers for cat food. It also conveyed a distinctly American accent, overlaid by a British upper-class drawl.

"What are you doing to catch my son's killer? Anything?" she asked. The words might have been belligerent; the tone conveyed only shocked anguish. Her eyes struggled to bring into focus this bearer of bad tidings in the form of an oversized plainclothes detective.

It was possibly St. Just's least-favorite question from the public, and he was not yet ready to answer.

"All that we can," he said at last, adding: "I didn't realize you were American."

"Oh, yes. Well, of course, I became a British citizen years ago."

What she actually said could best be rendered as, "became a Brishish zhitizhen," but St. Just could just about catch the spirit of what she was trying to say. Good lord, the woman was boiled as an owl, and it was just on two in the afternoon. Even allowing for the extra rations allotted for grief, he felt somehow that with Chloe, this was no rare occurrence.

She was looking about the room now, as if wondering where on earth she'd left her British passport. Like St. Just, she found little to divert her gaze, and after awhile she dropped her eyes to study the contents of the glass she was now clutching like a crystal ball. Silence hung in the room, except for the faint, annoying tinkle of some chimes on the balcony just visible through glass doors.

St. Just might not have been in the room; Chloe had retreated into some foggy area where, possibly, she mulled the problem of interest rates, global warming, or the death of her son—it was difficult to tell from her battened-down expression.

"Fucking chimes," she said, finally, looking up. "The decorator said they would keep the bad spirits away. Guess not. Poncy little creep. I keep meaning to ... Would you like a drink?"

He surprised her by nodding. She seemed to want company, but he felt it would be a delicate balancing act to keep her just sober enough to answer his questions. Maybe if he joined her he could control the pace of her consumption.

"Drinking on the job? Good for you," she said. "That's precisely why the sun never used to set on the British Empire. Don't know what could have gone wrong. I'll just ring for Augusta." She lurched toward a bell pull at the side of the mantel. St. Just, who already had spied an elaborately carved drinks cabinet in one corner, stopped her. If Augusta was the woman who had admitted him, it would amount to cruelty to make her shuffle all the way back in here.

"Don't bother. I can manage." He walked over to the cabinet, which proved to contain a large array of bottles and glasses on the shelves inside, along with a recently filled ice bucket. He poured two weak ones on the rocks, ignoring her scornful look at the ice cubes as she accepted the drink.

"Cigarette?" She indicated the lacquered case on the glass coffee table.

He retrieved two, igniting them from the matching lighter. It had been months since he'd had a cigarette, and tended only to do so when trying either to annoy or relax a suspect. If it relaxed them enough to make them cough up the truth, so much the better. Chloe, although she seemed to him unlikely as a suspect, almost certainly held background information that might be useful.

"Lady—" he began. Then he realized he didn't know what to call her. Surely Violet was Lady Beauclerk-Fisk now; there couldn't be two of them holding the title at once. He wondered how Debrett's would handle this one. He decided to err on the side of respect.

"Lady Beauclerk-Fisk," he began.

"Oh, for God's sake, call me Chloe."

That settled that.

"The correct form of address would be Chloe, Lady Beauclerk-Fisk, it you want the whole shootin' match," she added. "That other one is now Lady Beauclerk-Fisk." She flicked cigarette ash in the general direction of the tray on the coffee table. "I read somewhere that during the thirties, when divorce was all the rage, there were something like three times as many Duchesses as Dukes in the land. It must have been tremendously confusing for everyone."

"I see. Interesting. Well, Chloe, I take it this means you knew about your husband's—your former husband's—remarriage?"

"Yes. Ruthven called me that night. Thank God I'd had the sense to stay away from that wretched dinner."

"What time did he call you?"

"I don't know. Ten. Eleven. Afterwards."

St. Just imagined that time for Chloe was rather elastic, one hour warping into the other.

"What did he say, exactly?"

"Exactly? I couldn't tell you *exactly*. Just that he—Adrian—had got them all up there using this engagement ploy, but that the deed had already been done some days before in a registry office in deepest Scotland."

"Gretna Green, actually."

"Ah, yes. The Las Vegas of the United Kingdom. The whole thing is classic Adrian. I should have seen this one coming, but he always could surprise me. Seldom pleasant surprises either, I assure you."

"Did Ruthven mention his suspicions regarding Sir Adrian's new, er, wife?"

"They were hardly suspicions, Inspector. Ruthven dealt in facts. Yes, he told me what he'd dug up."

"And?"

"And what?"

"What was your reaction? His?"

"Similar reactions, Inspector. If you want the truth, we were both rather hoping she'd do a repeat performance. Serve the old bastard right."

"You don't feel there's any possibility it was, well, a genuine attachment?"

"True love, you mean? No. You'd get more affection from a goldfish than from Adrian. The whole thing—it's preposterous."

Or perhaps, so she needed to believe.

"You received an invitation to the wedding? Or the post-wedding event, as it turned out?"

"Oh, yes."

"That's a bit unusual, isn't it?"

"I don't know the etiquette of these things, inviting the ex-wife. In California, I imagine it's standard procedure."

"But here?"

"Here I imagine it's not."

He waited for her to say more—there must have been more she had to say on the subject—but whatever damage had been done to her pride she was not going to invite sympathy by sharing it with him. He found he admired her for her reticence, or was it caution? Perhaps, she just had other things on her mind now.

"You were here last night?"

"I was at the theater. That play about the white painting."

"*Art*. Yes, I've seen it as well. Quite a short play, isn't it?"

"Yes, Chief Inspector," she said, eyes suddenly in focus, the churning sadness behind them diverted by anger. "Quite a short play, leaving me plenty of time to nip up to Cambridge and kill my own son and scamper back home. I can't imagine what the motive would be, though, can you?"

No, he couldn't. But it was clear that no matter how far blootered Chloe might become, she was more than capable of quick reaction. He wondered if Albert shared, along with her capacity for drink, her capacity for sudden focus where needed.

"Tell me a bit about your other children. How did they all get along?"

He knew the answer, but was curious as to whether the mother's point of view in this case would be objective. It so seldom was.

But so far, oddly, she had evinced no curiosity as to the reactions of her children to being on the scene of the murder—or even as to their safety. Or their possible guilt.

"When Adrian wasn't busy setting them all against each other, you mean? I hardly know. You'll hear sooner or later that I left my children, for the most part, when I left that wretched marriage. But I don't myself recall a day when they all got along, even as toddlers. Constantly fighting from the day they could wave a spoon about; quite vicious they were. George probably still has a scar from when Albert brained him with a choo-choo." She sighed, tapping varnished nails against folded arms. "Where to start? I can tell you Sarah, the youngest, was the strangest of the lot. Fey. What the kids today would call a nerd, I imagine. Her school's headmistress told me once Sarah would sit in chapel every Sunday and take notes on the sermon—didn't half get on the minister's nerves. She also tends to weigh every thought until she's completely paralyzed herself into inaction. Hardly a chip off the old block, mine or Adrian's.

"Then there's Albert. Those two at least seemed to get along: he and Sarah. Both of them—all of them—jealous of Ruthven, of course. He was the favorite and no mistake. Dynamic, gifted, charming. Well, charming when he wanted something, but whatever else is the point of charm? Anyway, parents do have favorites, Chief Inspector, although they may try to hide it. Ruthven was mine."

"I see. And Albert? You say he was jealous of Ruthven?"

"Albert." Sigh. "He really does have talent, you know, but he seems to spend his life forever snatching defeat from the jaws of victory, in both his career and his private life."

156

"You've seen him on stage?"

"Yes," she said reluctantly. "I snuck into several of his plays when he was performing in London."

"Snuck in?"

"I relinquished my rights to him long ago, so, yes, I snuck in. I just wanted to see how he was doing."

St. Just, catching a glimpse of the despair in her eyes, thought: *Needed to, more like.*

"As for George—I haven't seen George in an age, so I couldn't tell you. I doubt he's up to much good."

Off his look, she said:

"You're surprised, are you? To hear a mother speak this way about her own brood? Sentimental lies from me won't help your investigation—but then again, neither will the truth. I'll tell you what: I don't think you'll ever be able to prove who did this. Because they *all* could have done it, any of them, killed my boy. That includes Adrian, that includes this Violet person, that even includes Lillian, although she must realize Ruthven's death is the end of all her wild dreams of avarice. Adrian won't leave her a cent with Ruthven gone.

"But whoever did it, that bastard Adrian was behind it; you mark my word on that. Go on, investigate all you want. But even if you do think you can prove something—if you can't bring Ruthven back, I don't much see the point."

"You speak of Sir Adrian with … dislike. Yet you had four children by him."

"Four," she repeated, wonderingly. She might never have stopped to count them before. "Yes. Hard to understand, I imagine, if you weren't of our generation. Worse if you were raised by

157

nuns, as I was. Raised by wolves would have been better. Took me years to slake off all that nonsense." She peered into her nearly empty glass—"Years," she repeated—before drinking off the last inch in one go.

By now most of her lipstick had been washed away, except for a trace around the edges of her mouth. Her lips were trembling— pale, nearly white. She looked as if a child had drawn the outline of her mouth in crayon but forgotten to color inside the lines. He remained quiet, hoping she would continue, that letting her run on would at best tell him more, at least release the pressure she was under. The jangling chimes filled the silence, diverting his attention out the balcony window; he could see storm clouds chugging steadily across a sullen sky.

"God, but that racket drives me crazy," she said.

She suddenly beelined toward the balcony. Before St. Just could reach her, he heard the sound of tearing wood, the shattering of glass. He caught up with her just in time to see the mangled chimes land in an ornamental pond in the front garden below.

Chloe stood dusting off her hands, sobbing as if her heart would break.

RUMOR MILL

St. Just had been reluctant to leave Chloe. He doubted the antiquated dog or housekeeper were much company, even though he had left her in their protective circle. They'd paused in their ministrations only long enough to glare at him (*What have you done to her?*) on his way out.

He sighed, riffling through the notes Sergeant Fear had provided him. He had Manda Croom to talk with next. She was Ruthven's girlfriend and corporate comrade-in-arms, as his e-mail account on the laptop had revealed.

St. Just was feeling the sting of urgency on this otherwise quiet Sunday—a full awareness that the clock would not stop while he interviewed suspects at leisure. It didn't help that there were so *many* suspects. Something had been unleashed in Waverley Court, and although he had left the place guarded like Buckingham Palace, his policeman's instinct told him the something was not over yet.

He navigated central London, making a deliberate pass in front of the offices of Ruthven's company, which were housed in an Orwellian structure of what appeared from a distance to be an enormous ice tray propped against a pyramid, but on approach resolved itself into an intimidating structure of reflective silver glass cut by exposed steel beams. It was on occasions such as this St. Just felt Prince Charles' anti-growth stance was possibly more than the dilettantish messing about of the underemployed. St. Just pictured himself being hoisted skyward in the outside lift that would carry him to the top floor, where Ruthven had been king of all he surveyed. Inside, St. Just imagined, would be a rat's maze of cubicles housing hundreds of people toiling in front of computer screens, to what object St. Just could only guess.

He found Manda living nearby this structure in a penthouse flat in Maida Vale, albeit in quite a different part of that community from the one in which Sarah lived. The flat was modern, in that polished-industrial-steel way St. Just particularly disliked. It looked the perfect place for alien medical experiments to be carried out on unsuspecting humanoids.

Manda herself was a surprise, not matching any of the various mental pictures sorted under the general category of "mistress" which he carried in his mind. For such, Ruthven's treasure trove of a laptop had revealed, she was, or had been.

She wore her thin hair cropped as short as a man's. On another woman it might have been youthful, pixyish; capping Manda Croom's somewhat heavy features it looked as if a large black spider clung to her head for dear life. And, why, oh why, did all these modern young women dress as if they were setting out either to sue someone or attend a funeral? Perhaps she was in mourning; as she led him into the flat he could hear an all-news radio broadcast rehashing the sensational news about the murder of the famous mystery writer's son. But she did not seem unhappy. Her face as she turned to him was composed, her manner businesslike.

She had, he saw, alert, dark-gray eyes behind steel-framed glasses that matched the furnishings. Her pronounced overbite became more pronounced when she pursed her lips with displeasure, which was often during the interview. He was reminded of a rodent listening for the approach of the neighborhood tomcat. What could Ruthven have seen in this pudding-plain woman? Simply a change from Lillian—and St. Just was willing to admit, a change from Lillian seemed perfectly justified—or something more?

But if Manda reminded him of anyone, it was Chloe, albeit a younger, slimmer version. Had not Ruthven noticed the similarities?

"I really don't see how I can help you, Inspector, and I don't have much time, anyway," she said by way of greeting. She walked over and turned off the radio, cutting off the announcer in mid-gasp. "It's quite a busy time for me. I've summoned the staff for a meeting tomorrow morning. To announce redundancies, I'm afraid."

St. Just thought she didn't look in the least afraid. The excited blinking behind the glasses, the arch delivery, spoke more of relish than reluctance.

Since he had not been invited to sit down, he did so, fearing immolation as he gingerly lowered himself into the shining arms of the steel-framed leather sofa, but finding it surprisingly comfortable.

"Even in spite of what has happened to Mr. Beauclerk-Fisk?"

"Especially in light of that. Life must go on, Inspector. Ruthven would have wanted me to forge ahead. I would say it's the least I can do to honor his memory."

If she was aware of any irony or anything misplaced in these sentiments, she didn't show it. She regarded him steadily, willing him to leave. He sat as far back as the chair would allow, displaying his intention to settle in for a nice long chat.

Discounting this, she walked over to the dining table in the large, open-plan room and began sorting papers into a large leather briefcase. Talking over one shoulder, she said:

"One doesn't just walk in and discharge people, Inspector, you know, so I've quite a lot of paperwork to attend to. One has to be prepared."

Again, he parsed her words for signs of either humor or compassion. Again finding none, he said:

"I'm relieved to know such things are not just done on the spur of the moment."

"Oh, no! There are many solicitors involved."

St. Just reflected that he and Miss Croom had so much in common in their professional lives—solicitors jamming the doorways at all hours. He would have spoken the thought aloud, but it was evident that banter was not going to be one of Manda's strong suits.

"It is often helpful in a murder investigation, Miss Croom," he said patiently, "to gain some insight into the state of mind of the victim. I believe, as Ruthven's right hand, so to speak, you can be of help to us there. You mentioned the need for redundancies. Were there any business problems he was worried about?"

"There are always business problems, Inspector." She sat down at the dining table (as far across the room as she could get from him without actually jumping out the window), made a minute and unnecessary adjustment to the alignment of the folders at her elbow, pushed her glasses higher on her nose, and folded her hands in a "Will that be all?" manner. St. Just found himself bristling. Given what he knew about her relationship with the deceased, he would have expected to see a tear, some show of emotion. Beneath the woman's cold exterior was, apparently, a colder interior. He said, slowly, carefully, in a way that Sergeant Fear would have recognized as pre-volcanic:

"I meant, was there anything in particular that may have been preying on his mind—something related to the business?"

"I wouldn't be able to divulge proprietary information."

Christ.

"In a murder investigation, you would do well to divulge whatever I tell you to divulge, Miss Croom. A charge of obstructing justice would bring about an unwanted and perhaps unhealthy dose of publicity for your organization, don't you think? With only you to thank for it."

"Ms.," she said automatically. Still, it thawed her. By a minute amount, a mere drop of sweat on the ice cube, but she was clearly weighing the consequences of answering his questions now against the inconvenience of not getting this over with so she could get on with her business. That her business seemed to consist of little more than routine rounds of redundancy announcements made no difference. He was getting in the way of progress. Her efficiency expert, no doubt, would have advised her to throw him a crumb. She went with that advice.

"All right, although I don't see how this could possibly be of interest. The truth, Inspector, is that we're in somewhat bad shape. Shockingly bad, in fact. The economy, the stock market, the dwindling audience for print products—it's all been a disastrous climate for the publishing industry for some years. The old formulas don't work. So we tinker with the formulas. That doesn't help, so we tinker some more. We've asked more and more of our employees, the ones who are left. Those who can't put in the extended hours required to keep the ship afloat are let go. Still, it's not enough.

"Mr. Beauclerk-Fisk was not unaware of all of this. It preyed on his mind, the sinking profits, and the effect it would have on our long-planned merger. What it could have to do with his murder, I couldn't say."

And couldn't care less—was he expected to believe that? Ruthven's death meant more for her to cope with, and that was all? On the other hand, his death created some job security for her, however temporary, so that was all to the good—someone, after all, had to pick up the slack left by his demise. The rest of her speech could be translated as: People with lives outside their jobs are out. It's making matters worse, but stockholders have to be deluded into believing that it helps. If we don't have an act, we can at least wear a costume.

"What about Mr. Beauclerk-Fisk's personal life, outside the office? Any problems there?"

To his utter astonishment, she blushed violently at that. Not a soft, pink, maidenly blush, but a blotch of red that spread like sunrise from her throat, engulfing her face.

My, my, he thought. All that could be hoped for by way of a reaction.

"Now that, I really wouldn't know." She riffled the folders at her elbow, not willing to meet his eyes. She checked her watch, as she probably did a hundred times a day, and began twisting the cap of a pen. He was definitely putting a crimp in her composure; her redundancy speech might not go as smoothly as it should, despite all the rehearsals. Good.

"He was, of course, married."

"I know that," she snapped.

"Happily, would you say?"

"Oh, for God's sake, Inspector. What do you imagine? That he and I sat around swapping love stories? It was a business. We operated on a businesslike level. I've no idea what his personal life was like, apart from what I read in the papers. Like everyone else."

That there was more going on than a business-like relationship, he already knew. That she had harbored hopes of something more permanent than their clandestine relationship, judging by her reaction, he no longer doubted. Was it possible there actually had been more, on Ruthven's side as well—or had he only led her to believe so? Had she removed her glasses one night as they pored together over the spreadsheets and, seeing her sharp little eyes, had he suddenly been overcome by unquenchable passion? Had he realized then that of all the people in the world, he had most in common with Manda Croom?

No, it was absurd. And perhaps therein lay the problem. She must have enough self-awareness to know it was absurd, hopeless, that she would never receive more from Ruthven than a pat on the head for being so convenient—such a good assistant in every way. His wife's income from a trust established by her father, St. Just had learned, was small by Beauclerk-Fisk standards, but reliable; no doubt Ruthven had come to count on it during the downswings. But it appeared such practicalities hadn't stopped Manda's daydreams.

Yet another feature of his job St. Just disliked, he reflected now, was reading other people's love letters, which he had occasion to do with astonishing frequency. They were—with a few exceptions, when they were chilling—so boringly, predictably the same.

Manda's letters, once the I.T. expert had broken Ruthven's laptop code so the police could read them at their leisure, proved to be simply painful to read. Manda wrote like a woman pleading for her life. Ruthven, it seemed, was her life. The earlier letters were either coy or beseeching, desperate, numbingly repetitive. So much so, St. Just imagined Ruthven had not bothered to read them after the first half dozen or so and clearly had not bothered to reply. The later ones were manipulative, calculated, and at times threatening, implying rather than stating that she had a tale to tell his wife, if she chose. The most recent had reached an agonizing pitch: a screed of vituperation, followed by abject, abasing apology.

St. Just didn't want to admit to her he had read every word, but he didn't see another way to cut quickly through the line she was feeding him.

"Miss Croom," he began.

"Ms."

"Ms. You were having an affair with Ruthven Beauclerk-Fisk."

She pulled off her glasses, the better not to see him.

"Whoever told you that?" The attempt at indignant outrage was one of the poorer efforts St. Just felt he had ever witnessed.

"Er. Certain letters—e-mails—you sent him have come to our attention."

She froze for a long moment, no doubt sorting out the possible responses. But at last her shoulders slumped, as if a puppet master had cut the strings tying her to the controller.

"You had no right," she murmured. She fumbled her glasses back in place but wouldn't look him in the eye; her gaze focused on nothing as she, no doubt, recalled certain choice words and phrases that she'd sent over the Internet for all the world, and the police, to see.

He trotted out the stock phrase:

"In a murder investigation, you will find we have quite a few rights. We obtained his wife's permission to search his belongings, in any event."

"Lillian? You didn't—"

"There was no need for her to see them, no. This, Miss—Ms.— Croom, is, again, a murder investigation. We're not interested in spreading gossip or stirring up trouble to no purpose. We're interested in the truth. Your e-mails to the murdered man …"

"Yes, I can imagine what you thought after reading them. So I'm the prime suspect, now, am I?"

"You need to be eliminated as a suspect, it would be more accurate to say."

"By all means, let's be accurate. 'Where were you on the night of the sixth?'—is that it?"

"Yes. I enjoy speaking in clichés wherever possible. So, Ms. Croom, where were you?"

"I'll need to speak with my solicitor," she said, all business again.

"Why? Does he know where you were?"

"Inspector …"

"Detective Chief Inspector St. Just."

"All right, DCI St. Just, my solicitor is Reginald Carr-Galbraith, Esq. And I am certain he would advise me to arrange a time at our mutual convenience for me to talk with you in his presence."

"You're not under arrest, Ms. Croom."

"But I am a suspect, Inspector, by your own admission."

By *my* own admission? Just who was being questioned here? Still, he felt he'd learned what he came to know. She had no real alibi, or she'd have come out with it. The blameless telly-watching alibi was his guess. And despite everything, he believed that was even quite possibly true. Possibly.

"Tomorrow morning, eight AM, Cambridgeshire Constabulary, then," he said, handing her his card.

"Eight AM? You must be mad. There's no way we can arrive that early. And I have a meeting with—"

He shrugged.

"Then face a charge of refusing to cooperate with the police, Ms. Croom," he said rising. "It's all the same to me. Eight AM sharp."

But it was an appointment he was destined not to keep.

DEAD END

By six pm, Mrs. Romano was concerned. By seven, she knew something was wrong. As the clock edged closer to eight, she knew something was very, terribly wrong.

At five she had followed long-established custom and surged her leisurely way to the door of Sir Adrian's study, bearing a tray with a silver tea service and a Waterford decanter of whiskey. She knocked. No response. Knocked again. This time there was a bark. At least, a bark is what it sounded like. On reflection, she realized the bark was human: Sir Adrian, demanding to know what she wanted.

What she wanted? *What she wanted?* Every evening at five the ritual was the same: tea with a drop of whiskey for Sir Adrian, against doctor's orders—Sir Adrian followed no one's orders—and a half-hour or so of conversation, usually on banal topics like the weather, Watter's lack of progress on the garden, or the wide-ranging folly of elected public officials. Only rarely did the conversation veer to the personal; that was not Mrs. Romano's style, nor Sir Adrian's. But these chats were Sir Adrian's reward to himself for another day of isolation at his desk, a decompression period before his solitary dinner, or before cocktails in the drawing room with visitors, as tonight.

"Your tea, Sir Adrian," she said. The "of course" was silent.

"Not now!" came the bark.

A crease formed in the otherwise flawless skin between her arched, black eyebrows. This was strange. This, in distant and recent memory, was unprecedented.

Then she realized what must be happening, remembering what had changed in recent days in her small world of Waverley Court, even apart from this unspeakable murder. Had she not been holding the tray, she would have smacked her hand against her forehead: *Stupida!* Of course. Sir Adrian was married. He was, in fact, on his honeymoon, in a manner of speaking, but, unlike the usual run of newlyweds, thoroughly enjoying himself by staying close to home to torment his family. Violet must be in there with him. Lady Beauclerk-Fisk, she corrected herself—she must get used to that. And they were—oh, God, it didn't bear thinking about. But that's what they were up to.

Put out with Sir Adrian, and somewhat embarrassed, she turned and made her thoughtful way back to the kitchen.

As usual, Watters was there, his tea and a plate of homemade biscotti before him. He was dipping a slice carefully in his tea before gnawing on it with new, ill-fitting dentures, courtesy of the National Health Service. Something about the look of abstracted concentration on his face made her think of Paulo. When he had been at the teething stage, she used to offer him the same treat, sometimes with a drop of brandy mixed in the tea and milk so he would sleep. Paulo had never been an easy child.

"Well, you won't believe it," she said and, borrowing a phrase she had learned from Paulo, added, "They're 'at it.'" She set down the tray with more force than was strictly necessary. She hadn't meant to say anything, but she was so used to Watters' hanging about, it was exactly like talking to the walls.

"At what? Who? They all fighting again?"

"Sir Adrian and the new wife. They are at it like rabbits. In the study. Good heavens, he might have warned me."

"You don't mean it." Watters was all ears. "I never thought, at their age ... Well, well ..." He chewed his biscotti slowly as he pondered this geriatric exploit. "She's a dark horse," he finished.

"Indeed," said Mrs. Romano. "I am surprised. Well, I mean that I am surprised that I am surprised. They *are* just newly married."

"Aye, but we none of us thought it were a love match, like."

Mrs. Romano, who rather thought it was, at least on one side, kept her own counsel. The jury, she felt, was very much still out on that subject.

Mrs. Romano held no illusions about her relationship with Sir Adrian, which was a little more than that of employer and employee, and a little less than a friendship. He needed her; she felt sorry for him and was grateful to him. She also did not approve of him. She thought him childish. But then, she thought all men childish.

Still, she was thrown off by the event, and what it might portend for her. What realignment of her position in the household was taking place—had already taken place. And like any female displaced by another, she did not like it. She did not like what was clearly happening, at all. Sir Adrian, when he was at home, had never missed their evening hour.

First a body in her cellar, and now this.

In some vague attempt to realign the order of her firmament, she sat with Watters and, as he gnawed his biscotti like a bone, distractedly drank two or three cups of Sir Adrian's tea, adding a dash of his whiskey for good measure. After awhile, she set about finishing the dinner preparations, going through the motions perhaps a little more woozily than before.

It was seven the next time she looked, and now she really did not know what to do. Watters had left for his cottage in the village some fifteen minutes before, and Paulo had appeared, ready for his stint serving at table. The adenoidal Martha arrived, late, just after Paulo.

Most of the meal Mrs. Romano had prepared ahead of time— she was pleased with the afternoon's culinary experiment, which included thickening the chicken gravy with carrot she'd puréed in her new Cuisinart—so she considered sharing another glass of whiskey with Paulo. She hesitated to share with him her news; she suspected he wouldn't have believed her. He was still at the age where sex between partners over fifty he thought of as an impossibility, if he thought about it at all, like the conception of the Minotaur.

She decided she had better forego the whiskey; it wouldn't do to have Paulo breathing fumes over the dinner party. She set about making the salad dressing, whisking olive oil, mustard, and vinegar together, creating rather more of a mess than usual. After awhile, she sent Paulo out to the drawing room to report on how things were progressing. He came back.

"They're all there, except for Sir Adrian," he told his mother.

Again, unprecedented. Then she realized what he was actually saying.

"His wife is there?"

Paulo nodded, not much interested, busy with getting the dishes ready for their journey to the hot plate—in actuality, a large black cabinet that resembled a bank vault—in the serving room. The distance of the dining room from the kitchen, separated from the family area by a long, winding corridor designed to keep cooking smells from traveling into the main part of the house, necessitated this holding stage to keep the food from cooling by the time it reached its final destination. It made meal preparation difficult on the best of days, and this day Martha was even less help than usual, nervously dropping knives and serving spoons that then had to be rewashed.

"Oh, give over, do," snapped Paulo at last. "Let me do it; it will save time."

Martha took this display of bad temper as a sign of Paulo's gentlemanly and helpful nature. Tittering, pleased—for in her mind Paulo resembled the swashbuckling heroes, cross-eyed with lust, depicted on the covers of the romance novels she read, and he featured in more than a few of her daydreams—she sank into a chair by the wooden work table. For the first time, she noticed Mrs. Romano's abstracted look.

"What's wrong then, Mrs. R.?"

By way of answer, Mrs. Romano said to Paulo:

"You're sure he's not there?"

"It's not like you can miss him, is it? I told you, he's not there. The rest are. That Albert came in last, as usual. But they're all there."

"Something is wrong," she said. "When have you ever known him to be a minute late for the cocktails? I should go …"

But the memory of her earlier rebuff at Sir Adrian's door stilled her. She couldn't risk it. Still, according to what Paulo said, Violet wasn't with him. Perhaps he was changing for dinner—yes, that must be it. He was just thrown off schedule by the novelty of the evening tryst with his bride.

But by quarter to eight, when Paulo reported back with Sir Adrian's continued non-appearance, she could no longer contain herself. Her dinner would be ruined, for one thing. And if this was the way things were going to be with her Ladyship in charge, Mrs. Romano felt she was going to have a few words to say on that subject with her employer.

She stood up.

"I'll go see what's the matter," she said, in the manner of a gladiator stepping into the Coliseum. Unscheduled visits to Sir Adrian's study, even by Mrs. Romano, were another item in the "unheard of" column. He would bellow, he would rage. She didn't care. Her chicken was going to be overdone.

Again she made her way down the long connecting corridors into the family area. She would one day attribute her long life to the exercise afforded by the floor plan of Waverley Court.

She stopped outside the massive double doors of the study. She knocked. Louder. Nothing. He must be upstairs. But just in case ...

Because she didn't believe he was upstairs dressing. She believed he was behind these doors—every instinct told her this was so—and not answering. Something wrong, wrong, *wrong*; the word reverberated as she slowly turned the handle and peered through the opening.

Sir Adrian sat at his desk in his smoking jacket, as always, with his pen and papers and the other accouterments of his profession spread out before him. But he was slumped forward on the desk, head atop a sheaf of blue onionskin paper, eyeglasses askew, and with his hands spread out before him as if he had tried to brace himself from a blow, or made an effort to raise himself to confront his assailant. He had knocked over the poinsettia plant on his desk in his fall; for a moment all she could focus on was the damp black soil scattered across the green blotter.

But sticking out from Sir Adrian's back, impossible to ignore, was a long, black, ornately carved object. It took Mrs. Romano's brain, cushioned as it was by shock and whiskey, full seconds to register this as a handle attached to a knife, the handle dark against a large, spreading stain on his back that could only be blood.

She threw the door open wide, inching into the room. No, she thought, not a knife. Bigger. *Spada*. No, no, no: sword. Her brain scrambled for purchase in two languages as she processed what she was seeing, as if finding the words for what she saw would make it all come right. Sir Adrian, he was pretending? *Si*, it was one of his jokes. She inched closer. No, not, pretending: Dead! Dead! *Morta! Dio mio!* Dagger!

Mrs. Romano staggered a few more steps toward the body, her hands pressed tightly against her mouth. Then she dropped her hands and screamed. She screamed until she fell, unconscious, to the floor.

———

They came running, a jostling stampede from the direction of the drawing room, led by George, Albert bringing up the rear. Just inside the door they stopped as one, like a panicked herd brought up short by an electric fence.

They nearly trampled Mrs. Romano before they noticed her crumpled form on the carpet.

George spoke first, but Sarah's screams had already begun to provide background music to his words.

"What the devil? Are they both dead? What's going on in this house? Goddammit, Sarah, will you shut up?"

She would not. He drew back his hand and slapped her with all his considerable strength—something he'd seen done in films to quiet hysteria. Unlike in the films, it made her scream louder. Natasha, with a fierce look at George, grabbed Sarah, held her massive form against her own reedlike one, stroked her hair, and tried to soothe her. When she saw Natasha staggering under Sarah's collapsing weight, Violet took the other side, sandwiching Sarah like a second slice of bread.

Meanwhile, a hubbub of exclamation rose around them as they all, like Mrs. Romano, tried to comprehend what had happened.

Only Albert, perhaps from what was beginning to seem like long practice, knew what to do. With no small sense of *déjà vu*— again playing the messenger part he seemed doomed to play—he ran to ring the police.

He thought of ringing the family doctor, or an ambulance. But what was the point?

Albert even knew what the weapon was: a Scottish dirk, one that had formerly hung in the hall, its lethal blade about a foot long. The weapon had been precisely inserted between the ribs, into the heart. No one could have survived that. Any fool, even one only trained in stage combat, could see Sir Adrian was dead.

———

The call, even though it bounced around Parkside Police Station a few minutes, reached St. Just in near-record time. He happened to be still at his desk, sitting amidst a clutter of takeout cartons and discarded "fortunes" from Wing Dynasty (*"Beware the dragon of desire disguised as fear. Lucky numbers: 1, 6, 10, 24, 36"*) mixed with piles of case files becoming overripe from neglect.

He had sent Sergeant Fear home to his family hours ago, and now sat staring once again at the scene-of-crime photos of Ruthven, hoping for a clue, seeing only a cold dead man in a cellar.

The Beauclerk-Fisk case had been stamped "priority" by the Chief Constable, who was tired of what he called "the hounds of hell" (the press) nipping at his heels. More than that (for St. Just was the type to say "yes" to his boss and then do as he pleased, for as long as he could get away with it), St. Just felt without any prodding that the situation at Waverley Court was only going to worsen the longer it took him to wade through the examiner's report and Fear's interview notes.

So it was that the call that reached him at seven fifty-eight this Sunday night came as little real surprise. In some subconscious way he had been expecting it, all the while helpless to prevent it. Something more had been due to erupt at that household, in spite of the police presence stationed inside and outside the gates, and here it was. It was as if someone had lit a fuse in that house with the killing of Ruthven Beauclerk-Fisk.

He swung by Fear's house on the way, interrupting a family meal, which earned him awe-inspiring glowers from both Emma and Mrs. Fear. He and Fear took the dark narrow streets of Cambridge, its outer burbs, and the surrounding countryside at reckless speed. At the entry to the manor house, St. Just slowed just enough to signal Constable Porter, stationed outside the gate, to follow them in.

They arrived in a screech of tires and sirens that brought Paulo angling more rapidly than usual to the door.

And there he was, the famous man in the study that had been the scene—at least in his imagination—of countless poisonings, shootings, head coshings, and other acts of malicious mayhem.

"You've touched nothing?" barked St. Just to Paulo, who slouched in the doorway in a manner that managed to combine impertinence with idle curiosity. The rest of the family had hiked off at some point to various places of safety in the house, after the nearly senseless Sarah had been dragged to a sofa in the drawing room by Paulo and Albert and deposited like a sack of undelivered mail.

"I know better than that," said Paulo.

"Good. Your prior knowledge of police procedure no doubt served you well. He was just found?"

Paulo raised an eyebrow, somewhat anxiously. Were they going to stir up that old dust again?

"Just now, by my mother. She's in a right state."

St. Just stepped delicately around the desk, taking in the scene: the scattered papers; the soil from the tipped-over pot; the ghastly, medieval weapon, reminder of a time that was more violent—perhaps—than his own. At least we've done away with the pots of boiling oil poured over the ramparts, he thought. Highly inefficient compared with nukes.

"Forensics on the way?" he asked Fear.

"So they said. On a Sunday Malenfant may have more trouble than usual rounding up his team."

St. Just didn't appear to be listening; he was bent over sideways trying to peer at the papers Sir Adrian had been working on. No hope from this distance; at any rate, the pages were largely covered by his round head. St. Just did a token check for pulse and saw that a poinsettia leaf was crushed in Sir Adrian's hand, the milk from the broken leaf sticky in his grasp.

He turned and surveyed the rest of the room, once again taking in the linenfold paneling and packed bookshelves. The dying embers of a fire glowed faintly in the handsome old fireplace, but there was nothing else to show him how long Sir Adrian may have lain there.

Easy enough to see where the killer had gained entrance: One of the French doors behind the desk where the body lay stood slightly ajar. He walked over; it hadn't been forced. Outside in a melting mush of snow and ice were the barest outlines of what seemed to be largish boot prints. He doubted forensics would be able to make much of that. Still, someone had been out here, that was clear. Someone who had been able to sneak up on the man as he sat engrossed in his work. Someone who walked softy and carried a big knife.

He turned back to Fear.

"Go see what's missing from that goddamn display in the hallway. Hang it all, I guess we should have seized all of that crap in the first place."

"There's a kitchen full of knives. It wouldn't have mattered—"

"Then go and find out where the bloody family's got to."

It took Malenfant nearly another twenty minutes to arrive, just ahead of the forensics team, peevish in an entirely Gallic way because his own leisurely Sunday meal had been interrupted. He spent a few minutes on a cursory exam, then turned to St. Just and said, "Yes, he's dead. He's been stabbed. A few hours but don't press me for a time yet. Anything else you want to know?"

"The last one was bludgeoned to death. What do you think we have on our hands here? A multi-talented killer? Or two different killers?"

Malenfant shrugged.

"You're the detective. How should I know? Although two killers seems unlikely, doesn't it?"

"You haven't met the family yet, have you? Nothing in this crowd would surprise me."

"No forced entry?"

"No need. Either Sir Adrian let the killer in himself—which seems unlikely; he to all appearances was absorbed in his work—or he helpfully left the French door off the latch."

"The ever-popular 'Murder by Person or Persons Unknown' will of course be my recommendation."

Malenfant made it sound as if Sir Adrian were being put forward for membership in some exclusive London club. But the also-popular 'Death by Misadventure' was certainly out of the question—legal jargon St. Just had always thought made it sound as if the victim had hopped on a plane for Paris and somehow ended up in a Turkish prison.

Malenfant added, "There were no prints the first time, and I doubt there will be any this time. Is there a criminal alive today who doesn't know from viewing *Crime Watch* to wipe up after himself? Still, there was a fireplace handy for destroying whatever evidence—gloves, say—the murderer wanted destroyed."

Fear's head appeared in the doorway.

"There's something missing from the display, Sir. There's a gap in the wall where there's a collection of knives and daggers, and two bare brackets that once held something. There's a sheath still hanging near the empty space. It would seem the killer just helped himself to what was handy."

Malenfant was peering at the object protruding from the back of Sir Adrian's body.

"It's a dirk. Scottish. The kind of thing you see in museums. Appears to be the real thing. Nasty piece of work. The blade will be about a foot long unless I miss my guess, triangular in shape. See the ballocks?

"The what?"

"The ballocks. The bulges between the handle and blade. Supposed to represent testicles. Ay, 'tis a manly weapon, forsooth."

"You don't think a woman …?"

"Oh, a sturdy child could kill someone with a sharp blade like this. No problem. Just like cutting through butter."

"Ugh. Well, thank you for widening the field: just what we needed. When will you be able to give us a time?"

"I'm never able to give you an exact time and you know it. Especially if that door was banging open and shut, which it probably was, and the fire dying down to nothing. I'll be able to give you an estimate sometime tomorrow. But what you need to know, you know already. He's been dead awhile, and somebody killed him."

"Thanks," said St. Just. "We'll just sit around and wait for someone to confess, then."

WHERE THERE'S A WILL

REPEATED SIGHTINGS OF THE majestic gothic spires of King's College Chapel cannot dull their impact. As the visitor to Cambridge ambles south from St. John's Street into Trinity, Trinity into King's Parade, the Chapel never fails to catch the eye unawares, often bringing the stroller to a standstill, reminding him of his ant-like status in the grand design. The enormous structure stretches forever overhead, in summer piercing blue sky, in winter blending into the gray, its carved stone spiraling into an ever more elaborate frenzy of fifteenth-century devotion.

St. Just could never pass the Chapel without thinking of the slow, painstaking decades it had taken a series of medieval stone-masons to fashion it, their names now lost to history. He doubted such a prayer to heaven and mankind could be reproduced in this pre-fabricated, jerry-built century. Whoever had built the horror that was Ruthven's office wouldn't have had a clue.

At this time of year, the tag end of full Michaelmas term, Cambridge had been largely depleted of students, and the few pedestrians joining him as he neared Trumpington Street, judging by their clothing, were non-natives of England. He imagined they were mostly graduate students, far from home, shivering, trapped here by penury and distance to work on dissertations on obscure topics that few outside their tutors—and often, including their tutors—would ever read. A man of African descent who appeared to be in his thirties passed St. Just, muttering something under his breath about nuclei.

St. Just turned to cut through Market Square, filled this morning with vendors offering Christmas ornaments, sprigs of holly and mistletoe and pots of poinsettias, and handmade toys and sweaters. He paused by a tray of small, gaily painted wooden trains, wondering if they would make a suitable gift for Sergeant Fear's baby, due in mere weeks. He felt somehow that Fear's wife would question the safety of the red and yellow paint, or worry that the baby would swallow the caboose whole. It was difficult on the whole to know what to buy a child in these days of highly educated mothers. A safe room, perhaps.

The offices of Quentin Coffield, Esq., were located down a cobblestone alleyway that snaked out near the right wall of the Cavendish Laboratory. They occupied the first and second floors of a squat, beamed Tudor building, whitewashed and bow-fronted, with dormer windows that seemed to date from a later period; on the ground floor was a shop catering to the tourist trade, selling sweatshirts, T-shirts, and coffee mugs bearing the heraldic emblems of the University and of its various colleges. A sign over narrow wooden stairs to the left of the shop announced he was entering the premises of Coffield, Grant, Crisp, and Barley. St. Just wondered how they all four could fit into the cramped space which revealed itself as he gained the first floor and stooped to enter the dark-beamed doorway.

The young assistant sitting in the antechamber behind a small oak desk was, he imagined, a moonlighting law student. She wore the severe black suit and starched white shirt that was becoming the uniform of young professional women everywhere, her hair tied back in a sleek knot by a stretchy black fabric that looked like a man's sock. All that was missing to complete the dress-for-success effect were the official black robes and a powdered periwig.

She peered at him suspiciously over thick, horn-rimmed glasses, an accessory making a comeback among the young, he'd noticed, the difference being that she wore them without a trace of the irony he found so touching among most of the students with whom he came in contact. This one would be head of chambers one day, he thought. That, or a hanging judge.

"You would be Detective Chief Inspector St. Just, would you not?" She might have been interrogating a witness in the box.

Perversely, he considered denying it. Instead, he settled for briefly flashing his warrant card and a smile.

"Mr. Coffield is, of course, expecting you," she said. "Shocking business, this."

"You knew Sir Adrian, did you?"

"Only in a manner of speaking. I just fill in here during the vacs, you know." As I fast-forward my way to the Inns of Court, finished St. Just for her silently. "But Sir Adrian was a frequent visitor. Mr. Coffield used to jest that he saw Sir Adrian more frequently than he saw his own wife." She broke into a wide grin, then, recovering herself, pressed her lips into a stern line. He supposed laughing at the boss's jokes was Chapter Four in whatever manual she was reading to help propel herself to the top. He just had time to note she had a lovely smile that he felt might take her even further than the starchy black suit might. She couldn't have been more than twenty, he judged.

"When did you see Sir Adrian last?"

"It couldn't have been even a week." She flipped open a calendar diary, running a polished nail over the appointments list. "Here it is. Wednesday."

Just after his wedding then.

"I gather Sir Adrian made rather a habit of rewriting his will," he said.

He immediately saw he had overstepped her bounds. Smiling approvingly at Mr. Coffield's little quips was one thing; betraying client confidentiality was another. Or perhaps her legal training was already teaching her that to say nothing whatsoever to the police was always the best policy.

"Now, that I wouldn't know." Slapping shut the calendar, she said, "Let me just see if Mr. Coffield is available."

The offices of Coffield, Etc., apparently not running to the modern convenience of an intercom, she squeezed her slight frame out from behind the crowded confines of the desk and walked the few steps over to a door at right. Knocking, she peeked her head in and announced his arrival. The answer apparently being in the affirmative, she turned and waved him in. As he thanked her, he was again rewarded by a smile as brief as summer.

The man who rose to greet him was somewhat a surprise, much younger than St. Just could have imagined to have his name listed first in the roster of his lawyerly colleagues. Perhaps thirty-five, no more than forty, with a full mane of dark blonde hair sweeping across a high forehead in accepted Hugh Grant, matinee-idol fashion. In spite of his comparative youth there was a hard glint to Coffield's eyes as he rapidly took the measure of his visitor. He waved him wordlessly into a leather chair before his massive polished desk. St. Just thought a person could have hidden several large torsos in its side drawers alone, if he were of a mind.

He wasn't sure he was going to like Mr. Coffield, who had pushed aside his coffee and now sat anticipating St. Just's first question in a studiedly dispassionate way. Far too polished by half, he thought. He also noticed Coffield didn't bother with the formality of offering refreshments, one upholder of the law to another. Nor did he offer any of the requisite expressions of regret at Sir Adrian's "passing." A small thing, but it bothered St. Just nonetheless. Coffield's manner seemed to say that the sooner the police could be gotten rid of the sooner he, Coffield, could return to more urgent business. And just what could be more important than murder?

Mentally steeling himself, St. Just sat down, causing the old leather chair to creak in protest.

"You were Sir Adrian's solicitor, I take it?"

Coffield nodded regally, straightening a pen against a sheaf of papers on his desk.

"For the past three years, yes."

"I see. I'd gathered from the family you'd handled his affairs for rather longer than that."

"They'd be thinking of my father, I expect. Passed away three years ago, which is when I took his place in the firm."

"But you are fully conversant with his affairs? Sir Adrian's, I mean?"

Here Coffield hesitated. "To a large extent. My father was meticulous in his record keeping—one has to be in this line of work, of course. I gather he and Sir Adrian went back donkey's years together, which helps explain—in part—the voluminous nature of the files on Sir Adrian." Here he gestured to a wall to his left, filled with neatly labeled legal boxes. A disproportionately large number bore the name Beauclerk-Fisk.

"I see. And the nature of Sir Adrian's business with your father?"

"My father was an expert on wills, probate, death duties." He allowed himself a small smile, visibly expanding. "As am I, even though I read Greats at King's College. I wanted an academic career, you see. My father convinced me not to be such a fool. Thank God—I think. Being the last word on Plato really doesn't pay all that well."

"I was at Peterhouse, myself. It was positively stiff at the time with students reading law."

Coffield barely troubled to conceal his surprise. How—why—would anyone go from Peterhouse to a career in the local police force? St. Just felt it would be pushing rudeness to counter-productivity to explain he had felt his passion for law and order would be better served in investigating crime than in exculpating it as a barrister. And to be a solicitor had struck him as the very height of boredom.

"I gather Sir Adrian was—a frequent customer?"

At this Coffield laughed. It was nearly as unexpected as the smile of his severe little assistant out there in the reception area. Perhaps knowledge of the old university tie had softened him a bit.

"Our best customer. One might think it was in the nature of a game he liked to play, this constant fiddling with his will. He did like to torment his family with it, or at least use it as a stick. But he was, I always thought, deadly serious about this 'game.' He was determined that no one who had won his disfavor would be permitted to gain from the sweat of his brow, as he liked to put it. Unfortunately, that left almost no one to leave anything to. At one point—this was probably the first will I made out for him—he'd left the bulk of his estate to some home for wayward girls. Rather as a joke, I think." He shrugged, palms upward, in a "Who knows?" gesture.

"Personally, I was amazed to learn there was such a thing in this day and age," Coffield went on. "It was a convent school in London. St. Drudmilla's or some such, I believe. But he couldn't be talked out of it. He believed in his heart of hearts—as we all do, I daresay—that he would live forever, so he could put anything he damned well liked in his will and it wouldn't matter. At the same time, as I say, he was quite *serious* about it all. Worried, would be a better word. I think it really tormented him that—well, that his family had turned out the way it had. That he had no one he trusted or liked enough to leave it all to. Rather sad, when you think of it."

But Mr. Coffield didn't look sad, thought St. Just. Puzzled, yes, but not sad.

"You didn't like him?" he asked.

"It was neither here nor there whether I did, and after our first encounters I gave up trying. For his part, he was confident I was competent to draw up something airtight and incontestable and that's all he cared about. But no, I can't say I did—like him, that is. My father—well, he spoke of him infrequently, but he indicated once that Sir Adrian had greatly changed over the years. That success had changed him, is what I suppose he meant."

"How did they meet, Sir Adrian and your father?"

"In Paris, he told me. In a café, most likely, while my father was doing the Grand Tour. That would be about ten years after the war, when Sir Adrian was establishing himself as a writer. No doubt hoping to get in with some remnant of the Hemingway/ Fitzgerald crowd. I doubt he had much success at that. Didn't have a pot to piss in, for one thing, until his marriage, and even then, Sir Adrian was so … competitive, he wasn't likely to be welcomed by any group of writers, cutthroat as they themselves may have been. My father rather took him under his wing, and may have given him a pound here and there to keep body and soul together. At least Sir Adrian wasn't entirely ungrateful, we must say that for him. More likely, he saw my father's potential usefulness. In any event, he maintained the relationship for all the decades that followed, and, of course, became a favored client."

"I see." St. Just made a concerted effort not to shift about in the leather chair, which protested like an old saddle with his every movement. "For the moment, let's go back to your most recent meeting with him. He always visited your offices, did he? You weren't invited out to the house?"

Again, that brief, harsh laugh. "Tony Blair would have been more welcome. No. It may have been partly that I was regarded more as hired help. But beyond that, I think he liked his little visits here kept secret—until he was willing to announce them to fullest effect himself."

"Was there any one beneficiary who seemed to be in favor more often than the others?"

"I think Sir Adrian rather regarded Ruthven as a chip off the old block," Coffield answered obliquely. "For the most part, yes, he had stayed at the top of Sir Adrian's personal honors list more often than the rest of them. But his last will and testament—his *very* last—changed all that. The estate was divided equally, this time, among his new wife and his lawful issue, excepting Ruthven—a new wrinkle. The wife gets the use of the house, which is then to pass to George. The staff were well done by, as always. Yes, surprising, what? Oh, and that secretary chap of his was made literary executor of his most recent manuscript—something about Scotland. The royalties from that were left to his ex-wife. Interesting also, I felt. But it all didn't matter, in a way. He'd probably have just changed it again, before too long."

"Given the chance. But ... how peculiar. For a start, I didn't gain the impression he was on the outs with his eldest son."

"It's not really peculiar. At least, not by Sir Adrian's standards, not peculiar at all. He'd done similar things before. The last will but one, his daughter was cut out completely; I forget why. Something about Middle Eastern *foie gras*. Before that, George, when he got involved with a rock group or something of which I gather Sir Adrian disapproved. It was all quite feudal. They none of them knew at any given time who was in, who was out of favor. And somewhat akin to Russian roulette, as it turns out, for Sir Adrian himself."

Ignoring the question behind Coffield's last words, St. Just said, "He sounds like the kind of man who'd enjoy making a *tontine*."

Coffield cocked a brow in amused appreciation.

"Quite illegal these days, you know. It creates too much temptation for people to bump each other off in the hope of being the only remaining beneficiary. Sir Adrian sailed very near the wind on that score on several occasions, or tried to. It quite suited his proclivity for promoting fierce competition amongst his heirs. Fortunately, I was able to talk him out of it. As I say, *tontine* schemes are illegal in this country, although I understand they survive in some limited way in France."

"Could any of them have gotten hold of a copy of the will?"

"Highly doubtful. Sir Adrian was most particular about that. Of course, I tried to give him a copy in the usual way. He declared he would just burn it like he'd burned all the rest—he didn't want it lying about for prying eyes to see. No, the will was lodged with us here, on the premises, with a further copy kept at the bank for safekeeping. "

"It's not impossible someone could have broken in here to have a look?"

Coffield's reply was chilly. "It's not completely without the realm of possibility, of course, but I would say it's highly unlikely. Extremely. We've never had a burglary of any kind."

"I meant no criticism of your care in handling your clients' affairs," said St. Just evenly. "But you must see that this will, especially the ... peculiar ... way Sir Adrian messed about with it, may be vital to solving the case. This marriage, for example—"

"I was the last to know about that, apart from his family. He slipped off to Gretna Green, mind made up on that score. I doubt I could have talked him out of it, even had I been given the opportunity to try."

"And now, weeks later, his new wife inherits a large share of— What sort of amount are we talking about, Mr. Coffield?" He didn't expect an answer, and so was all the more surprised when Coffield said:

"Upwards of seventeen million pounds. And that's just the ready cash."

Off St. Just's look, he said equably:

"Sir Adrian was a canny investor. Quite a lot of motive to go around, perhaps you're thinking. Yes, indeed. Except for Ruthven, of course. Not that any of that matters now. To him."

"No, Ruthven won't mind any more, will he?"

DOWNSTAIRS

St. Just stood admiring Mrs. Romano's gleaming stainless steel kitchen, which at first glance blinded the eye much like an operating room. Row upon row of pans and kettles; several enormous restaurant-caliber ranges, and a refrigerator large enough to store cadavers, should that become necessary. The way this case was going, he thought, it just might.

He had stopped by the station to see how Sergeant Fear was progressing. Fear handed him a stack of files: coroner's reports, background checks, and further downloads from Ruthven's computer, heavily annotated by Fear with exclamation marks and star ratings in the margins. The tracks in the snow had led nowhere, literally.

"The weather was changeable that night," said Fear. "It mucked the tracks enough they can't be sure, but the person wearing the wellies may have 'borrowed' them from someone with a larger foot. Nothing helpful on the carpet or floor, either. They could say more, they tell me, if the person had helpfully stepped in mud."

"On the telly, they're always sure."

"Real life is more ambiguous-like, don't you think, Sir?"

"I do. What's all this?" asked St. Just, peering closely at a sheaf of faxes.

"Ruthven's research on this Violet Winthrop, as she was, Sir. We've done a bit of research of our own. She inherited a bucketful of money from Husband No. 1, since she got off scot free for that."

"Please, no puns, Sergeant. Even though, as I understand it, scot free has nothing to do with Scotsmen."

"Sir? Oh, right, the Winthrop murder: Scotland. Sorry, Sir. But she seems to have run through the cash over the years. Sir Adrian came along just in time, in her view, you ask me. This Ruthven had a lot of the old files about the Winthrop murder on that computer. You ask me, there's plenty of motive there."

"Thank you, Sergeant. I was just about to ask you." He flipped through more of the pages. "Get on to this Agnes person, the cook who testified way back when. Assuming she's alive, still."

"On it already. This Violet, Sir—she's in this up to her tiara, I think."

"You don't think she's being a bit … obvious? Killing him so soon, in what is nearly a stunning replay of her first supposed crime? She must have realized she'd be the first person we'd look at. More likely, it seems to me, that someone wanted to put her in the frame. Still, I've just come from the solicitor's. She made a nice income for her brief time with Sir Adrian. Neatly enough, they all did, except Ruthven, who isn't around to collect, in any event."

"He was cut out of the will, was he? His lady wife won't be pleased about that."

"No. And if she knew about it, it certainly would remove one of her motives—the profit motive. But not all of them. There's revenge, for a start. As to Ruthven's death—Could anyone be as indifferent to a husband's affairs as she pretends? But there's no sign any of them had a clue what was going on with that will."

"'Who profits?'"

"All of them, except Lillian. We're back to square one."

"Not quite, Sir. Here's the background on that Paulo fellow. I took his statement and all, after both the killings. No better than he should be, was my impression."

St. Just flipped through the report, again bleeding red in the margins with Fear's commentary.

"He's been involved in the usual town-and-gown fracas. Broke a bloke's nose once in a fight over a woman. Mostly seems to specialize in receiving stolen goods, with a little small-time drug dealing thrown in for good measure. Clean the last few years. Still…"

"Yes, I rather thought we might find something there," said St. Just. "I think it's time I had a chat with the staff, don't you? Meet me over at Waverley Court when you've done here. My apologies to Emma, but we'll be working late."

———

Mrs. Romano and Watters were seated at what appeared to be customary positions at a large wooden table in the center of the kitchen.

Murder in the manor house seemed to have had a rejuvenating effect on Watters. His rheumy eyes strained to twinkle, like stars behind a cloudbank, as he sat bolt upright, hands folded expectantly. He looked like a wizened schoolboy awaiting a question to which he might have the correct answer.

Mrs. Romano, on the other hand, seemed less delighted to see St. Just: perhaps wanting to be of use in catching whoever was responsible, but fearing—or so St. Just interpreted her nervousness—her son's involvement. Had she or he any idea of the kind of money they would enjoy with Sir Adrian out of the way? Was it enough for Mrs. Romano herself to do the old man in?

Looking at her handsome, still-youthful face, he somehow didn't feel money would be an overriding motive. Passion, yes. Killing to defend her young. That type of crime. Cold-blooded killing for money was a different crime, and a different type of murderer. Still, three hundred thousand pounds—a total of six, for both her and Paulo ...

She looked at him warily. It was Watters who seemed to have something he wanted to get off his chest.

"Them boots," he said. "I told that young copper, someone else used them boots of mine. Put them back wrong, too. He took 'em away. You want to see?"

More out of politeness than anything, for he had seen Sergeant Fear's meticulous report on them boots, he followed Watters into a utilitarian mud-cum-storage room between the kitchen and the kitchen garden. Here among the raincoats, scarves, and assorted outdoor gear stood several well-worn pairs of green, black, and bright yellow wellies.

"I left them just here," he said, pointing to an empty spot in the row of shoes, evidently a collection of paired sizes and colors that had gathered in no particular order over the years. "When I came to use them the next day, after Sir Adrian was killed, they was mixed in—tossed in, like—with the others. I would never of done that. Mrs. Romano is most particular. I put them boots away careful like and then the next day they was all tossed about."

Watters peered up at him to make sure he was taking all of this in. St. Just nodded.

"Right there, they was."

"Yes, Mr. Watters. That was really most helpful of you to notice that. It would seem whoever killed Sir Adrian borrowed your boots, to obscure his or her own tracks. The ice makes it impossible to say for certain who might have borrowed the boots, and there were no prints on them, but forensics are still running tests."

"That's what I thought," said Watters, pleased at the acknowledgement of how he, single-handedly, was helping solve the case, but at the same time deeply affronted. "Pure evil, 'tis, whoever done that. Trying to make it look as if I had sommat to do wit' it."

"Or just finding the boots handy to cover their own shoeprints. You, yourself, heard or saw nothing on the night of either murder—leading up to either murder—that would help us?"

"I was snug at home, thank the Lord. Mrs. Romano didn't hear nothing either, did you?" He turned to her. "Not until she found him, Sir Adrian. She ain't been right since, have you, Mrs. R.?"

"For the love of God, Watters. Do be quiet."

"Yes, well, thank you so much, Mr. Watters. I can't tell you what it means to us to have the active cooperation of the public. If you wouldn't mind, I'll have a word with Mrs. Romano alone."

It took Watters a moment to realize he was being asked to leave.

"She had nothing to do with it, no more than I done," he said.

"I just have a few questions. Mrs. Romano was in the house more often than you were."

While that was patently untrue—from what he could tell, Watters spent most of his time hanging about the kitchen—the old man gathered his things and with a supportive little wave at Mrs. Romano, took his leave.

"He means well, Inspector. And it was a nasty trick to try to involve him, whoever did this. Watters wouldn't hurt a fly."

He had to agree, it was difficult to picture Watters worked up to a murderous fury. He sat down in Watters' place across the table and regarded her.

"You'd worked for him a long time, Sir Adrian, hadn't you?"

"I knew him for years. Decades. I never thought I would live to have such a shock, finding him like I did. Poor man, he did not deserve this. No one does. Ruthven, either. Whoever did this is wicked and cruel. I will not believe ..."

She stopped, evidently fighting back tears, her mouth working.

"Not believe what, Mrs. Romano?" he asked gently, willing her to look up from the tea cup that held her enthralled.

She raised her fine eyes to look at him squarely.

"I'll not believe any of them did this," she said evenly. "It's monstrous. Cold-blooded. And what did it gain them? He was an old man; he would have died soon enough, anyway."

"Maybe someone just couldn't wait."

She nodded. Clearly she had been thinking along the same lines.

"Were you aware that both you and your son were mentioned in the will?"

"Paulo? Paulo, as well? No. No, I had no idea, no expectations. Not for either of us. That would have been wrong, to even think of it. Paulo had no idea either," she added, staring at him unblinkingly, willing him to believe.

"Three hundred thousand pounds. Each."

"*Buon Dio.*" Her hand flew to her heart. "*No.*"

"Not as much as was left to his family, of course."

"Of course," she said hastily. "Of course. Of course not. Three hundred thousand? Six hundred thousand for us? Are you sure?"

"He was a wealthy man, Sir Adrian."

"Wealthy. *Sì*," she said. "In some ways. He had so much, but ... Inspector, I have something to ask of you."

"Go on."

"I would ask you this: Do not tell Paulo about this money. Money like that, it can ruin a man, but especially—Let me be the one to tell him."

Nodding, not even knowing why, St. Just saw no harm in agreeing.

As if making the decision as she spoke, she said slowly:

"I will return to my country. Sir Adrian, he must have known: That is what I most wanted. To be with my family, to live my old age where it is warm."

She might have been speaking of her people or the weather. As he watched, the tears in her large almond-shaped eyes escaped. She made no attempt to wipe them away, crying as openly as a child.

She turned away toward the kitchen window. Outside was the iced-over garden, fallow until spring. Suddenly, everything around her seemed foreign; Sir Adrian had been the only anchor holding her here. She thought of her pre-Paulo days and traveled in her mind the long road back to where she had met her feckless young husband: he a handsome footman with big dreams, she a girl in service. It was he who had convinced her to move south to Cambridge, believing it would be warmer. *Sciocco*, she thought, fondly.

"God rest his soul," she said.

St. Just assumed she was still speaking of Sir Adrian. It was the first time he'd heard him spoken of with affection.

———

He found Paulo nearby in the butler's pantry, to which Mrs. Romano, now dabbing her eyes with a dish towel, had reluctantly directed him. The pantry lay just inside the brass-studded baize doors that led into the servants' quarters. It was a large room that seemed to serve as both a supply area and Paulo's personal sitting room, the furniture a mismatched jumble apparently accumulated at random over the years. Two plump armchairs in clashing plaids were drawn up close to the hearth. On a side table lay a stack of magazines, largely concerned with the opposing worlds of women and rugby.

Paulo was in mufti: artfully torn jeans and a Stanley Kowalski T-shirt. He gazed up out of doe's eyes as beautiful and long-lashed as his mother's. He struck St. Just as one of those men who had little use for other men and was fully aware of the effect he had on women (unlike St. Just, who was always taken aback). Still, he was friendly enough as he offered the policeman a drink.

"Whiskey, if you have it."

"We have everything you could want in this house," said Paulo.

"And more in the cellars besides?"

St. Just could almost hear Paulo's brain whirring as he parsed the remark for hidden implications.

"Frightful, it was, what happened to Mr. Beauclerk-Fisk. To both of them."

"Yes. About that cellar," said St. Just, accepting the glass which Paulo now reluctantly handed him. "I've been wondering how a man in Sir Adrian's condition could have managed those stairs."

Paulo weighed loyalty to his former employer against the unwanted scrutiny of the Cambridgeshire Constabulary, with whom he wanted no repeat dealings. Common sense and a strong sense of self-preservation tipped the scales. No contest: After all, the old man was dead now. Dropping the accent he normally assumed for his role as butler, he continued in his more normal mode of speech, a match for his street clothes.

"He asked me to start hiding this book he was working on down the cellar, a bit at a time," said Paulo, settling back in his chair. "It was the only place he could think to hide it where his snoopy family might not trip over it somehow."

"When was the last time you were down there?"

"The day before Ruthven was killed. Honest. Look, I don't want trouble; it's not as if there was anything wrong in it. Sir Adrian, he'd give me the pages, a handful at a time, like I said. You'd think I was transporting diamonds, the way he carried on about it. 'Don't lose a page. One page missing, it's the end of you,' stuff like that. Tell me to hide them down there, he would—add them to the stack already there, and be careful to keep them in order. The night Ruthven was killed, I started to go down very early in the morning, when I thought they would all be asleep, like. I hadn't counted on Albert. There he was, in the middle of the bloody night, stumbling down the stairs. I guess headed to the cellar. Because not long after that, he started the holy hubbub about finding his brother."

"We haven't found any manuscript down there, and the room's been sealed since the crime."

"Well, then, I figure Sir Adrian, he hadn't counted on that Albert. Said, 'Albert won't find it if you put it in with the beer; he always drinks up all the good stuff when he's home.' So smart, he'd cut himself, that was Sir Adrian. Thought he knew them all so well. He hadn't counted on Ruthven, either. That one would move heaven and earth to know what the old man was up to."

He leaned forward confidingly.

"I can tell you this. Them two were plotting. Or, more exact-like, Ruthven wanted Albert to go to Violet—threaten her—with what Ruthven had dug up on her. Albert wouldn't have no part of it. They fought. I heard them—just happened to hear them."

More likely, eavesdropped until he heard them. Still, St. Just didn't care how he came by his information. Eavesdroppers were always useful.

"And what else?"

"That's all I heard. Albert, he blew him up; said Ruthven could do his own dirty work or get his men to do it for him."

"And the manuscript? What was that about?"

"I wouldn't know, would I? I reckon the old man trusted me with it because he figured I wouldn't bother reading the thing. Even if I could of made it out, which I couldn't."

"You did try, then?"

"Well, sure, all right. I was curious. But there was no hope. I'm what they nowadays call dyslexic anyway, but a genius couldn't read that scratch. So I just did like he told me. Every day or so, I'd collect more pages, and take them down there to hide. If they're missing I don't know bollocks about it. But you'd do well to ask that Albert. Or that Jeffrey bloke. He'd know, you mark my words."

"Thank you, Paulo," he said, putting aside his glass and rising. "What excellent advice I am getting on this case. I think I'll do just that."

FINE PRINT

"I haven't seen the current manuscript in several weeks, Inspector. I've just kept busy updating files, answering correspondence, and so on. I did rather start to wonder..."

He spoke in a flat American accent reminiscent of a young Jimmy Stewart talking to his horse, but with twice the animation. St. Just found himself leaning forward as he listened, wishing for sub-titles, as he often did during American films. Fear, who had caught up with St. Just in the garden after his interview with Paulo, edged his chair closer.

Looking around Jeffrey's flat, St. Just said, "This is quite a nice arrangement. Self-contained, I see, and separate from the house, so you have some privacy."

"Yes, I must say, I'm pleased as punch about the arrangements." He hesitated, unsure whether "pleased as punch" were a British or American saying. Was it perhaps, "pleased as Punch?" It was important that the Inspector understand him completely. Hands across the water, and all that.

"I'm very pleased with the arrangements," he amended. "Very, very pleased indeed."

"Good. Now, about this latest book of his …"

"I only saw the very early chapters, you understand. But I can tell you that it was different from the others."

"How, different?"

Jeffrey squinted, diving into deep thought. After a moment he said:

"Better, for one thing. His books tended to be very plot-driven, low on characterization. He was often accused by the critics of using cardboard figures. They were right about that. Stick figures. You know, the absent-minded cleric—often the murderer—the sharp-eyed but sympathetic parson's wife, the horsy county matron, the pukka sahib Colonel, all the rest. They were quite interchangeable, these characters, from book to book. This time was … different. It was almost as if he were describing real people. Which he wouldn't have done," Jeffrey added hastily. "Much too careful about being sued, was Sir Adrian."

"Did you mention any of this to him?"

"Good heavens, no. He'd have taken my head off and had it for stew. I rather got the impression sometimes he thought I was stupid. But then, he held most Americans in the lowest possible regard."

But Jeffrey's analysis had St. Just wondering whether Jeffrey was anywhere near as silly as he appeared. Take away the ridiculous attempt at an English accent and the puppylike exuberance—the man couldn't seem to sit still, but St. Just wasn't certain whether this was nervousness or just an excess of energy—and you might just find a high degree of intelligence operating behind those guileless calf's eyes.

"What seemed to be the plot?"

"Well, the title was *A Death in Scotland*, but the beginning chapters are about an ambitious, talented, sensitive young boy from a mining town in Wales who longs for fame and pines for acceptance into the upper classes. At first I thought he was borrowing from the life and times of Richard Burton, and he may well have been. Anyway, this boy hares off to London, leaving a curt farewell note for his mother, and on the strength of a few short stories published in the newspapers, finds himself taken under the wing of a society matron who sees herself as heading up a salon in eighteenth-century fashion. He—Sir Adrian—devotes quite a few pages to a mercilessly cruel portrait of this woman, while it is evident, reading between the lines, that she was the soul of kindness to a penniless—penceless—young writer. That part, or at least the spirit of it, you can bet your last dollar—pound—is true. Then, one day, said penceless writer is invited to a house party in Scotland by someone he's met at one of this lady's salons. He realizes he hasn't the clothes for it, and has no idea how to comport himself in such a setting, and he winges on about that for a few pages. Finally, he convinces this salon lady—the one he holds in such contempt—to sponsor a new wardrobe. That's about it."

"That's it?"

"That's as much of it as I saw. When last spotted, our hero was on the overnight train to Scotland, new wardrobe tucked away in new luggage, courtesy of his sponsor, whom one strongly suspects he dropped like a rock as soon as her usefulness had been served. Now he's worried that he doesn't have a valet, and spends the journey thinking of a story to cover for this embarrassing state of valetlessness in which he finds himself. He's also frightfully worried because he's never been on top of a horse and to get out of the hunt he's wrapped one of his ankles in a bandage. Read on one level, it's rather amusing, but I don't think Sir Adrian intended that. How it would have gone over as a book, I've no idea, but the fact is he could get away with printing the deed to this house and it would fly off the shelves."

Jeffrey now sat forward on his typist's chair, regarding them both eagerly.

"I must say: I'm finding it quite, well, intriguing, Inspector, to be in the middle of a murder investigation. Not exciting, exactly—well, yes, ok, I have to admit: It *is* exciting in a way. I've been bored silly the past few weeks—one can only write fictitious replies to fan mail for so long, you know. 'I am delighted by your comments and will certainly take them under consideration for my next book.' Baloney. Or as you might say: fish and chips. He never read the things—the man couldn't stand the slightest hint of criticism. His books were loaded with factual errors and gross improbabilities; as a result, he got quite a lot of mail. I winnowed out the flattering letters and reviews and hid the rest from him. God knows, he wasn't willing to *learn* anything from anyone; his success had taught him not to bother.

"Now," and here finally he took a pause for a breath. "Now, I've given this whole situation quite a lot of thought. For example, have you thoroughly investigated the triangle angle?"

"The what?"

"Just a thought. I wouldn't want to presume. But, well, Sir Adrian was known to have bits on the side, wasn't he?"

"You mean to say, women friends?"

"Isn't that what I said?"

"I do wish, Sir, you'd stick with American expressions, and let us translate," said St. Just. "But yes, to answer your question, I gather there were affairs here and there. But more so in the past, and Violet apparently prevailed in the end. Why do you ask?"

But Jeffrey was now off on a new train of thought.

"Then there's that Paulo. His mother is a nice woman but I'd trust him as far as I could throw him. Always skulking about. Up to no good whatsoever. By the way, you might want to have a look in the shed back there." He pointed out his small window in the general vicinity of the back gardens. "Unless they've suddenly started storing trash—rubbish—there for no reason, he's up to something with that."

As they walked away from the stables, having firmly refused Jeffrey's offer to "get to the bottom of the rubbish situation," St. Just said to Fear:

"I imagine he came here to search for his roots. With a name like Spencer he's bound to climb up several wrong branches of the family tree. Still, Americans do seem as delighted to think their forebears were yeoman as they are to learn they were ladies and lords of the realm."

"He was sod-all use about the manuscript."

"Do you think so, Sergeant? I'm not sure I agree. But I can think of two explanations: Either he knows everything about the rest of the tale and is being coy about it for some reason, or else he knows nothing at all, as he says.

"Let's see if our lads have even had a chance to look at that shed he mentions."

———

Tracking down Mrs. Butter had proved to be far easier than Albert had imagined, for, much to his surprise, she was not ex-directory. Albert had remembered her as a private person, but perhaps she had turned into one of those lonely elderly ladies who enjoyed the intrusion of salesmen's telephone calls on her dinner hour.

Getting out of the house proved a far more difficult matter than locating Sir Adrian's former secretary, for the press had dug in without the gates and could occasionally be spotted lurking in the trees or patrolling the perimeters of the house in the hope of a photo opportunity—or, better yet, another murder to report.

While St. Just had warned the family not to leave, Albert told himself what he meant was that they should not depart permanently for the Costa del Sol. But they were effectively held hostage anyway unless they were willing to run this gauntlet of reporters and photographers. Albert, usually ravenous for publicity, decided that there were, after all, occasions when bad publicity was worse than none, and that this was one of those occasions.

He kicked himself for not having brought his full stage makeup kit with him, but in the end, he felt that a minimum of disguise was safe enough: a hat pulled low over his forehead and a scarf muffling his nose. He would have borrowed Watter's wellies, to aim for a more rustic effect, but Watters had been complaining yesterday that the police had now "run off" with all of them. Thus minimally shielded from photographers, Albert headed toward the opening in the fieldstone wall at the back of the estate, an area so overgrown, so untouched by Watters since time immemorial, that Albert felt certain no city-bred journalist would venture there.

Sergeant Porter, meanwhile, spotting him through field glasses from the roof, radioed Sergeant Fear to ask if he wanted him followed, or stopped.

A half-hour's walk brought Albert to the village in time to catch the chicken-stop train that would take him into Cambridge. From there he traveled to Ipswich and, after a slight delay, to Felixstowe, on the way passing endless farmland and little else. At another time of year, fields of corn would have enlivened the gray scenery. Albert peered somberly through the rain-spattered, fogged-up window of the train as it approached the resort town, perched at the tip of a flat peninsula standing fast against the North Sea. In summer the beach and pier served as a backdrop for the full catalog of the human form on parade, wearing all the possible hues of sunburn. During winter, no one seemed to have business at the seaside—indeed, Albert began to regret that his costume had not included another layer of wool, for the wind at water's edge once he arrived at Felixstowe was fierce, stinging as it spat saltwater in his eyes.

He took a taxi to the other end of the bay, to the little fishing town of Felixstowe Ferry, a village consisting of little more than a cluster of cottages, a pub, a doll-sized church, and a boatyard resting on low-lying land at the mouth of the River Deben.

He had taken the precaution of phoning ahead from the station at Cambridge. Mrs. Butter greeted him warmly at the door.

"It's lovely to see you, my dear," she said, taking his coat. "I don't get many visitors. Of course, that was the point in moving way out here."

Like Jim Tanner's cat at the Thorn and Crown, she seemed untouched by time. The room she led him into just off the hallway was of the kind where stacks of books and furnishings upholstered in a riot of chintz patterns seemed to proliferate of their own accord. Green and red dominated the color scheme—in the plaid at the windows and in assorted garden prints on chairs and sofa. It was, apparently, Christmas every day at Mrs. Butter's house.

The ceiling was painted a deep goldenrod that reflected back an Aubusson carpet on the flagstone floor. The bright colors in such a small room should have been unsettling but, once the eye adjusted, were oddly restful, with flames from the Tudor-style fireplace casting flickering light and shadow against the ceiling. Two brass sconces, one on either side of the hearth, provided further soft illumination.

A lovely blue-point Siamese dozed atop a copy of *The Rise and Fall of the British Empire*. As Albert walked in, it stirred, opened one eye, stretched one paw in what looked like a friendly wave, and went back to sleep.

Presumably there had once been a Mr. Butter, but he was nowhere in evidence.

She bustled about a bit, offering tea and an assortment of little cakes and sandwiches that Albert was certain had been purchased specially for his visit. Mrs. Butter, despite the implications of her name, was neither large nor particularly plump. Age had followed its tradition of redistributing her weight a bit more around her waist, making her even more sparrow-like in appearance— rounded and brownish gray with black-button eyes that missed nothing. He imagined she kept herself fit with brisk, healthful walks at water's edge.

Albert hoped she could afford the lavish little spread for tea, and was torn between consuming everything offered to show his appreciation for her effort and eating sparingly so there would be something left for her the next day. In the end, ravenous hunger won out—he had had nothing to eat all day but the dry crust and cheese sandwich wrapped in plastic on offer from British Rail.

After awhile she finished fussing. Sitting back and fixing him with those shiny dark eyes, she asked:

"So, what was the old devil up to, then?"

Taking the signal that they were now getting down to business, Albert looked around for a place to set aside his plate.

"Oh, put it on top of Mathew Arnold. Do him good to be used as a tray," she said. "Tedious man."

Albert placed the remains of his fish paste sandwich on top of the *Collected Works* to his left and delicately brushed his fingertips.

"As I mentioned when I rang you," he said, "I've what appears to be a partial manuscript written by my father. It was something he was working on when he … died."

"Yes, of course, I've seen the newspaper accounts. Even allowing for the usual sensationalism, it does seem to me quite a … well, quite a sensational occurrence. Terribly sordid. And extraordinarily strange. I suppose one can't blame the press for taking a quite unhealthy interest. To be killed by an *axe* …"

"Knife, actually."

The newspapers had been particularly excited by the choice of weapons used in the murders, which had been the occasion for a sidebar on medieval armaments. Malenfant not having been forthcoming with precise details, the papers had decided Ruthven and Sir Adrian had both met death by battleaxe.

"But, yes," continued Albert. "I couldn't agree more, really. Only natural on their part—it's like putting a sizzling steak in front of a cage full of starving tigers. But the problem it creates for the family—"

"Oh, yes, I quite see that. It puts all of you in a horrid position, doesn't it? Not just you, but the others staying at the house. Simply horrid."

She gave a little shudder to demonstrate the horridness of it all, but in general, Albert thought, she was having a hard time concealing her rabid interest. Only natural, as well. Not only did the story have elements of irony—two members of a family whose name was synonymous with bloody murder being done in by foul play—but there was the added frisson of the opportunity for the press to drag Violet's historic old crime—alleged crime—across the front pages yet again. And in Mrs. Butter's case there was an added thrill: She knew two of the victims at first hand, and one of those quite well.

She seemed to be following his train of thought, as her next words revealed:

"Of course, knowing Sir Adrian as well as I did does make a difference."

"Of course."

She turned, stretching her hands toward the fire. After a long pause, she said musingly:

"Ruthven and Sir Adrian." Albert noticed it was not the conventional "poor" Ruthven or "poor" Sir Adrian.

"Both," she continued. "It's very strange, that."

"The whole thing is strange," said Albert.

"No. No, what I meant was—and I hope I'm not being too indelicate, but—what I meant was, Ruthven's death was a surprise, in a way. Sir Adrian's was not. I can't begin to tell you why I feel that way about it, but I do."

Albert, who felt it was a case of six of one, half a dozen of the other, held his tongue.

"I used to blame you children. At first, you know. I hope you'll forgive me. But I was astonished at the lack of family feeling. Few visits, fewer letters. I thought his isolation sad, inexplicable. Then later, of course, I came to understand."

"You were there some time, weren't you?"

"Five years, to the day."

"Remarkable."

"Yes, wasn't it? I wanted to leave after three months. But Sir Adrian had promised me—in writing, thank heaven—quite a generous pension for which I would qualify after five years. With Mr. Butter gone—well, you won't want to hear all of that. But I rather desperately needed that pension. Of course, he tried to renege on the agreement when I left—I knew he would. Which is why I had quite a vicious solicitor lined up before I gave notice. My nephew," she added, smiling.

Albert laughed.

"You must be one of the few people who worked for my father who have a success story to tell."

"I imagine. I survived by avoiding him as much as possible. As I came to realize all of you children did, as well."

It was a sad but true commentary on the family dynamic, thought Albert.

She had resumed her study of the flames in the fireplace.

Into the pause, Albert said, "Why did you say earlier you were surprised? About Ruthven?"

She turned to him.

"Hmm? Oh, just because, it's rather obvious, don't you think? I can quite see why he might be killed by even a casual acquaintance—forgive me, I know I'm being blunt—but to kill him during a family gathering, when the suspicion would quite naturally fall on the family … It's so risky, don't you see?"

"You think a more public setting, something designed to look like an accident, perhaps …"

"Something like that, yes. Someone pushing him under the Bakerloo Line, perhaps. Something that would point the suspicion a bit away from the family, not right toward it. I must say, none of you children ever struck me as stupid—even George, if you will forgive me, has a certain animal cunning. You were all bright and talented, in your different ways, in spite of it all."

Albert did not quite know what to say. On the one hand, she was complimenting him—all of them—on being too bright to commit murder, at least in an obvious way. "Thank you" didn't quite meet the situation.

"Perhaps the manuscript will shed some light?"

"Oh, yes. That's why you're here, isn't it? Dreadful things. I never needed reading glasses until I worked for your father. Part of the problem, of course, was that he could barely see what he wrote, having writ, so to speak. Let's take a look."

She pulled out of a knitting basket at her side a pair of thick spectacles on narrow gold frames and proceeded to attach them to her ears. She reached to accept the pages Albert had pulled from his rucksack.

"Good heavens," she said, riffling through the pages. "Worse than ever. This will take awhile."

"I am quite willing to pay for your time. I realize this is a huge imposition on you."

She laughed, a little chirping sound that rippled through the room and (nearly) woke the cat.

"This is quite the most exciting thing to come my way in an age. You did say when you rang this was not, perhaps, his usual run of manuscript."

Albert wondered how much he could take her into his confidence, but felt he had little choice.

"I really can only go by the title, but I think there's bound to be something in there that sheds some light on … something. Something he knew. Perhaps the something that got him killed."

But she barely noticed what he said. She had begun to read, slowly, tracing the manuscript line by line, occasionally pausing to hold a page closer to her lenses. He could hear a clock ticking in the background, punctuated by the sound of the village church bell tolling the quarter hour.

For a man whose minimum daily requirement of calories tended to come from alcohol, it was a shock to the system to have butter and sugar and flour coursing through his veins. His stomach seemed to have nearly forgotten the formula for converting these ingredients into energy. The unaccustomed exercise of the day—he was more used to spurts of manic activity on the stage than steady walks through the woods—acted, on top of the recent stress, the hot tea, and the fire, as a soporific.

At one point, a second Siamese wandered in, a missing bookend to the first, and settled itself on a pile of periodicals near the hearth before gazing off, cross-eyed, into space.

"There you are, Cly," she said, looking up. "I wondered where you'd got to."

"Sisters?" asked Albert, his mind elsewhere.

"Mother and daughter. Clytemnestra is slightly smaller than Leda. It's the only way I can tell them apart."

After awhile, Albert asked her permission to replenish the wood in the fireplace. Then he sat back down and watched the *Roman Empire* cat, it's back rising and falling with sleep, and soon, inspired, began nodding off himself.

It was a long time before Mrs. Butter removed her glasses and looked up from her task. Albert, by this time, was sound asleep, gently snoring. She studied him awhile, remembering a younger Albert, before time and drink had left their handprints. She wondered very much what was best to do.

There are people in this world who, while they hold to a high and strict moral code, include in that code the necessity for lying once in awhile in the service of a greater cause. Mrs. Butter was of this flexible school.

Finally, she reached her decision. She cleared her throat. Then again, louder. Albert started awake.

"I don't know how to tell you this, and or whether to tell you at all," she said. She looked at him closely to be sure he was awake enough to take in what she said. His eyes were clear, focused. She realized with some surprise that she might never have seen him sober before.

"What is it?" he said. "You're worrying me now."

"I am sorry; I don't mean to. We have to remember we don't know, never will know, probably, if your father was writing fiction here, or fact. But if he's done what I think..."

"Go on!"

"Were you aware, Albert, that Ruthven was only your *half*-brother?"

UPSTAIRS

St. Just and Fear found Sarah in her rooms on the first floor, dealing cards from the bottom of a tarot deck.

"I've seen your book in the stores," he said, pulling up a chair opposite. "You don't find all of this a bit at odds with Christian beliefs?"

She looked up abstractedly from her task.

"The path to enlightenment is One," she said. "It is the ancient teachings that carry the most undistorted truth. Ah, the death card."

She showed it to him—the card depicting a grinning skeleton on horseback—before slapping it down on the table. She sat back, surveying the arrangement.

"Not too surprising, is it?" she said. "It's all around us." She sat back more heavily in her chair. "I want to leave this house. We're all in danger, you know."

"We've men stationed inside and out, not to mention you have the press guarding you. You're safer here than you would be in London."

Sarah shook her head.

"Can't you sense the evil here?"

"As a matter of fact, I can."

She had been experimenting with makeup, so it appeared, with mixed results. Or perhaps the blue-eyed panda look was the result of frequent swipes at her eyes with the stained handkerchief that lay near her hand on the table. Was she merely eccentric, he wondered—a quality much cherished by the English, after all—or was she barking?

Catching his look, she took up the handkerchief again and began vigorously dabbing the corners of her eyes, making matters rather worse.

"Natasha has been trying to indoctrinate me into what she calls the 'feminine arts,'" she explained. "It gave us something to do while we're all stopped here. Trouble is, I think I'm allergic to the stuff."

Not crying, then, as he had thought. Not a tear for Ruthven or Sir Adrian?

"You'll never catch who did it," she was saying now. "Anyway, 'Justice is mine, saith the Lord,'" quoth Sarah.

"'Vengeance.'"

"Excuse me?"

"I believe the quotation is 'Vengeance is mine.' And quite right, too. I'm looking for justice on behalf of the victims of these crimes." And trying to prevent another, he wanted to add, but she seemed disturbed enough already. "I'm quite happy to leave vengeance to a higher power, and I wish more people would. It would save the world, not to mention the police, a lot of bother."

She turned up another card.

"Ah. The Empress. Representing fertility and motherhood."

"Representing Natasha?"

She seemed to give the matter serious thought.

"I doubt it. But that reminds me: With Christmas coming up, you really can't hold us here. It is the most important birthday on the calendar, after all. And Albert—he has to earn a living. George, too, I suppose. I saw him this morning and he was quite distraught—although he'd probably just run out of styling gel or something. But I know Albert must be worried; all this may have put his rehearsals in jeopardy. They'll be looking to replace him; he has financial worries enough without that. You know, it's quite true that 'the lack of money is the root of all evil.'"

"Love," he said automatically. It seemed no one had bothered to tell her that none of them would have financial worries the rest of their lives. Had Sarah not troubled to ask? Or was all the sudden disinterest in money an act?

"Sorry?"

"The saying is that the love of money is the root of all evil. Although, Sarah, I think you may be onto something there."

———

George settled himself on his spine, crossed one elegantly shod foot over one knee, being careful to maintain the crease of his silk trousers, and glared insolently at the two detectives. Pointedly, he looked at his Rolex, in unconscious imitation of his father.

"I'm due in London in two hours," he said.

"That's too bad, Sir," said St. Just. "I have several questions for you regarding what went on in this house that may have led to the murder of your brother and your father. I'm certain you're as anxious as we are to get to the bottom of this. Let's start again with this family dinner. There was some kind of altercation between you and Albert."

"Albert? No. Not particularly. That was more a ding-dong between him and Ruthven. He was, as usual, somewhat over-trained, so whatever he said I long ago learned not to mind."

"I beg your pardon?"

"He was drunk, Inspector. Three sheets to the wind; lashed up; pissed as a newt—however you wish to say it. One didn't tend to take him seriously when he was like that. I didn't."

"And your father?"

"Didn't take him seriously either, I would imagine. The dinner was the same as always, not particularly pleasant. Maybe a little worse than usual this time. Look, I've been over this with you, with your men. What exactly is it you want to know?"

"I want to know who would have killed your brother, for a start, and why. And your father. Greed? Hatred? I want to know what *you* think."

"In Adrian's case, unless dislike of pretentious bad taste is a motive, I don't have any theories in particular. My father—Adrian—was a first-class phony. You've only got to look around you to see that. Half of this crap"—and here he waved an arm to encompass the room—"is nothing but a load of cheap reproductions. The rest, most of it, is expensive reproductions. Once in awhile he'd get hold of an honest dealer—that commode over there, for example, is genuine Louis XV, or I miss my best guess—but the rest of it is just rubbish. I tried to advise him, warn him—it drove me wild to see him spending money in that way—but he'd have none of it."

"Surely, it was his money to spend as he wished?" asked St. Just.

The look George shot him was surly: *You* would think so.

"It was mine. My inheritance. Potentially," he finished lamely. Realizing he'd just stamped "Suspect" on his own forehead, he hurried on. "Not that I could ever count on that, of course. I was out of the will as often as I was in it."

"That was true of your siblings as well, of course."

Oh, them.

"Yes, I suppose so." It really was as if he had forgotten they existed. "The difference, in my case, is that I'm already well-off, you know. Pots of money of my own. I'd no need of his money. Certainly, not enough to kill him for it. You'll have to do better than that, Inspector."

St. Just wondered. If what his sources were telling him they suspected were true, it was a fact that George had pots of money, much of it made from selling a pharmacopoeia of illegal substances. No form, but Vice gossip was seldom wrong. They were anxious to get their mitts on him, but George Beauclerk-Fisk had proved frustratingly elusive.

Could it be George had decided it was time to go straight—and killing his father looked like a way to get the cash influx that would allow him to do so? There was a certain weird logic to it that St. Just decided he wouldn't put past George.

"There was also the title—"

That brought a short bark of laughter from George.

"Yes, well, the 'Bart.' was hereditary. And it's mine now. But you don't seriously think I'd kill anyone over that? Let me tell you just how valuable that title is: It was bought and paid for. You see what I mean? He was a phony, to his fingertips."

"He bought the title?"

"You can arrange that, you know, if you have the ready cash. Some distant, elderly, impoverished relation—very, on all counts—with no direct heirs, got in touch with father some years ago. Or maybe it was the other way around. But he wanted money for an operation or some such. Father forked over—he must have borrowed the money from someone, because it was before he came into the serious cash—in exchange for being named heir to the title in the old man's will. There were a few other potential and equally minor claimants in America, so his being British born became the deciding factor. Obligingly, the relation didn't survive the operation."

"I see." St. Just regarded him. Something George was telling him, he felt, was important to the case, but he couldn't think for the moment what it could be.

"Did you see your father often?"

George hesitated slightly before answering. St. Just detected the familiar indecision of an interviewee debating whether or not telling the truth were the best course.

"Not often," said George. "No more often than the others."

St. Just nodded in Fear's direction, a nod that told Fear to put a mark by that statement for later verification. Ostentatiously, Fear licked his pencil and drew several big stars on the page. As if suddenly realizing Mrs. Romano would surely be able to put the lie to his statement, George amended:

"Oh, fairly often, I suppose, in recent years. It depends on what you mean by often."

"You tell me, sir," said St. Just. Sergeant Fear noticed the familiar frown forming, the one that could make St. Just's eyes nearly disappear beneath his brows. Young George here, he felt, would do well to notice it, too.

"I made rather a determined policy to stay in his good graces, that's all. I think the old man was lonely. It rather explains this stupid marriage, doesn't it?"

"The marriage acted as some kind of catalyst, didn't it? You must feel as I do that none of this would have happened but for the marriage?"

Dishonesty having failed as a policy, George made a further attempt at open frankness.

"It was part of his usual shock treatment. But we were used to it, Inspector. In a way. 'Numbed by it' might be a better expression. Isn't there an animal that eats its young? Being around him—it was like that for all of us, except Ruthven, perhaps."

"There were bad feelings between you and Ruthven because of this—competition—your father encouraged between you."

It was a statement rather than a question.

"There were no feelings at all, Chief Inspector. I tell you, we were simply numbed by it. Ruthven might be on top one year, but it was simply a matter of waiting my turn to catch the King's eye."

After fifteen minutes in which George reiterated his indifference, and his alibi for Ruthven's murder—none of them had a verifiable alibi for the time of Sir Adrian's death—they left George preening before a mirror.

"Alibis are a two-way street," said Sergeant Fear as he shut the door, just loudly enough to be sure George could hear.

"With a roundabout in the middle," said St. Just. "Yes, I realize that if George and Natasha are both lying for each other about being together, it means both have no alibi for Ruthven's murder at all. I am glad to see you were paying close attention during your interrogation training."

They walked farther down the hall, pausing near an alcove holding a dusty stuffed crocodile, jaws ajar, in a glass display case. St. Just shuddered and turned away.

"Interesting morsel of information about the title," he said. "Perhaps Sir Adrian was an even bigger phony than George had sussed."

"St. Drudmilla's, you mean."

"Yes. You and I know now that Sir Adrian was raised in an orphanage—the place Coffield mentioned to me—so we can discount the part of Sir Adrian's novel where the sensitive young boy left his family behind in Wales. Looks like it was the other way around—someone abandoned *him*—and it was still very much a sore spot. Since St. Drudmilla's is a home for unwed mothers, he must have flat-out purchased the title in an even dodgier deal than George believes. I doubt 'Sir Adrian,' as we may as well continue to call him, could have learned of some remote blood tie to the Beauclerk-Fisks—the 1976 Adoption Act hadn't been passed at the time. How did he manage it? Forged documents—had to be. In any event, he was willing to tell the truth about other people's secrets, but he still couldn't bring himself to come entirely clean about his origins. He'd look a fool after so many years of passing himself off as to the manor born.

"More than that, I think that coming from a poor background was one thing, but being born on the wrong side of the sheets, to someone of his generation, was another. He would have wanted to take that one secret to his grave."

Sergeant Fear shook his head in disbelief.

"Who would care, in this day and age?"

"Sir Adrian, apparently. No wonder he felt that nothing would do but that Natasha and George had to get married, and the sooner the better. Well, what next? The lady of the house, I think."

———

They found her in the sitting room that separated her bedroom from Sir Adrian's, flipping through a fashion magazine as thick as a telephone directory. Perhaps she felt the occasion of the murder of her new husband called for a freshening of her wardrobe.

She looked up and smiled wanly. There were signs of strain around her eyes, perhaps a smudge of shadow beneath that hadn't been there before, along with a fine etching of wrinkles, but she was remarkably composed for someone who had sustained such a shock. Her hair was pulled back in the gleaming black, sleek chignon that was apparently her trademark, her lips were carefully lined in dark red, and she wore a dress of soft, dove-gray wool. Perhaps there were degrees and shades of mourning, and pale gray was the best she could manage.

St. Just greeted her and accepted her invitation to sit down. Sergeant Fear took up a position at the window, apparently just watching snow melt against the panes, but listening closely.

"According to Mrs. Romano, you and Sir Adrian were together in his study before he died. But according to our examiners, he was dead well before five, when she heard you in there together. Can you explain the discrepancy?"

"Quite easily. Mrs. Romano is either lying or she is mistaken."

"You claim you were not in Sir Adrian's study the afternoon or evening that he died?

"I was not, Inspector," she said flatly. "Adrian in his study was like a tribal chief in his hut. It was well understood by all that he was not to be disturbed, without permission, which I gather was seldom granted. If he wanted to see anyone, he commanded them into his presence. One did not just casually drop in."

"Even his wife?"

"Rules of the house. I was no exception, Inspector. Mrs. Romano was granted more leeway than most. She's been around since the last ice age, and seems to think she owns the place. Perhaps she has her own reasons for implicating me. Not the first time, as you must know by now, that I've been in that position."

"Your first husband—"

"Was murdered. Yes. But not by me."

Suddenly she smacked the magazine down on the table in front of her, looking straight at him.

"Not by me," she repeated. "Let me tell you, Chief Inspector, something about Winnie Winthrop and myself, since you're so curious: No matter what you read or hear, or what you choose to believe, that was a love match. He was rich and I was young. People put two plus two together and came up with four, or so they thought. But I can tell you Winnie was the kindest man who ever lived. Anyone would tell you the same. Also, they would tell you I was devoted to him. He was my best friend, Inspector. I trusted and respected him. To my astonishment, he felt the same, for which I will always be grateful to whatever God allowed me that brief time of happiness. I simply adored the man. Do you have any idea how rare that is, for two people to feel that way about each other?"

St. Just, long a widower, said quietly, "I have some idea. Yes."

"No one else has ever taken his place for me. No one."

"Not even Sir Adrian?"

She laughed.

"Especially not Sir Adrian."

His face must have registered his surprise.

"Does my honesty shock you, Inspector? If you want the whole truth, you will find I am capable of nothing but. I have nothing more to fear, you see. Those of us who have been unjustly accused of a crime can fear nothing, ever again. The truth is I did not murder my husband. *Either* of my husbands. Believe me or not; I don't care what you think or what I say to you. I am quite used to being called a liar, ever since Winnie ... I don't care. Because you see, whoever killed Winnie, killed the best part of me as well."

"Why did you marry Sir Adrian, if you felt that way about him?"

"Do you really need me to spell it out? He promised me security. A retreat from the probing eyes of the world. More money than Zeus, he had, and that was the kind of money I needed to escape the notoriety once and for all. You may think it a terrible reason to marry, but I had no other reason. He loved me, so he said. That I did not love him, he was well aware. I told him so, many times, when he proposed. He said many times it didn't matter. Somehow, I doubted that and I doubt it still. Don't most people want more than anything to be loved? But he took me on my own terms. That was our bargain. Life was hard for me after Winnie ... died. All the accusations, the suspicions. Sir Adrian offered me not just a refuge, but a comfortable old age, and an unassailable position. 'He who laughs last,' after all. If you see anything wrong with my wanting that financial shield against the world,

Inspector, you are not a realist. Perhaps, you are just not a realist when it comes to women."

Somehow, St. Just didn't doubt that for a moment. What she said about this marriage of convenience struck him as true. What that said about her character, he could only imagine. As to the rest of her story...

"Here is another dose of reality for you," she was saying. "Sir Adrian was in failing health. He knew he would not live many more years. That was part of his calculation, part of the deal he struck with me. I had no reason to kill him. The odds were he would be dead long before I was. He knew this, even if you do not."

"And Ruthven?"

"Ruthven was no threat to me," she said, a tinge of exasperation in her voice. "Not once Adrian and I were married. There was plenty of money to go around, and Adrian was always generous—with me. I am many things, but greedy is not one of them. You want a motive—I'm the only one in this bunch *without* a motive."

Her *sang-froid* was admirable, he had to admit. But was it the poise of innocence or the arrogance of a woman born without a conscience? St. Just had long ago given up believing he could, at first go, tell the difference.

BOOK OF REVELATIONS

"You were told, Sir, to keep the police apprised of your where-abouts," St. Just was saying. "Imagine my surprise to learn you were in Felixstowe yesterday."

Paulo had telephoned the station with ill-concealed delight to report the prodigal's return to Sergeant Fear.

"Trying to escape and changed his mind," was Paulo's verdict.

"He'd be hard put," Fear told him. "We had a man trailing him the entire time. But thank you for your vigilance, Sir. We'll put a gold star on your form."

Now a tired and somewhat chastened Albert was being questioned in his room by St. Just and Fear, under the embroidered eyes of Cain and Abel.

"I understand there was a plan in the offing between you and Ruthven to go to Violet, offering an inducement that she leave the field."

Albert answered wearily.

"I am not an organizer, a joiner, nor a leader of men, Inspector. I left all that to Ruthven."

"It was your brother's idea, then?"

"Of course."

"Would you say that was a plan likely to meet with a great deal of success?"

Albert wouldn't say; he simply shrugged.

"I understand, Sir, you've had some little trouble with the law."

"I've had some trouble with alcohol, if you want to be strictly accurate. About which I've been giving considerable thought the past few days. Do you know, Chief Inspector: I've decided I'm through with roles that are all wrong for me, now. Aging gracefully might be the toughest role of all, but I'm willing to give it a try. Somehow, Adrian's being gone allows me to breathe for the first time. Not—*not*, I hasten to add, that I would have done anything to hasten his end. I'm just finding it surprising—astonishing— how freeing it is, his being gone. Awful thing, the truth, isn't it?"

Frequently, thought St. Just. And it seemed that Albert was not alone in finding Adrian's death to be a breath of fresh air. Of course, having more money than Croesus was wonderfully freeing, too. Had Albert been in touch with Coffield, he wondered? He made a mental note to find out.

"What I am learning about Sir Adrian hardly fits with what I know of his public image."

Albert laughed.

"It is odd, that. He wrote what are called in the trade 'cozy mysteries.' He felt, especially as he grew older, that it was essential to his image to be perceived as this gentle, grandfatherly type, a male Miss Marple, if you like, with superhuman powers of deduction, doddering harmlessly about the village solving crimes in between sips of tea and sherry."

"And this was not accurate?"

"You do have a gift for understatement, Inspector. No, this was not accurate. It was simply the image he wanted, or needed, to project. At first, I imagine, to bolster his sales. Eventually, I think, because he bought into his own bullshit. No, not by the furthest stretch of the imagination could the word 'gentle' be applied to him. Or 'grandfatherly.' Although I sometimes felt he had ambitions in that regard."

"He wanted grandchildren, you mean?"

"His immediate offspring being such a disappointment, yes. Not so he could dandle them on his knee, of course. Heaven forbid: He detested children. I imagine it was more along the lines that he had dynastic ambitions. You know the sort of thing. Perpetuating the House of Beauclerk-Fisk was becoming a bit of a mania with him. All the more reason, I was not a top contender in the 'Grab for the Gold' sweepstakes in which we seemed forever to be engaged. Really, George's announcement was a stroke of genius."

"The first grandchild. Yes, I can see that might win him to George's side."

"It's rather strange, you know, when you think of it. The four of us, with no children. For whatever reasons, Ruthven and Lillian never had them. I suspect that was Lillian's doing. Just as well, no doubt. In my case, it would certainly be a new and different kind of miracle birth. Sarah? Always possible, but unlikely, at least in Father's estimation—which is what we're talking about, isn't it? Father's all-important estimation. Yes, he was bound to look at

George with new eyes, if he thought George was his only hope of carrying on the famous family name and title. That *silly* title. Also, keeping the estate intact was the kind of thing Father tended to worry about. Entail, and all that rot. Still..."

"Still?"

"I rather thought the old man had hopes of Ruthven's getting a grander title of his own one day. Becoming one of the 'Press Barons,' so to speak. Anyway, so it went, back and forth, year after year, Father constantly changing his mind which horse to back—sometimes hedging his bets, sometimes putting it all on the nose to win. Exhausting. It exhausted us all. George seems to have hit on the method that would settle it, once and for all."

"Rather a cruel game, wasn't it?"

"George's or Father's?"

"Both."

"George learned from the best, you forget. My father had a self-regard that was truly Shakespearian in its dimensions. It was always, always, all about him, and if it wasn't all about him, he would accuse whoever was ignoring him of being self-involved. One really could not win, up against that monstrous ego."

"He was a vindictive man?"

Again, Albert laughed, a harsh, mirthless sound.

"Let me tell you a story by way of illustration, Inspector. Every once in awhile, some reporter would write a profile of him for one of the Sunday papers that accurately captured his personality and attempted to probe his background, rather than regurgitating the nonsense Father routinely fed to the gentlemen of the press. Said accurate reporter would soon find him- or herself out of a job. I always rather suspected Father would enlist Ruthven and his Fleet Street connections on these occasions."

"How does this manuscript of his you say you found fit into what you're telling me?"

"In keeping with his personality, I'd say he planned it as his last joke on the world. He knew when he died there would be a crush of authors—university types as well as popular authors—wanting to write the definitive biography. One of them might have the audacity to publish the truth, and he would no longer be in control of that. He decided to take the wind out of their sails by getting his own version out first, is my guess."

Albert stood up and retrieved the manuscript pages from his desk.

"I had to leave the rest of it with Mrs. Butter. This is as far as she got. It's all in there. Ruthven was not his son. Ruthven was not my brother. Doting father that he was, he had no idea Ruthven was completely the wrong blood type to possibly be his offspring. It's something he discovered by accident that time Ruthven was in hospital. He saw the medical chart somehow; probably it was clipped to the end of the hospital bed."

St. Just pulled out his gloves to handle the pages, knowing it was probably a waste of time. They'd been too manhandled by too many people by now. He turned over the pages, trying to make sense of it.

"You'd need a Rosetta Stone to decipher this," he said. "I wonder how that American secretary managed it."

He looked over at Albert.

"You've had this from the beginning. I know you didn't feel it worth mentioning to us. Did you tell anyone about it?"

Albert shook his head.

"I needed time to try to decipher the handwriting. Judging from the title, the book held implications, good or bad, for Violet. I needed time to decide how best to play my hand. The possible ramifications of this were huge, I'm sure you can appreciate, but I wasn't sure I could anticipate all the fallout."

"The ramifications were possibly also deadly," said St. Just.

"I don't follow."

"Effectively, Ruthven was cut out of the will from the first moment Sir Adrian discovered that Ruthven was not his son."

"True. But that removed Ruthven as a threat, don't you see?" protested Albert. "At least, as far as the rest of the family is concerned."

"But by your own acknowledgment, you didn't know about this until Mrs. Butter told you. And you told no one the manuscript even existed."

Seeing too late the trap into which he had fallen, Albert mentally kicked himself. Too late to save Sarah, or any of the rest of them, for that matter, with a lie.

"I did hint to Sarah that something was up. Something important."

"That's not the same as telling her her brother was really her half-brother, and not Sir Adrian's flesh and blood. As far as your sister knew, your news might have been that you'd found a cure for dandruff."

"I didn't know exactly what the manuscript contained, that is true. But I knew it was important. I knew that from the way Adrian was skulking around the house with it—or, to be accurate, having that Paulo skulk around on his behalf, unless I miss my guess. I think you underestimate the strength of the bond between my sister and me. It's almost … well, telepathic. She wouldn't have made a move without first finding out what—if anything—I had learned."

"Hardly likely to hold up as a defense in a court of law, wouldn't you say, Sir?" said Sergeant Fear.

Alarmed, Albert turned to him.

"Oh, I say. You're not serious? Sarah is incapable of this, I tell you. It doesn't matter in the least what she knew about Ruthven's real relationship to her. The entire idea is preposterous."

St. Just was thinking that given Albert's predisposition in favor of his sister, he was not the most impartial witness they could have found.

"In any event," Albert continued, "there was always the possibility Father was lying, just making things up to cause mischief. Even Sarah would have known that, known *him*. It could all have been just another of his outlandish plots. It certainly has all the earmarks so far. Nothing about the man was real, beginning with the 'Sir Adrian.'"

"You knew about that? And of course, didn't feel it worth mentioning…"

"That he bought the title? I didn't mention the Battle of Hastings, either, Inspector, which seems every bit as relevant. But, yes, one of Ruthven's people sussed that one out. He let it slip to the rest of us during one of the phases when he was on the outs with Father. But that's not entirely what I meant."

"Go on."

"One of the more interesting suggestions in the book is that the protagonist—someone loosely based on Father himself, and I do emphasize the 'loosely'—had other conditions attached to gaining the title than just cash. The name Adrian goes back many centuries in the Beauclerk-Fisk clan. My father has his protagonist, born Joseph Evans, change his name to Montague Ruskin-Pall or some such rot, as a condition of being named heir. Do you see what I mean? It's very possible all of us have a real surname of Bollocks or Dumbprat. You never knew what was true, not with Adrian. Not even if your name were your true name."

Just then St. Just's mobile rang. Holding up one hand to still Albert, he pulled it from his pocket and hit the answer button. Fear watched as the Chief Inspector's face drained of color.

He walked to one end of the room, holding a hushed conversation. Ringing off after a few moments, he thoughtfully put the mobile away.

"Yes," said St. Just, turning slowly to Albert. *What in the world is the matter?* wondered Fear. *The man looks like he just heard his granny died.* "I do begin to agree that nothing here is as it seems."

———

Martha had been barred from cleaning the bedrooms until the police had completed their search, and her lack of attention was evident. While some attempt had been made to keep the clothes under control, a frilly cluster of bras hung from a bureau knob like a brace of grouse.

This one was probably called the Green Room, thought Fear, looking around at the gathered draperies looped extravagantly at the windows, the satiny tufted chairs near the fireplace. It was decorated in a shade he supposed his wife would call celery, but Fear felt it came perilously closer to the color of baby spit.

Natasha sat at a writing desk, evidently sketching a diagram of some sort. Sergeant Fear had had a race to keep up with St. Just as he stalked down the corridor from Albert's room. Whatever had his superior upset, Sergeant Fear knew better than to say anything for the moment.

She glanced up from her work.

"George isn't here, I'm afraid," said Natasha.

"It's not George we've come to see," said St. Just. "I had rather an unusual call just now. Someone named Sir Michael Cheek, of Scotland Yard."

He looked at her closely.

"Who are you, really, Miss Wellings?"

She smiled.

"If I told you, Inspector, I'd have to kill you."

I SPY

"Sorry, Chief Inspector. Bad joke. Detective Natasha Landeski of the Art and Antiques Unit at New Scotland Yard. That, as you know, is part of the Metropolitan Police Specialist Crime Operational Command Unit, or SO6. At your service."

She held out her hand. St. Just looked at it as if a toad had sprouted in its palm.

Sergeant Fear, who had automatically flipped open his notebook, had heard enough. He shut his eyes tightly. When he opened them again, he drew a firm line under his notes and wrote beneath it, in large capital letters: FUCK.

Later, back at the station, he would take pains to blot this out, but for now, he let it stand. She really had led them up a garden path.

"I see my superior has finally notified you. I don't have my real identification on me, for obvious reasons. My hands were tied until he gave the go-ahead to put you in the picture."

St. Just stared at her coldly. If anything was more irritating than Scotland Yard on one's turf, he had just decided it was Scotland Yard on one's turf, incognito.

"What's all this in aid of, then?" he asked.

"George, of course. Finding out what he's really up to. And he's up to quite a lot."

"We ran a background check on George Beauclerk-Fisk. He came up clean—no form, at any rate."

"He would. In your files, there would be little to implicate him—at least, not in the area of his activities in which we're most interested. You can be certain the *real* investigative details aren't in the shared database."

"Why weren't we told, dammit?" he demanded. "This was—is—a murder investigation."

"I'm telling you now. It wasn't my decision to make, it was Sir Cheek's. My marching orders were to keep my cover, no matter what, and in my line of work, that means no matter *what*—I don't have to tell you that. But now, as I say, my hands are untied. Let me give you a hint—"

"Thank you. That's most kind. A hint from one of the professionals from London. Do take this down, Sergeant Fear; perhaps we can study it and learn from it later. Let's have it, Miss Landeski, the whole story. If George so much as returned a videotape late, I want to know about it."

"All right. Here you go, the short version: Almost nothing in this house is what it seems. I don't mean the personalities—although heaven knows there's a gold mine of dysfunction there—I mean the surroundings. The furnishings, the paintings. It's a mixture of truly extraordinary art and antiques mixed in with the most extraordi-

238

nary crap. It's a bit hard to sort out because Sir Adrian had appalling taste to begin with, but—"

"But you think some kind of exchange has been going on."

"Precisely."

"The real goods, so to speak, substituted with fakes."

"Precisely." She beamed at him, a teacher acknowledging a promising student.

"George's art gallery..."

"Those who can, do. Paint, that is. Those who can't, buy art galleries. Those who really can't make a go of that, steal, paying a starving artist to create passable substitute paintings or bits of furniture. Adrian was quite near-sighted; I tested him on that myself. He never knew the difference. If anyone else noticed, they assumed he'd been ripped off by a shady dealer, or that he was just exercising his naturally appalling taste."

An electronic bleating erupted once again from the direction of Fear's jacket.

"Jingle Bells," laughed Natasha. "I say, that is jolly."

"I thought I told you to get that thing seen to, Sergeant."

"I tried, Sir. I.T. couldn't figure it out, either."

"Get Emma to change it back then."

"She refuses, Sir."

"For God's sake..."

Turning again to Natasha, he said:

"How long has it been going on?"

"Since George developed expensive habits, at a guess. Drugs being the most expensive. He's rather frugal when it comes to women. I have a theory—not yet proven—that in addition to the art theft, he's found some of the furniture leaving the country is

239

extremely useful for concealing whatever one wants to conceal. The earlier centuries were very clever about hidden compartments, for which the modern drug dealer has found much the same uses."

"It's Chloe Beauclerk-Fisk, Sir," said Fear. "She's been calling the station all morning, wanting to talk with you."

"Later, Sergeant. So you've insinuated yourself with George, winning his confidence, to find out who the receivers are."

"Precisely."

"This deception includes having a child with him? Are you quite mad?"

"Of course not, Inspector. 'All in the line of duty' can be taken too far. That was George's harebrained scheme, to get in good with his father. To stay on George's good side, I had to play along. I was appalled, but what could I do? God, this family. When Ruthven was killed, I knew I was in over my head, but even then I couldn't risk calling for instructions, not with your men crawling all over the house. You must realize, it was almost certainly George behind that, but I don't know why or how he did it yet. I can promise you I'm working on getting it out of him. As far as I *knew*, he was asleep all night next to me when Ruthven was killed. As long as I can keep his confidence, he might just let the truth slip. I had to keep playing the game. It was too important—and I was closer to unraveling the case than anyone had been able to get—to blow my cover. We're talking about two men killed over this, not to mention millions of pounds in stolen treasures, taken not only from here but from museums all over the world. We're closer to the truth than ever before, now."

Sergeant Fear was wishing she'd be quiet. He got it, got it, *got it*. It was known that Scotland Yard had its own agenda, and sometimes played by its own rules when it suited them. It wasn't the first time they'd elbowed the "provincials" out of the way over an international case deemed to be of overriding priority. He just resented being made to feel like some kind of fucking Cambridgeshire goatherd.

"Look, Chief Inspector; Sergeant. I know you're angry at being left out in the cold. I would be, too. I couldn't help it; I had no control, no real authority. This is not your average smuggling scheme. We still don't know all the receivers in Europe and the Middle East, let alone all the suppliers. It would seem George was not only stealing from his father, but using this house as sort of a warehouse for incoming goods. Paulo is in on it with him, I'm sure, but I doubt Paulo knows the magnitude of what he's involved in."

"Natasha, I would suggest, with all due respect, that neither do you."

MEMORY LANE

THE TWO POLICEMEN CAME stomping down the staircase into the hall to find Paulo taking Chloe's fur coat at the main door. Just before Paulo kicked the door shut, St. Just glimpsed the black limousine that had transported her in state to the house.

The Hollywood-style sweep of staircase left him nowhere to hide. Inwardly, St. Just groaned, imagining she was there for a hand-holding session for which he had little time or inclination.

"God, but the press is vile," she informed him. "One of them practically flung herself on the bonnet trying to stop us on the way in." She took off her leather gloves, flapping them in his direction. "Needed to talk with you. And Mohammed wouldn't come to the mountain."

She marched into the library. At least, judging by her sturdy progress, she was relatively sober this time. Reluctantly, after a whispered conference with Fear, he followed, closing the door behind them.

"Seem to have been a few changes here," she said, hands on hips, taking in the vast room. "All that military crap in the hallway is new since my time. As for this—" she waved one arm, taking in the paintings cramming the walls—"Adrian never could tell a racehorse from a plug mare. That much hasn't changed. Speaking of plug mares, why haven't you taken that one into custody yet?"

"I assume you are referring to Lady Beauclerk-Fisk."

"Of course I mean Violet. What does she have to do, come running in here waving a poison-tipped spear and threatening to run us all through?"

"There's no evidence..."

"Evidence? Her first, wealthy husband dies under 'mysterious circumstances.' She no sooner has her hooks into wealthy Adrian than he's dead. What more evidence do you need? Oh, I see the truth now. Poor Ruthven. He probably got wind of what she was planning, so she killed him. She should have been locked up years ago, but all she had to do was bat those baby blues at male officialdom and off she flies to Gstaad or Monaco or wherever it was she disappeared to."

"'Baby blues?' Had you met Violet before, then?"

"It's just an expression." She shrugged. "Oh, all right. I did know her, in the way one did know people in those days," she said vaguely, not quite willing to meet his stare. "All the same crowd at the same wretched parties every weekend. Violet was always included because of the way she looked; I because of my money. I knew, and I didn't care. Daddy sent me to England to snag a title and, by golly, I did."

Her round, plain face brightened momentarily. Was marriage to Sir Adrian the singular accomplishment of her life, in Daddy's eyes? And what would Daddy have said if he'd known the background to that title?

"You must have recognized her name on the invitation."

"That's exactly it, you see. I did *not* recognize the name Violet Mildenhall. I knew her as Violet Winthrop. You think I wouldn't have mentioned that to Ruthven, if I'd put it together in time? I might have warned him to stay away from her, from this house, at a minimum."

"All right." Here St. Just felt it was time to divert the conversation into more procedural paths. There was still the looming question of what she had been doing when Sir Adrian met his demise. Feeling like a BBC news announcer forced to lurch from headline to unrelated headline, he put the question to her.

"At home, of course."

"Can anyone vouch for you?"

"Mrs. Ketchen, of course."

From what he had seen of Mrs. Ketchen, he thought it unlikely she had any idea whether on any given day her employer was at home, pinned under a lorry, or planting gunpowder in the basement of Westminster.

"All right," he said patiently. "Tell me what you know, now, about that weekend in Scotland. And I mean, *all* that you know: gossip, facts, and innuendo. Let's start with Violet. Everything you can remember. She was popular with men, Violet was, I take it?"

"Popular? *Pop*ular?" Chloe, who had been peeking at the ending of a Graham Greene novel, swung on him, astonished, in an "is-there-no-limit-to-your-ignorance?" way. "Good God, man. People nearly brought back dueling for Violet's sake. She was a force of nature, no question about it. Pamela Harriman had nothing on her. Pam, of course, was *older*, but there was an enormous competition between them, at least on Pamela's part. Quite deadly.

Oh, yes, indeed. All the kiss-kiss in public, gloves off in private, if the rumors were true. I remember Averil—"

"Were you jealous of her? Then, I mean?"

"Then and now: no," she said flatly. "You could really only gaze in dumbstruck awe where Violet was concerned, as at ... oh, I don't know. A thunderstorm. Or a train wreck. Somehow, she didn't inspire jealousy, only wonder. Oh, there was the expected cattiness over her marriage to that old lizard Winthrop. But do you know, the more I saw them together, the more I came to believe that was a love match. Didn't she have *me* fooled."

"You were not in the camp that believed she killed him, then?"

"I wasn't then. I am now. Do you really believe this is coincidence? Everywhere she goes, there's a trail of bodies, or hadn't you noticed? The problem was ..." She didn't seem to want to meet his eyes. "The problem was, I couldn't imagine why she would kill him. It's not as if he held her captive, you know. She was free to ... you know ..."

"I don't know."

Again the look of surprise. "To have discreet affairs, of course," she said. "If she wanted them. It was quite the done thing in that crowd. I never got the impression that she did. Want affairs, I mean. Rather cold-blooded, she was, I always felt. All the men hoped differently, but I don't think any of them got too far."

In spite of her denials, St. Just wondered if there weren't just a bit more jealousy here than she was willing to own to. And more than a shade of bitterness. She was taking Sir Adrian's death with less hand-wringing than might have been expected, given the manner of his death, if nothing else. But then, it had been decades since their divorce.

He sat down, first leading her by the arm away from the bookshelves in front of which she'd planted herself and repotting her in a seat across from him.

"You weren't entirely truthful with me when we first met, were you?"

"As truthful as the situation warranted. She killed Adrian, all right, but for the life of me I don't see how Ruthven was a threat to her. Unless he knew she was planning to kill Adrian. And how could he? And—why wouldn't she have waited a decent interval before killing him, if only to make it *look* good? Oh, I don't know. I go 'round and 'round about it in my mind, and I can't see the motive there. Not unless she's insane. Do you think that's possible?"

Again feeling like a news announcer, skipping now to the tabloid news, he said:

"You didn't feel we needed to know that Ruthven was not Sir Adrian's natural son?"

She could make a quick recovery; he had to hand that to her. Hesitating only for a second, she said defiantly:

"No, I didn't. What possible bearing could it have?"

"Quite a lot, I should think."

She shrugged her shoulders, spreading open palms before him. Think what you like.

"How did you find out?" she asked at last.

"He was working on a book when he died. A work of nonfiction thinly disguised as fiction. *A Death in Scotland* was the title."

He was watching her closely for a reaction. She blinked several times, but otherwise her expression remained frozen.

He kept pitching, hoping to catch her in contradiction. And now for news from the publishing world…

"Are you aware Sir Adrian had already made arrangements to leave you the proceeds from this manuscript?"

"No," she said slowly. "No, I wasn't ..." She paused, clearly thinking through the ramifications, then said, "But it was precisely the kind of joke he enjoyed. *A Conception in Scotland* might be a better title, for his purposes. For that, of course, is where Ruthven was conceived. By quite a dashing young man with a title who dashed off and left me holding the baby, literally. Said young man had decided this was all getting much more serious than he had intended, you see. And not long after that I met Adrian, who ... shall we say ... turned his attentions to me.

"I honestly didn't know—to an absolute certainty, Chief Inspector—whose child it was. God—*that* didn't quite come out the way I meant it to sound. What I *mean* to say is, I didn't *know* I was pregnant when I took up with Adrian. Then later ... perhaps I suspected Ruthven wasn't his, but I didn't *know*. As the years went on, and I came to the point I couldn't stand to be in the same room with Adrian, I came to believe Ruthven wasn't his, because I preferred to believe that. Then, the first time Ruthven had to have his blood typed, when he was sent off to school—then ... Well. I said nothing to Ruthven at the time—that came later—and certainly not to Adrian. You don't know how it was in those days. Although I don't suppose that kind of announcement would go over big today, either. So that's what Adrian chose to write about in this wretched book: How I trapped him into marriage, and with a child that wasn't even his."

"That was part of his topic, certainly,"

She wasn't listening. He imagined she was trying to piece together, as he had been, the implications of the rest of the family's learning of Ruthven's true parentage.

"I wonder how Adrian found out?"

"When Ruthven was in hospital. Ruthven was type A. Sir Adrian was type O. You had to be type A yourself for Adrian to have been the father of Ruthven."

"Which I'm not. However did he?—wait. That explains what he was doing, coming to visit me. I carry a medical card in my purse—I'm a diabetic, as Adrian well knew, so all my information is there in case they have to tow me out of Harrods on a stretcher one day. Sneaky, creeping little bastard. Adrian paid no attention to Ruthven while he was growing up; it doesn't surprise me it took him this long to tumble to it."

"The book seems to have been some form of revenge, from what I know of it, or of him, yes. He seems to have started on it right about the time of Ruthven's operation."

"And then made sure it was going to be left to me. I suppose he thought it would place me on the horns of a dilemma, giving me the choice of destroying the manuscript—which would be worth a fortune—or publishing it for the proceeds, and destroying my own reputation in the process. I can see how he would love that, knowing he'd put me in a position where I was damned whichever choice I made."

"Would you publish it?"

She didn't hesitate.

"Of course not. I have money of my own, Inspector. This was probably his twisted way of leaving me something essentially worthless. On the whole, I think I may douse it in oil and set fire to it."

"I'm not certain that option is in your hands. It's the proceeds he's left you, not the decision whether or not to publish. He made his secretary the literary executor."

"The American chap? How extraordinary. I'll have to have a word with him, now, won't I?"

The news didn't please her, he could see. Had she known what Sir Adrian was writing? And if she had—what might she have done to stop him?

She paused, looked around her.

"God, how I hate this house. Do you know how many years since I set foot in here? And I never would have, if he weren't dead and gone. Very freeing, it is."

"That seems to be the common sentiment."

"For the children especially, yes. For us all." She sighed. "It wasn't always quite this bad, you know. I thought I'd made a good bargain, at first. But it all went pear-shaped after the children were born."

Catching his involuntary glance, she laughed, that attractive, deep-throated chuckle that had no doubt, at one time, been part of her attraction for Sir Adrian.

"I didn't mean that, Inspector. Although that certainly went pear-shaped as well. I meant the marriage. It's hard to trace these things back to the single, defining moment when you know you have to get out for the sake of your sanity, when you can stand no more, when the whole thing just comes unstuck. With Adrian, there were so many such moments."

"But you stayed with him, all those children …"

"It was what one *did* in those days, Inspector."

"Was he always so …?" An array of possible words presented themselves. Malicious, vindictive, and petty topped the list.

"Adrian?" A faraway look came into her eyes. She might have been surveying the ravaged, war-torn past, looking under pieces of wreckage for signs of life. "No. No, he wasn't. Or he didn't appear so, at first. Oh, he was always selfish and full of himself. Confident, in the extreme, of his talents. I used to admire that. So much."

"What happened?"

"To turn him into a monster, you mean?"

"Something like that, yes."

She considered. "I used to think it had something to do with his chosen profession. After all, how often can one contemplate murder by poison, stabbing, pushing someone off a cliff or throwing them down a well, et cetera, et cetera, without it all starting to work on one's mind? Then I started to meet his competitors. What he would call his imitators. He didn't have colleagues, of course. And they were lovely people—most of them, at any rate. Wouldn't say boo to a mouse. In the end I decided Adrian was simply born the way he was. Preprogrammed to get nastier with each passing year. His profession had nothing to do with it. In fact, it may have prevented him from doing actual bodily harm to someone."

"He sublimated his murderous impulses into writing about murder?"

"Hmm. Yes, something like that. Though if someone told me he actually had killed someone, I wouldn't doubt it for a moment."

In spite of her words, her face still held a look of melancholy.

"You loved him very much, didn't you? Once?"

"Once," she said, but now with the finality of a book slammed shut. "It must be hard for you to imagine, looking at him as he became. But he was ... beautiful ... once. All the women were after him—there was a lot of the working-class hero about Adrian that was very appealing, in spite of his ridiculous attempts to cover it up. But he singled me out, for some reason. Well, who am I kidding? For my money. And, as you know, I needed a rescuer right about then. Would that he hadn't. Singled me out. But Adrian was a force of nature."

"He remained so. A force of nature, I mean."

She laughed, nearly a shout of surprise. She was perhaps thinking of tornados, floods, and earthquakes—every form of unstoppable destruction known to man.

"Just like Violet," was all she said.

A dawning suspicion had begun to emerge in St. Just's mind.

"You say the same crowd traveled in packs in those days. Were you actually there in Scotland at the time of the murder of Winnie Winthrop?"

"Didn't I mention that? How extraordinary of me. Yes, all that set were there, of course."

"Go on," he said carefully. How much more hadn't these suspects thought worth mentioning to him?

"Let's see. It was so many years ago, I hardly remember it all. Funny, what I mostly remember is that there was red tartan carpet all over the place, like they do in these old Scottish places. Really quite dreadful. I don't suppose that's of much use to you, though, is it?"

St. Just shook his head.

"Let's see," she said again. She settled back in her chair and looked at the ceiling, as if the past might be projected up there. "Well, there was a lot of alcohol involved, I can tell you that for a fact. Probably why my memory of events is a bit hazy here and there. I'm really not much of one for the country—it's so goddamn noisy. There were curlews screeching the whole time we were there, it seemed. I could empathize with Violet on that score—she hated the place and made no bones about it. All peat bogs and bags of poor dead animals. Really, what's the point when you can always order a good steak in London?"

St. Just sat back, letting her ramble. The oddest connections formed in people's minds if you just left them alone.

"They were all out shooting when I arrived and the staff were stood down," she said meditatively. "This mad little Scottish cook had to show me to my room, I recall. She wasn't half put out about it, either. I can nearly remember her name..."

"Agnes?"

"You know, I believe you're right. How odd you should know that. Restores one's faith in the British bobby. She must be long gone by now. But she was the one who nearly pegged the thing onto Violet. I wasn't there for the inquest—those of us who had nothing to contribute or had convinced the authorities that was so were quick to beat it out of there, let me tell you. But I read the newspaper accounts, of course."

"You wouldn't know where Agnes ended up, would you?"

"Good heavens, Chief Inspector. I mean really. Agnes was the *cook*."

"Let me get this clear. You were there at the time of the Winthrop murder. You weren't a suspect?"

"We were all suspects. But I had an alibi."

"Which was?"

"I was busy bringing Ruthven into the world."

This time at least, when he left her, she was smiling.

COMIN' THRO' THE RYE

THE TRIP TO ST. Ives took nearly all day, Great Western Trains not having yet come around to a view of Cornwall as a place people might want to reach in a hurry. St. Just's dog-legged journey deposited him at the far edge of England just around teatime, and he had still to find the Methodist Ladies' Retirement Centre where Sergeant Fear had assured him he would find Agnes Baker, née Agnes Burns.

Locating her had not, Fear had assured him, repeatedly, been an easy task.

"She's nearly ninety, Sir, and there was no guarantee she'd be alive. But what turned out to be the real problem was the fact she's been married five times and changed her last name each time."

"Five? And lived to tell the tale?"

"Apparently. All five of them died, her husbands—natural causes, although by all accounts living with Agnes might have been what you'd call a contributing factor. Anyway, she's now Mrs. Peter Baker, widow, retired at long last to one of those 'extended-living' facilities or whatever they call them now. A home for wrinklies."

"'Assisted living' is, I believe, the accepted euphemism, Sergeant. Well, have you been able to reach her by telephone?"

Fear shook his head.

"'Deaf as a post' is the matron's diagnosis."

"I think she's important in terms of sorting out how Violet fits into all of this. Someone needs to go and see her. At least I know the way to St. Ives by heart, and who knows? The sea air might blow the cobwebs out. We seem no closer to nailing this one shut than we were at the beginning. There's something we're missing, and it's right under our noses, too."

So on the Thursday he set out, clutching his ancient Gladstone bag, lightly packed for overnight, and armed for the journey with one of Sir Adrian's best sellers. He found he enjoyed it, far more than he would have expected. The whole, despite the litter of bodies at the end, recalled a gentler England—one which no doubt had never been, but which one wanted to believe had existed.

The train carried him across desolate gray moors, austere as a monastery in winter. The traveler's rewards for patience, however, were the panoramic coastal vistas of the shore at journey's end and the quaint old harbor town itself with its maze of narrow cobbled streets. The cliffs created a natural balcony overlooking the huddle of brightly painted fishing boats in the harbor.

St. Just wanted to linger, but instead, finding a taxi at the station, he was carried up and up one of the cobbled streets to the top of one of the promontories overlooking the town. On the way, they passed the old parish church with its tall tower; the well-worn nativity scene near the entrance looked nearly as old as the church itself. Only Joseph and one of the sheep looked newer than the rest; it was likely they were replacement parts taken from another ensemble. In keeping with tradition, the crèche was empty—the plaster infant Jesus wouldn't make his appearance until Christmas Day.

The driver dropped him off near the top of the hill, pointing out one of the narrow, curving lanes that led even farther up from the harbor.

"As far as I can go, mate," he told St. Just. "You'll have to walk the last few yards. They won't let us drive up the service road at back, it's for the ambulances. And the hearses, here and there."

St. Just approached the building with no small trepidation. He had had a particular abhorrence for such places ever since he had spent every weekend for four months trying to find a suitable accommodation for his mother several years before, determined to meet her expressed wish "to die by the sea." She had in fact succumbed in a small, quiet, and fastidiously run establishment operated by Anglican nuns, not far from St. Ives. Still, he never could set foot in the door of any of these "assisted living" places without breathing a fervent prayer that he would die quickly, in his home, in his sleep.

He had taken enormous satisfaction, however, in getting one of these operations shut down by the local authorities; he periodically checked to make sure its former owner was still in his cage and likely to remain there.

This place was better than most, he could see right away. Quite pricey, too, from the look of things, although the decoration leaned heavily toward sentimental scenes from the Bible featuring a patient Christ dividing loaves, roughing up the money changers, or delivering the Sermon on the Mount. The place was spotless, with fresh flowers dotted about the hallway tables. Agnes must have done well for herself out of at least one of her husbands.

The woman who bustled up to him wore not the starched nurse uniform and cap of old, but a brightly colored smock over white nylon trousers, the smock covered with what looked to be bright yellow ducks roving happily in a field of red tulips at sunset. It would have been suitable garb for a preschool setting.

Catching his look, the nurse, who had introduced herself as Mrs. Mott, laughed.

"We try to do away with any reminders that they are effectively in a hospital and not, frankly, likely ever to leave under their own steam. Something cheerful to look at, that's the ticket. I don't much mind looking a bloody fool, although I do get some stares when I have to stop in the Sainsbury's on my way home. Right! Now, you're here to see Agnes. I've told her to expect a visitor, but I didn't go into the details. Thought I might leave all that to you. You'll find her on the tennis courts."

At his look of surprise, she laughed.

"I should say, near the tennis courts. This used to be a school, you see. We still allow people from the village to use the courts. She likes to watch the players. Colin, I believe his name is, is her favorite. You'll see. She's quite deaf, you know, and will only wear her hearing aid when men aren't around—terribly vain, but sweet, she is. So I warn you, you'll need to shout."

———

He found her in a wheelchair, knitting, her gnarled hands trembling slightly as she painstakingly worked the needles. Age spots had nearly turned the pale skin of her hands a uniform brown. She appeared to be working on one of those pointless decorative items people used, presumably, to keep their boxes of facial tissue warm.

Her eyes never dropped to her knitting, which no doubt explained the gaping holes in the colorful green and red object emerging from the needles. She greeted him with a brief smile, revealing that she had kept many of her teeth, before again fastening her gaze on the two handsome tennis players visible over the hedge that divided the nursing home from the courts.

"Isn't the blonde one a sight fer tired eyes, though?" she asked.

St. Just smiled, nodded. The blonde one looked like the model for a Viking invader—tall, slim, broad-shouldered.

"It keeps me yoong, being around yoong folk," she said. "There's nothing but *old* folk livin' here."

They watched the game in companionable silence awhile, the only sound the distant swoosh of the waves and the thunk of the ball as the boys batted it back and forth. Suddenly, she turned to him and said:

"The saicret to a long life is to die a vairgin, and so the Chairch would have us believe. Me last oozeband was a layer and a farnicator, God rest his soul. It shairtened me life, living with that man."

Again she gave him her Stonehenge smile. Looking at her, St. Just found her assertion difficult to countenance. She was one of the oldest living women he had ever seen, and if Mr. Baker had worn her down, there seemed little sign of it now. He would take odds she'd live to see a century.

During a break when one of the boys scurried off to retrieve a return that had gone wildly astray, he introduced his topic.

"Mrs. Baker." When she didn't respond, St. Just raised his voice several notches. "Mrs. Baker. I am a policeman investigating two particularly brutal recent murders that seem somehow to be connected with the death of Sir Winthrop decades ago. You were working for him at the time he was killed, weren't you?"

"'Course I was. And I never forgot one minute of them goings-on, neither. But what I want to know is why it's taken you so long to coom ask me aboot it?"

"I think, Mrs. Baker, because sometimes the wheels of justice grind finely but they grind exceedingly slowly. By coincidence or by design, Violet Winthrop, as was, is implicated in two very recent murders. I think it possible she's being set up. I would like to know by whom."

She peered at him out of the maze of wrinkles around her eyes, like a small prehistoric bird looking out from the undergrowth.

"What makes you so sairtain o' that? I give it as me opinion at the time, it was Lady pushed Sir Winthrop off his pairch. I know what I haird. Only the yoong man said daifferent, and she was let off. And that's an end on it. The truth o' that matter noon wanted known. Maybe someone wants her punished now for what she done then. It's a wicked thing, to be sairtain, but I dunna see how I can help you with it."

Losing interest, she turned from him to resume watching the game. Colin thundered up and down the court on powerful legs. He was too big a lad to be agile, but he demolished the ball whenever by chance it caught his racket. His small, dark opponent scampered lightly back and forth, easily outmaneuvering him with precisely aimed returns.

Why had he come? he wondered. Surely, she was right. What-ever she knew of that, by all accounts, badly managed case was so lost in the mists of time as to be irretrievable as evidence now. He'd seen the reports, the statements taken by those "investigating."

But every instinct told him that the Winthrop murder held the key to recent events. Anything else was coincidental beyond belief.

Eventually, Colin lost the match on the serve. The boys were packing up their gear when Agnes turned to him and announced she was cold. He unlocked the brakes of her chair, and, following her directions, took her up in the lift to her room, a small but cheerful private room with flowered wallpaper, overlooking the front of the building where a small ornamental waterfall spilled over into a rock garden. Perhaps a bite to eat in town while he put in time, he was thinking, waiting for the late train ...

"I have a photo of the castle as it was then, you know, if you care to see?"

He feigned curiosity, more out of politeness and deference to her age than anything, and followed her arthritic, pointing finger to the bottom shelf of a painted yellow bookcase against the wall. There on its side lay a large, velvet-covered photo album, of a type he hadn't seen since his grandmother's day. He hefted it over to the table where she sat and placed it before her, rather fearing a protracted stroll through all ninety years of Agnes' memories. Indeed, she paused at pages bearing a photo montage of husbands one through five, and took a moment to introduce them all. But then she flipped back to near the beginning of the book.

He saw what looked like a professionally composed photograph of an imposing gray castle set against thundering gray skies. But what caught his eye were the people in the photo on the opposite page.

She pointed to it.

"The architect took that after he finished renavatin' the castle kitchen. Lady Vi wasn't half in a state over that, gettin' it doon before the party arrived. There, that's me, holding the book."

The black and white photo showed a cavernous room with stone walls, feebly lit by a skylight levered open for ventilation. The five of them, four women in their twenties and thirties and one solemn young man, stood captured in various studied poses, not looking at the camera, apparently absorbed in their tasks. A much younger Agnes consulted her book of receipts; one woman sliced a potato as another stirred something in a large metal bowl, a bowl so deep one of her hands disappeared inside it to the elbow. Something about their stilted posture and calculated avoidance of the lens told the viewer it was not the casual shot it appeared to be but one carefully arranged by the photographer, right down to the props. One could almost hear him shouting directions at them down the century: "Try to look natural, for God's sake! That's it! Hold it!" Only the young man, one hand on an enormous metal canister, was turned slightly toward the camera as he stood near the cooker, spoiling the effect of industry caught unawares as he stole a sideways peek at the photographer. The fourth woman, holding by the neck a dead fowl with about half of its feathers left intact, spoiled the effect as well by staring off blindly into space as if wondering how on earth the thing had flown into her hand.

He took the album from Agnes, holding it close to his eyes for a nearer look, to make certain he was right.

It couldn't be the same woman. It couldn't. But it was. Among the array of old-fashioned ranges, cookers, and spits stood a very young Mrs. Romano, wearing a long white apron tied about her waist, and holding by the neck that bedraggled wildfowl.

"Who is this?" he asked carefully.

"The undercook, Maria. She left shairtly afterwards, run off with the footman. Told me she'd seen somethin' that night, the night of the mairder. Said folk wairen't in their beds as they claimed. Any road, many did leave aboot that time. I asked her was it the mairder upset her. She said, no, it was the haggis. But I think it were the mairder, just the same."

He felt as if the more he peeled the layers off this case, the further he was from the center. Mrs. Romano had been there, Chloe had been there—who else had failed to mention their starring roles in that long-ago murder case?

He asked her to name the other people in the photo.

"Spencer, did you say?"

"That's right. I don't know I ever knew his first name. He left shairtly after, too. They all did, myself and oozeband number one included."

"How did you come by these photos?"

"I told you, the architect took 'em. For posterior, like. They'd set him up with a little room to work in, to make the photos. A darkroom, they called it. I asked him could I have it, the photo. It was me kitchen, after all."

He turned a page. This time, another black and white group, but of a very different kind: a gathering of about thirty people, all dressed formally for dinner, posed stiffly on a carved wooden staircase. He scanned the faces, many of them of people probably long gone. There … there was a diminutive Chloe, looking like a girl playing dress-up in her mother's finest, her neck and wrists encircled with massive diamonds intended for the larger woman she had become.

"After the mairder, the castle wair shut oop. Lady Vi was gone, the master dead." Defensively, she added, "Well, that photo was just sittin' there, and no one to mind me having it."

The photographer had arranged them so that the guests fanned out behind what were clearly the hosts of the party, a distinguished man in his sixties, a beautiful, much younger woman at his side, one hand resting on his arm. Sir Winnie Winthrop and his lady. The women's stiff bouffant hairstyles and fulsomely petticoated dresses identified it as a scene from the fifties. Violet was instantly recognizable, sleek in classic, form-hugging black, her hair pulled back into the chignon she still affected.

But this was a different Violet, one unaltered by fifty years and a surgeon's hand, and there was something about the hands, the eyes ... He held the photo closer.

Agnes was saying something about eyes, as well.

"The goings on, weekends in that house, you wouldna believe. Accairding to what the maids told me, noon stayed in the beds they was given, not for long. Scampering aboot half the night, they was. There—that's the gentlemon there the weekend of the mairder, the one who said he was with Violet. Any road, he was making calf's eyes at Violet all the weekend. Right behind her on the stair, see? Could hardly stand to be more than a foot away. Handsome, was he. But she'd 'ave noon of it, not me Lady Vi, not she. I dunna recall his name. Welsh, he was, though he tried to put on airs like he ware fooling someone aboot that."

"John Davies."

"What?"

He'd forgotten her infirmity. "John Davies," he shouted.

"Aye, I believe you're right. The one who told such tales later at the inquest."

"And went on to make a living at it. Telling tales, that is."

———

Being driven back down the hill some time later in another taxi, St. Just sat looking again at the photos Agnes had let him borrow, turning over the possibilities in his mind. Now he had all the pieces to the puzzle, but could not for the life of him see how they fit together. The driver, launched on a monologue about the local rugby match, seemed not to notice his passenger wasn't listening, might indeed have been miles away.

Competing images crowded St. Just's mind, but what he kept coming back to was the look of pride and accomplishment on Chloe's face when she told him of capturing a title for "Daddy." A rose by another name, he thought. Davies. Beauclerk-Fisk.

Some rose. That second-hand, shopworn title of Sir Adrian's. Had she funded not only its purchase, but the forged identity that must have been necessary to attain it?

He looked again at the photos. The faces, young and old, passed before him as in an identity parade: Mrs. Romano. Chloe. Violet. Sir Adrian. All at Waverley Court—by design, or by chance? Spencer—a common enough name. Jeffrey's father?

They passed again the church with its nativity scene, his thoughts on crimes, old and new, on births, miracle and otherwise.

And suddenly, he saw the truth, unfolding before him like a bolt of shimmering cloth. Finding his mobile, St. Just punched in Sergeant Fear on speed dial, smiling as he imagined the receiving instrument bursting into the happy strains of "Jingle Bells."

TOO MANY CROOKS

SERGEANT FEAR DROVE TOWARD Waverley Court at a speed sufficient to peel the paint off the car. St. Just jostled against his seat harness in a way he felt reflected his fettered thinking on the case from the beginning.

"Three murders," he was saying. "Two of them growing out of the first. All of it, Fear. All of it woven together."

Fear slowed just enough to be able to talk over the straining engine.

"Hang on . . . What could any of this have to do with the Winthrop case?" he asked. "If anyone wanted revenge against Violet for that, they certainly waited a long time."

St. Just answered indirectly, his mind still retracing the steps that had led him to the solution. Had he missed anything? Lost the trail somewhere? No. The "who" was clear; the "why," if he had it right, was astounding.

"I thought the motive was confused," he said, "an explosion of years, decades of spite—an explosion going off, as explosions by definition do, in all directions. Where there is years-long suffering, the desire to make your enemy suffer includes the wish to prolong his pain, the way yours has been prolonged. A quick kill isn't enough: the demolishing of your enemy's dreams, before his eyes, must come first. Perhaps, too, anything or anyone remotely associated in your mind with your enemy becomes a target. But making the enemy pay, suffer, that is paramount, and by any means at hand. What was at hand was Sir Adrian's investment in Ruthven as his heir."

"But Ruthven—"

"Yes. What the murderer didn't know was that Sir Adrian's dreams for Ruthven had already been demolished. How frustrating—maddening—it must have been, to learn all the 'effort' of killing Ruthven had been wasted. Sir Adrian had already stopped caring about Ruthven—instantly, in the way a man of his nature could turn his limited affections on and off. No matter that Ruthven had been raised as his son; he was not his flesh and blood. He ceased to matter once Sir Adrian learned the truth."

St. Just closed his eyes as they nearly ran the car up into the back of a lorry.

"Slow down. It can all wait. Some of them have waited years, after all."

Fear, after talking with St. Just in Cornwall, had telephoned ahead to Waverley Court, telling Maria that the inmates were to gather and await the pleasure of the Chief Inspector. The car having returned to a velocity somewhere below the speed of light, St. Just continued:

"We know that Sir Adrian liked to play games with his will. A game of Russian roulette, as his solicitor called it. Perhaps a better comparison would be that his heirs were all perpetually riding a Ferris wheel. When one of them was at the top, it meant the rest were below. They'd almost become used to this over the years, resigned to it. What, after all, could they do about it but hope, when the old man finally did go to his reward, they'd be the one who happened to be riding at the top when the wheel stopped?

"But then, the unexpected happens. He's added a new player, yet another person to ride this infernal wheel with them, reducing the odds in their favor even further. That, I thought, was what made them—made someone—finally snap. Sir Adrian had fatally underestimated the extent to which his lack of feeling might finally, fatally, antagonize one, or all, of the members of his little family."

"That explains why Sir Adrian was killed, perhaps, but it doesn't explain Ruthven's death—unless, as you say, that was a mistake on the killer's part," said Fear. "But if one of them wanted to kill off the competition, so to speak, surely the most likely target was Violet—the newcomer?"

"Of course, you're quite right about that."

"And?"

But, again, St. Just didn't appear to be listening. At times like these the DCI could be maddening. If he, Fear, was so right, why was Violet still hanging about? Fear slowed the car just enough to fishtail into the drive.

St. Just continued thoughtfully:

"Adrian, as we have sensed from the beginning, was the catalyst for murder. He certainly had everything to do with setting in motion the machinery that led to Ruthven's death. And eventually, even inevitably, he became the catalyst for his own death."

"With his remarriage, you mean."

"We have to keep in mind that Sir Adrian's character combined the wanton destructiveness of a child with all the untrustworthiness of a detective novelist. He was bored. He was old and he was bored, jaded and discontented, in fading health. Disappointment over Ruthven may have driven him over the edge, who knows? So he spins the wheel again, just for mischief's sake.

"He has to do something that will make them all come running. He knew if he announced his wedding *after* the fact it was unlikely to cause a stampede to his door. Quite the opposite, in fact, was likely to happen. Oh, they would carry on and gnash their teeth, but they'd all stay in London to do that—and where was the fun in that? Eventually, curiosity might have brought one or two of them to Waverley Court. But not all—and perhaps not the one he most wanted to see: Ruthven. I think what he had in mind was to disown him publicly, a final, dramatic humiliation—on top of his remarriage—for Chloe.

"In any event, he stages this phony engagement or pre-wedding party, whatever you want to call it. That, he knew, would bring them all on the run. Especially Ruthven, the control freak. There was still a chance, you see, of changing their fates, preventing the wedding. Or so they thought."

A final spurt of gravel, and Fear brought the car to a halt at the door of Waverley Court.

St. Just gazed balefully at the coat of arms over the imposing door.

"'Blood alone moves the wheels of history.' But I don't think blood lines are quite what Mussolini had in mind."

———

Something about the golden light shimmering off the dark mahogany fittings onto the group made him think of spiders trapped in amber.

They were arranged in an artful tableau, like stage actors holding their poses just before the curtain went up for the next act, clustered in pairs or groups reflecting their current, no-doubt constantly shifting, alliances.

Natasha stood near the mantelpiece, wearing a clinging gray dress that made her look as ephemeral as one of the puffs of smoke going up the chimney. George was at her side in one of his studiedly casual slouches designed to display his Armani to best effect.

Mrs. Romano and Paulo had tucked themselves into a far dark corner, standing, just the pair of them, distancing themselves from the rest. Her hand, he noted, lay protectively on her son's arm.

Sarah had acquired a new partner: She sat on one of the sofas, flanked by Albert on one side, Jeffrey on another, an arrangement that served to point up the physical resemblance between the two men.

Violet, Chloe, and Lillian, all now in black, sat together in silence in a triangular grouping of chairs, watching him warily as he took up a position before the fireplace. The smoke from their cigarettes created a literal screen in front of them. Natasha and George withdrew at his approach, taking up a position behind the three women.

He paused, taking them all in, sizing them up, like a washed-in-the-blood minister about to exhort them to repent before it was too late.

It was Violet who spoke first. After all, he thought, it was her house, now.

"Do you have any idea of the hour, Inspector?" She stabbed out her cigarette in an angry gesture, swatting away the smoke. "Don't you think we've been through enough?"

"I do indeed, Lady Beauclerk-Fisk. But I felt certain you would share my interest in solving the mystery of the murder of your husband, whatever the hour."

"Have you solved it?" She wouldn't meet his eyes; she might have been asking the ashtray.

"I have indeed. Although I doubt you will care to hear what I've learned," he said.

He saw her large hand freeze in the act of lighting another cigarette, an infinitesimal hesitation that told him the arrow had struck home. As she tensed for further attack, he turned instead to Chloe.

"There is a tradition in this country of which I am certain you are aware: Lying to the police is deemed a crime. You failed to mention during any of our interviews Adrian's involvement in the Winthrop murder. You even failed to mention he was *there* at the time."

"You didn't ask, Inspector," she said. Her low voice was even, unconcerned. "Do you really imagine it had anything to do with Ruthven's death? It couldn't have done. And his death is all I care about, certainly not Adrian's. I'd like to pin a medal on the person—"

"What if I told you your son's death sprang directly from the death of Winthrop?"

A slight start of distress, followed by her usual quick recovery.

"I would say you were mistaken. Yes, Adrian was there. It was how we met. He was laid up with that 'sprained ankle,' or so he said, so he was mincing about the house with the women while the others were out shooting. Always his preference anyway, the company of women." She angled a glance in Violet's direction. "In a strange way, that murder brought us together. When I ran into him again in Paris, later in the season, it gave us something to talk about, didn't it? Nothing like being suspects in a notorious crime to bring people together."

She looked across at Sarah, who, as if on cue, moved marginally closer to Jeffrey.

"You also didn't mention that his name was not Adrian Beauclerk-Fisk when you met him, but John Davies. Why?"

She said nothing this time, but he knew the answer, incredible as it was: rampant, bloody-minded snobbery. She kept silent because that damned title—the one she had had to subsidize for Adrian—meant so much to her. As she had kept silent in part to keep the scandal of Ruthven's parentage out of the headlines.

"You didn't want me digging around in Adrian's past," he said for her. "That is a wish you shared in common with at least one other person in this room. Mrs. Romano, for one."

He saw her grip tighten on Paulo's arm. "Sir Adrian said never to talk about those days," she said.

"You were certainly well-rewarded for your silence. I suppose the danger of your being recognized by Violet was minimal—it's not as if she would have remembered an undercook from her household of decades ago. Any more than she spotted Jeffrey's resemblance to her former scullery boy."

"Mine?" Jeffrey looked genuinely startled. Turning to Sarah, he said, "I knew my father had emigrated from England in the fifties. I had no idea there was a connection. None at all."

St. Just allowed his glance to rest on each of them in turn.

"As I was explaining to my sergeant on the way here, I thought at first the motive of the murderer might be muddled, indiscriminate—someone who wanted only to eliminate the family, one by one. And to some extent, that was true."

Involuntarily, Albert flicked a glance in Sarah's direction.

"The order in which they were eliminated did not seem to matter. Why kill Ruthven, when it was clear to anyone the real source of the conflict in this family was Sir Adrian himself? Why not go straight to the source—cut off the head of the snake?

"Then I thought, what if the choice of Ruthven were not random at all? What if there were a *reason* to eliminate Ruthven as heir? His death would point the finger of blame at the family, to be sure—at everyone in the house with a vested interest. Perhaps that was part of what the murderer wanted: to widen the field to such an extent no one person could be excluded as a suspect absolutely. And at the same time, to narrow the pool to be divided up on Sir Adrian's demise.

"So there was that possibility: Ruthven was an inconvenience to be eliminated, by a cold-blooded killer who would have killed anyone who happened to get in the way. But—what if the motive were even more ... personal than that?

"Ruthven was not well-loved, certainly, but the violent, brutal method chosen for his death spoke of something more frenzied than a desire to simply get him out of the way. That was when I realized the motives might be multiple—not muddled, multiple. Not random—multiple. I asked: What if someone felt *betrayed* by Ruthven? His wife, for example? The victim of his multiple infidelities."

He looked to Lillian, who turned away disdainfully.

"Or, was it perhaps one of his victims on the other side of that coin, so to speak? His mistress, for example."

Now he had captured even Lillian's attention. They all looked at each other, mystified.

"No one came near the house that night. You said so yourself," said Albert.

"Perhaps no one needed to. Perhaps the killer, the mistress, was right here. You, for example, Natasha," he said.

"Don't be ridiculous. You know perfectly well my relationship is with George. You even know *why* I'm with George."

George frowned, deeply baffled. What other reason could there be for a woman to be with him, apart from the sheer wonderfulness of it all?

"After Ruthven discarded you, you turned to George, that is true."

"I say…" began George.

"If you couldn't insinuate your way into this family one way, you decided to try another, didn't you? The child you're carrying is not an invention of George's, as you led us to believe, but quite real—or so say your NHS records. That was a silly lie; did you count on us not bothering to verify every word you said, just because you were with the Yard? It's not the kind of secret you could keep forever, now, is it? Perhaps Chloe here can give you pointers on that subject. But the one secret you could keep was that it is Ruthven's child, not George's—Ruthven's. And thus, a child that is no heir to Sir Adrian's fortune.

"When exactly was it that you met Ruthven, Natasha?"

She gave him a cool smile, but he saw her mouth slip, trembling just for a moment before she spoke.

"Last week, when we were all summoned to the Presence by Sir Adrian, of course."

"I think not. No, I think not at all. I think you met him in the course of cozying up to George for your investigation. Oh, your story on that score checks out. How was it your superior put it? That you were 'relentless' in pursuing a case, like a hound after the fox. I don't believe he meant that comment on your methods entirely as a compliment, either, even though it often brought him results.

"That is what threw us off course for a while—your story, insofar as what you were doing here, checked out. But the real story is that you met Ruthven and saw in him a finer catch than the one you'd landed. You had to continue seeing George, professional"— and he let his voice dwell on the word—"professional that you were. But it was Ruthven, with his power and money and fame you wanted, not the thief who was stealing from his own father and in due course was headed, with your assistance, for gaol."

George, his invincible stupidity penetrated at last, looked as if he'd been pole-axed. Sergeant Fear quietly stepped over behind him, blocking a move toward the French doors. He didn't fail to notice that Paulo had been edging in the direction of the exit, as well.

"Then, as in the nature of these things," St. Just was saying, "you discovered you were pregnant with Ruthven's child. You were elated. Here was the tie that would bind Ruthven to you. Now he would leave his wife for you. It's the same old story, isn't it? It doesn't change with the centuries. Far from sharing your joy, Ruthven was appalled. His wife's money was what had kept him afloat while he waited out his inheritance. He wasn't jeopardizing that for some commonplace affair. In any event, he knew the child wasn't Sir Adrian's grandchild. His mother had let him in on that secret. A child was of less than no use to him in this competition to be favored heir—it might prove to be a danger, in fact. At first he may have told you he wouldn't acknowledge it, told you to get rid of it. At least, that was no doubt what he was thinking.

"Then you—or was it he?—had a better idea. Clever Ruthven was full of ideas, wasn't he? Why not foist this child off onto George, ensure its "legitimate" claim to Sir Adrian's fortune? It was a case of the past repeating itself, wasn't it? His own mother had done the same, palming Ruthven off onto Sir Adrian. Ruthven must have appreciated that there was a certain symmetry to all of this. A grand joke to play on the old man."

"The child is George's. Of course it is. Tell him, George."

His virility at stake, George repeated manfully, "Of course it is."

"No doubt blood tests will confirm that," said St. Just calmly. "In any event, I would urge you, Mr. Beauclerk-Fisk, to investigate that option thoroughly."

While George mulled this over within the tiny confines of his brain, St. Just went on, speaking again directly to Natasha. She would no longer look at him, but seemed to be studying with great interest the gold bracelet on her wrist.

"Ruthven persuaded you to this scheme. Perhaps you pretended to go along. There was a great fortune to consider, wasn't there? And poor George would be none the wiser."

Sarah and Albert exchanged fleeting looks. They had never heard the words "poor" and "George" used together before in the same sentence.

"What did he promise you, Natasha? That you and he would be together once you'd established yourself as the second lady of this house? Did you fall for that? If so, what changed your mind? My guess would be the telephone conversation you overheard him having with his London associate: the other woman in his life. One of the many women in his life.

"Perhaps it was at that moment you accepted the reality at last. He cared nothing for you. You were indeed just the latest pawn in this game. And once you had decided you alone were going to win the game, Ruthven had to die. He knew too much; he was the only one who knew about this child of yours and his. George having sprung his announcement at dinner, there was no time to lose.

"You convinced Ruthven to meet you that night, for one of your usual assignations. You lured him that night to the cellar, stopping to collect your weapon from the selection in the hall, and then you killed him. You killed him, and then carried on with the plan to produce the next Beauclerk-Fisk generation, and collect the money that would go with it."

"Well, it's a fascinating theory, Inspector. Oh, and Sir Adrian? While I was on a killing spree I just decided to finish him off, too? Is that it? Before he'd had time to change his will in favor of the child? Silly of me to rush things like that, don't you think?"

"You didn't have to worry overmuch about the will—and you are the only one who can truthfully say that. George's inheriting from Adrian wasn't essential to this plan. One way or another, you and Ruthven's child were going to inherit—perhaps later rather than sooner, but eventually. From your mother. From Violet, the new Lady Beauclerk-Fisk."

MIRROR, MIRROR

ALBERT LOOKED AT NATASHA, at Violet, back to Natasha. Why the deuce hadn't he seen the resemblance? Hazy, like a reflection in a pond, but decidedly there. More obvious than the physical similarities, obscured as they were by Violet's age and Natasha's youth, was the way they both stood and moved with silent, feline grace. He was suddenly reminded of Mrs. Butter's Clytemnestra, the daughter a smaller version of the mother.

For his part, Jeffrey understood that from the first glimpse of Natasha, he, too, had registered the physical resemblance: in the planes of her face, in her walk, even in the ungainly hands that Natasha was at such pains to hide behind long, draping sleeves.

"I should have noticed from the first," said St. Just. "The similarities are evident, once one becomes aware of them. But I didn't become aware until I saw a photo of Violet taken decades ago. It was like looking at a photograph of Natasha.

"There was a clue Sir Adrian, the mystery writer, left for us," he went on. "He was found clutching the red leaf of a poinsettia plant, known as the Christmas plant. We assumed this was an accident, something he simply grabbed at, blindly, as he fell across his desk. But we were forgetting the way Sir Adrian's mind worked. He couldn't leave an obvious clue—the killer would have simply removed that from the room. But the subtle clue, the clue to the killer's name, we nearly missed altogether, as did the killer. What he left us was the name, 'Natasha.' Natasha, a common variation of 'Natalia,' meaning, 'born on Christmas day.' Only Sir Adrian's sleuth Miss Rampling, or his daughter, Sarah, with her interest in the derivations of names, would have realized what he was trying to tell us."

"I could have told you ... about the name ... You never mentioned the plant ..." began Sarah. She looked over at Natasha in wonder. Natasha, a killer?

St. Just nodded. "The plant was a clue straight out of one of his novels, and we nearly missed its significance. It was the only thing close to hand that he could use to point us to his killer, without leaving a clue so obvious the killer would realize what he was doing."

"Oh, come on, Inspector," said Natasha. "I mean, really. You'll have to do better than that. My birthday is December 25. That proves exactly nothing. Sir Adrian didn't know that; he didn't ask. Why would he?"

St. Just's look was piercing.

"He didn't have to ask. He knew as soon as he heard your name, as did Sarah. Among his hundreds of reference books are half a dozen of those baby-naming books containing the etymology of every name imaginable."

"He used those to come up with his characters' names," put in Sarah.

"Everywhere I went in this case," said St. Just, "I was nagged by the thought that it was connected with Christmas, and I couldn't think how. This time of year, we're surrounded with reminders. Even my sergeant's mobile, with its blasted 'Jingle Bells' ring."

"My name has nothing to do with this," said Natasha.

"Names, lineages, inheritances—they have everything to do with it."

She shrugged. "All right, yes, so Violet is my mother. What a brilliant deduction on your part, Inspector. You're positively wasted out here—we could use you in London. The rest is bollocks and you know it. You can't prove a thing." But her voice was harsh, strangled, no longer ringing out with quite so much confident authority as before.

Turning to Violet, St. Just said:

"When did you tell your husband just who Natasha was?"

Violet, eyes hooded, said nothing.

"We've had enough lies from you. The truth, now."

It seemed Violet didn't dare look at her daughter as she spoke.

"That afternoon he died, when we were alone together in his study—yes, I lied about that; haven't I had enough of the police in my life? But I told him then. Natasha had asked me not to, because she was working undercover. She didn't give me any details about George. I was used to that, all this skullduggery that went with her line of work. I never really knew what Natasha was up to—what was real in her life, and what pretend. But the longer the deception went on, the more awkward it became not to say anything, especially once Adrian heard about the baby on the way. He was over the moon. How could I not tell him that this grandchild and its mother were even more … special … than he realized."

She hazarded a glance at her daughter.

"I did swear him to secrecy, Natty."

Natasha returned the look of appeal with one of scorn.

"I should have known better than to trust you," said Natasha.

"That is just not fair." Violet might have forgotten anyone else was in the room. "Everything I've done I've done for you. I told you: He was talking about changing his will again. He had to know there was a double reason for—for arranging things totally in my favor and yours. This was not just his grandchild, but his and mine. And I was right about telling him, whatever you may think."

"Shut up," said Natasha.

"So you told Sir Adrian about your daughter, born of a liaison while you were 'in exile' on the Continent. One—" He turned to Sergeant Fear. "What was his name again, Sergeant?"

Sergeant Fear flipped back a few pages in his notebook.

"Count Madalin Landeski."

"Count Landeski. Thank you, Sergeant. Interpol has been most helpful, haven't they? Frightfully efficient. Yes, Miss Landeski, even country bumpkins like Sergeant Fear and myself know how to ring the experts at Interpol."

Sergeant Fear smiled at them all. It was rather a terrifying smile; he was enjoying himself immensely by this point. He fixed his eyes on St. Just with something like adoration.

"And then you told Natasha that Sir Adrian was in on the secret—that you had 'blown her cover,'" St. Just said to Violet. "Thus helping to seal his fate. Sir Adrian was anything but discreet, and Natasha knew it, even if you did not. The whole setup—a stranger in his house posing as someone else, Ruthven's murder, this pregnancy—was bound to make him suspicious, start asking questions. Sir Adrian knew all about false paternity, after all. And what proof had he—had any of you?—that all this wasn't just a typically short-sighted scheme on George's part?"

"What do you mean, short-sighted?" said George, thoroughly affronted. "The old man might have been dead long before we had to decide what to do about the kid."

"Thank you for illustrating my point so nicely. As it happens, the 'old man' was.

"Natasha wasn't planning to reveal her identity—at least to the necessary extent—until well after Sir Adrian was dead and the inheritance secure. But once her mother spilled the beans, she couldn't risk having Sir Adrian start snooping into her affairs. So she moved up the timetable for Sir Adrian's death, which I am certain she had planned from the first. When the time was right, she would strike. With Ruthven dead, George took his place as heir; her mother had already secured rights to the proceeds by her marriage. Everything was in place. Why not, then, strike now? She would win either way. But her relationship with George, cold and calculated as it was, must not be subjected to analysis.

"What did Sir Adrian do, Natasha, when you went for your friendly little chat with your new stepfather? Suggest a blood test, that very subject being so fresh in his mind? Just as I did to George, just now?"

Natasha held her silence, but her expression told him the game was up. If she hadn't chosen to tell so many direct lies—about the child, just for one—she might have gotten away with it.

Wonderful, he thought, what a good line of bluff can produce. Didn't she know: The National Health released medical records to the police only under threat of torture. And sometimes, not even then.

ST. JUST IS DENIED

As they drove away some time later, Sergeant Fear's mind was still following the strings that had led his superior to Natasha. He drove slowly this time, but distractedly; several times St. Just had to warn him off a ditch on the narrow drive away from the house. Natasha, George, and Paulo had been taken into custody on their various charges and been driven off to be sorted out on their journeys through the legal system. George would be out in a few years; there was little, so far as St. Just knew, to stop him inheriting Adrian's precious title, but he wondered how easy a time he and Paulo would have getting their hands on the money, under the circumstances. Somehow, he felt a good solicitor might be able to sort all that out. It seemed a shame, but there it was.

"Will it stick?" Fear asked at last.

"Oh, yes, I believe so. George, her 'alibi,' isn't going to stand by their mutual story for a minute. Then there are Ruthven's phone records, his credit card receipts, his appointments calendar—somewhere, I would be willing to bet, there's at least one waiter who saw this unforgettable beauty dining with Ruthven in London. But most of all, there's Ruthven's child. We've got her for lying straight down the line. Circumstantial? Some of it. But the prosecution will have more than enough to go on when George caves, which he will."

"There's one thing I don't understand, Sir," Sergeant Fear said at last. "Just who in hell did kill Winnie Winthrop?"

"You want my guess or my certainty? We'll have to wait in part for Mrs. Butter's complete translation to confirm it. But Violet, of course, with Sir Adrian's help in the coverup. You can put five stars by her statement regarding her deep love for Winnie Winthrop. She wanted out, and she wanted the cash to go with her."

"Sir Adrian's help?"

"Back in the days when he was plain old John Davies, yes. Madly in love with the delectable, completely unattainable Lady Winthrop, as he was all his life, but having to settle in the end for plain old Chloe. Adrian, as we are the last to know, was part of that whole crowd at the time. He'd fallen head over heels with Violet, who barely noticed he was alive, but found him immensely useful when he offered to testify he was in bed with her at the time of the murder.

"As I shall explain in great detail to Mrs. Romano, her vow of silence to him is now officially broken. She's coming to the station, and this time to tell all. She knew he was in bed with someone, just that it wasn't Violet."

"He paid her, all these years, for her silence?"

"And the big payoff was to come at the end. When he met Maria Romano again, years later, I think it was by chance. He realized: so much time had passed, but she hadn't told what she knew.

282

I imagine he considered her discretion made her worth her weight in gold, but it would be as well to assure her silence. He took her in, took care of Paulo, left them both extremely well off in the will, at least by Mrs. Romano's standards. If Paulo isn't yet another illegitimate by-blow in this case, I'll eat my hat."

"Good God, you don't mean—?"

"I do. Just a guess. But that would explain so much about her silence, would it not? Why not just tell me she worked at the bloody Winthrop castle? Mrs. Romano is basically an honest soul; it's the one thing she did that didn't add up, and the discretion of a good servant didn't entirely account for it. She doesn't even seem to resent, if she realizes it, that her cut of the will is a fraction of what the others got. Anyway, it's irrelevant to the case against Natasha, so I'm not going to press her on where Paulo came from— yet. Not if she tells me what she knows about that night: that it was she who was with Sir Adrian. Which of course she was afraid to tell the authorities at the time. I'd bet my last shilling she was in the country illegally, which probably answers to her silence, as well.

"As for Sir Adrian—are we really surprised? No one doubted for a minute he had the heart of a murderer, that he was a man of many guilty secrets, some major, some minor. He'd changed his name to get the title illegally, but who cared about that? Only he and Chloe. But, by the way, there's one other thing that got in our way: He was Welsh, which helped him even more in keeping his origins quiet."

"I don't follow, Sir."

"Davies is a common name in Wales. And, by tradition, children in Wales sometimes take different names from their parents, often a name evocative of the father's place of origin, creating even more of a muddle for anyone interested enough to try to trace his origins. I wondered why, according to Albert, Sir Adrian worked so hard to squash reporters not willing to swallow intact whatever he fed them. That whole title business—he was as big a snob about it as Chloe. In that regard, it was a match made in heaven."

"But, Sir, why in the name of all that's holy would he write a book about a murder that he himself had helped cover up?"

"Maybe because he thought he was so clever, no one would realize it was not a work of fiction. Or maybe he didn't care about anything but creating a stir that would guarantee his reputation would live on forever. Who knows, with an ego like that? I do know his instructions were explicit—that was the one book that was not to be published until his death, when he was beyond the reach of our law, anyway.

"Sir Adrian, as I have noted before, was a childish man, recklessly indiscreet. He couldn't resist the fun he was having with his ready-made plot, regardless of the fact he was telling a lot of tales in there that other people didn't want told. Yet another reason for Natasha to get rid of him, you know—if she knew about the book, which I think she did. She was, all her life, the daughter of that notorious, adulterous murderess, Lady Violet Winthrop. A book by Sir Adrian called *A Death in Scotland* could only be about her mother's case."

"I can see why she would want it not to come out," said Sergeant Fear. "But how would she learn about the book?"

"My guess is she saw it in Albert's room. I'm certain she spent half her time turning over the contents of the house—remember her training—to learn what she could learn. Even if she couldn't get past the title, the title told her all she needed to know—or all she needed to know to panic over it. Or perhaps she just chatted Jeffrey up about it; it wouldn't be hard to get anything she wanted out of him. Watch out for that branch!"

Sergeant Fear turned the wheel sharply onto black ice, fighting to control the skid.

When his heart resumed normal operations, several minutes later, St. Just went on, "That old dear, Agnes, had it right all along. But without Mrs. Romano's evidence—which we'll get—we'd never have been able to prove much of anything, after all these years. Basing a case on a book of 'fiction' would be next to impossible. They didn't believe Agnes then, they wouldn't believe her now. But the Devon and Cornwall Constabulary is sending someone to get her statement. Someone 'yoong.' We'll see if it does any good this time."

He sighed.

"Violet is one of those women capable of doing whatever is necessary, and getting away with it. She is, as Chloe said, about as cold-blooded as they come."

"Like mother, like daughter, then?"

"Very much so, in appearance, and in temperament. We all missed that, but shouldn't have. The callous manipulation, particularly of men, but of everyone—the kind of coldness I am certain is highly prized in the more secret corridors of Scotland Yard, by the way. Yes, I am certain Natasha learned all of that at her mother's knee. What is more, I believe Violet manipulated her own daughter, telling her it was Sir Adrian who was the killer, giving Natasha a healthy grudge to nurse all those years."

"And then, the money thrown in as a sweetener for revenge..."

"Violet inherited a fortune from Sir Winthrop, pretty much in line with the plan Natasha had for George. It took the pair of them decades to run through it all. And it wasn't until Violet had exhausted most of it that Sir Adrian's proposal—a form of blackmail, if you ask me—held any interest for her. As I say, cold-blooded, with money being the motivating force for both of them."

Sergeant Fear laughed.

"We really should have paid more attention to Sarah, Sir. In a way, she was right: 'The lack of money is the root of all evil.'"

———

Several mornings later St. Just was on his way to the train station to await the 8:02 for London and Heathrow. It was rare that he could get away for even a few hours; this time, he had wrangled four full days on the slopes. His cat, Deerstalker, was being spoiled by the neighbors. All was right with the world, and Sergeant Fear would have to cope with what wasn't right until he returned.

It was as the cab neared Trumpington that he saw them, Sarah and Jeffrey, power-walking, hand-in-hand, which rather impeded their progress. They didn't seem to mind. They looked blissfully silly, as only those newly, deeply in love can do.

He wondered if it would work, how they would get on together, Sarah with her grab bag of philosophies, and Jeffrey with his boundless, seemingly directionless, energy. He supposed what they really had in common was a sort of unfounded, blinkered optimism.

And perhaps, he thought, that was sufficient to be getting on with.

THE END

BOOK CLUB QUESTIONS

1. Mystery novels have been written from a variety of viewpoints—first person, alternating point of view, and so on. What point of view is used in *Death of a Cozy Writer*? Why do you think the author chose to tell the story this way? What are the drawbacks to a writer in using a particular point of view—for example, first person—to tell a crime story?

2. *Death of a Cozy Writer* has been called an affectionate send-up of the traditional or "cozy" mystery genre. The author calls it an homage to the golden age of the classic British mystery. What key elements do you think constitute a traditional mystery? How is this book different from a traditional mystery? How does it play off the traditions of the genre?

3. Of the four grown children of Sir Adrian, Ruthven appears to be the favorite (insofar as Sir Adrian favors anyone). Do you think most parents have a secret preference for one child over another?

4. How much do you think Chloe, Lady Beauclerk-Fisk is responsible for the failings, or the successes, of her various offspring?

5. *Death of a Cozy Writer* has several unlikable characters. Was there any one you particularly "loved to hate," and why? Which of the characters in *Death of a Cozy Writer* would you like to get to know better?

6. The novel has several red herrings. Were you misled by any of these? Were you able to guess "who done it," or did the author surprise you? If you were surprised, who did you think was the murderer, and what was his or her motive?

7. How does the weather reflect the atmosphere inside Waverley Court?

8. How important is the Christmas holiday season to the story? How would the story have been different if set in a different season?

9. *Death of a Cozy Writer* belongs to the "fair-play" school of crime writing. Once you learned who the culprit was, did you feel the author had "played fair" in providing you the clues needed to solve the crime?

10. Discuss the author's use of humor in the book. Is humor ever appropriate to a murder mystery?

11. *Death of a Cozy Writer* is also the story of a death in Violet's past. How successful is the author in bridging the past with the present?

12. In what ways do you think Sarah's future will be altered by the events of this book?

If you enjoyed reading *Death of a Cozy Writer,*
stay tuned for G. M. Malliet's next St. Just Mystery

Death and the Lit Chick

COMING SOON FROM MIDNIGHT INK

PART I——ENGLAND

I.

"WHAT DO YOU THINK? Poisoned Pink, or Pink Menace?"

The young blonde woman of whom this question was asked adopted a pose of deep concentration, weighing the matter with all the deliberation of King Solomon presented with two feuding mothers. That the colors under discussion were nearly identical to the naked eye seemed to escape the notice of both women. The manicurist held the two small bottles aloft in the late winter sunlight streaming through the window of the trendy Knightsbridge beauty salon.

"The Poisoned Pink, I think, Suzie," the blonde said at last. "The other is so, like, totally last year. Positively no one in New York would be caught dead wearing it any more. Besides, Poisoned Pink sounds perfect for a crime writers' conference, don't you think?"

Suzie nodded, bending to her task and laying about with an emery board. *Give me an old-fashioned romance book any time*, she thought. *Barbara Cartland, now: There was a woman who knew which way was up with men and all. Lovely hair she had, too.*

"I'm getting an award from my publisher during this conference, you see. Did I tell you?"

Only three times.

Kimberlee Kalder, the blonde, paddled the fingers of one elegant, narrow hand in a bowl of soapy water as she lifted one elegant, narrow foot to examine the hand-woven gold brocade of her £900 ballet flats. "And for that and, well, *other* reasons, I want to look, like, to die for."

So there's another man at the end of all this effort, then, thought Suzie. *Thought so.*

"Not that I don't *always* strive to look, like, really hot," Kimberlee went on. "Image is, like, everything in this business, my agent says."

"I'm certain he's right, Miss."

"She, actually. At least, for the moment."

Not really interested, Suzie asked politely, "When's the conference, then?"

"This weekend. I head to Scotland tomorrow. My publisher is treating his most successful—well, in some cases, just his longest-lived—authors to a few days at Dalmorton Castle and Spa during Dead on Arrival."

Seeing Suzie's look of mystification, Kimberlee said: "That's a crime writers' conference held in Edinburgh every year. And, as I say, he'll be handing out a special award to his most successful writer: Me."

"Me," as Suzie well knew, was a favorite word in Kimberlee Kalder's vocabulary. That and "I." She was a big tipper, though—writing must pay bloody well.

"I always wanted to write a book," said Suzie wistfully. "Maybe I will one day when I have time. I'd write about me gran, during the war—"

Kimberlee just managed to stifle a snort of derision, although she didn't bother to hide the contempt that lifted her beautiful, chiseled mouth in a smirk. If she had a pound for everyone who was going to write a book when they could find the time. Like they were going to pick up the dry cleaning or something when they got around to it. Really, people had no idea.

Cutting off the flow of wartime reminiscence, Kimberlee said: "No one cares about that old crap anymore. Don't forget—I want two solid coats of the topcoat. Last time my manicure only lasted two days. And watch what you're doing. You've missed a spot."

"Must be all that typing you do," Suzie said quietly. Kimberlee was her least favorite customer and there always came a point in their conversations when Suzie remembered why.

"What, me? Type?" said Kimberlee, as if to say, *I? Slaughter my own cattle?* "I guess you've been looking at my publicity stills. 'The Famous Writer at home, fingers poised over her laptop.' But I have *people* who do all that, where necessary. I just dictate."

Really? thought Suzie. *So what else was new?*

II.

News item from the *Edinburgh Herald,* by Quentin Swope:

> *Book lovers wait in thrilled anticipation of this weeks' Dead on Arrival conference, where fans and would-be authors can meet their favorite crime writers—in the flesh. Said writers will also be signing their books "by the truckload," conference chair Rachel Twalley tells this reporter.*
>
> *Among conference highlights is the anticipated appearance of hot young newcomer Kimberlee Kalder, who burst onto the mystery writing scene last year, quickly climbing the charts with her runaway "chick-lit" hit,* Dying for a Latte. *Kimberlee will be fêted before and during the conference by her Deadly Dagger Press publisher, Lord Julius Easterbrook, who must be thanking his lucky stars for leading him to Kimberlee. She may single-handedly have revived his moribund family publishing house.*
>
> *Other Dagger authors invited to push out the boat at Easterbrook's exclusive gathering at Dalmorton Castle include Magretta*

Sincock, Annabelle Pace, and Winston Chatley—the stars of yester-year. Rumor has it top agents Jay Fforde and Ninette Thomson, and American publicist B. A. King, are also on the guest list, along with ex-pat Joan Elksworthy, author of a detective series set in Scotland, and American spy-thriller novelist Tom Brackett. Also look out for newcomer Vyvyen Nankervis—a little bird tells me she's really Portia De'Ath, a Cambridge don, and the author of a delightful series of Cornish mysteries.

But it's our little Kimberlee who is stealing the other crime writers' thunder. Definitely, a publishing force to reckon with!

III.

Jay Fforde had come to the conclusion that the invention of e-mail signaled the imminent demise of mankind. Even though his agency Web site stated explicitly "No Email Queries or Submissions," every day his network server was nearly shut down by some berk trying to send him a 150,000-page manuscript by attachment. The ones that made it through went straight into his little electronic trash bin, unread. Even after fifteen years in the business, Jay was amazed at the number of people out there tapping away at manuscripts—each one, of course, a potential best seller, according to its creator.

The phone rang. A carefully screened call had been allowed through the bottleneck by Jay's assistant. Jay picked up the instrument, first pausing to fling back a strand of the longish, sun-streaked fair hair that flopped in accepted head-boy style from a center part on his patrician skull. Many thought his wide-set eyes, high cheekbones, and sulky face held a suggestion of Byronic decadence, a thought Jay liked to cultivate.

"Jay," came a confidant, female voice. A trace of an American accent flattened what would once have been called BBC English, before regional accents became the new Received Pronunciation. Immediately Jay sat up a little straighter. The voice of a beautiful young woman who happened to be a wildly successful, selling-in-the-millions author was a potent combination for any agent.

"Kimberlee?" he said. Frightful name; it must come from her American side. Well, no one was perfect, although Kimberlee came close. "What a delight to hear from you. How was the rest of your holiday?"

Just then, his assistant appeared in the doorway, carrying a sheaf of manuscript pages. Jay impatiently waved her away, miming for her to close the door behind her.

"... Bahamas are not what they were, but still—you should see my tan," Kimberlee Kalder chirped on. "I just heard you'll be at Dalmorton. How wonderful of Julius to include you. Of course, you rep what's-her-name, don't you?"

"Magretta Sincock? Yes. For a short while longer, at least."

"Oh *really*?"

"Yes. Damned shame about her books and all, but tastes change and poor Magretta will keep turning out the same old thing. I mean, seriously, how many women can there be out there married to some guy who—surprise!—turns out to have shoved his three previous wives overboard during their honeymoon cruise? Anyway, Easterbrook thought it would be a good opportunity to mix business with a little pleasure."

"Good," she said, lowering her silky voice to a purr. "I do think it's time you and I met for a serious discussion, too, don't you?"

Jay's heart took flight at the words. If he could land Kimberlee Kalder as a client, well ... He'd be running the agency in a year. The Troy, Lewis, Bunter, and Hastings Agency would become the Fforde Agency at last. And he could ditch his other clients, beginning with Magretta. Who would need *them*?

Reluctantly, he tore his mind away from empire building. Kimberlee was saying something about train connections and reservations at the castle.

"You'll have to call today if you want to get near the castle spa," she told him. "They'll be booked solid from the moment this crowd of scribblers arrives."

"I'll tell you what, Kimberlee. Why don't I book a massage for you, while I'm at it? My little treat, courtesy of the agency. I insist. What's that you say?" He picked up a pen and jotted notes as she talked. "All right. So that's a black mud envelopment treatment, an Aromapure Facial, a hydro pool session, and a sun shower treatment." Feeling like a waiter, he asked, "Will there by anything else?"

He rang off awhile later, Kimberlee having run out of special requests. Almost simultaneously, the door to the outer office swung open again.

"That was Kimberlee, wasn't it?" said Laurie. "She wouldn't identify herself, but the bossy tone is unmistakable."

"Yes. She's ready to dump Ninette and come over to the dark side."

"I suspected as much. You can tell her for me you can catch more flies with honey—"

"Before I forget, call Dalmorton Castle, will you, and book her into the spa for these treatments." He handed her the list. Laurie glanced at it, and sniffed.

"She doesn't want much, does she?" Laurie tucked the list in her pocket and began tidying his desk, gathering files, tapping papers ruthlessly into line against the antique mahogany wood.

"If you move that you know I'll never find it again," said Jay.

"That's what I'm here for, Jay. To find things for you."

Jay smiled. Laurie always made him think of the redoubtable Miss Lemon, Hercule Poirot's fiercely competent secretary, foil to the well-meaning but dim Hastings. She placed a stack of papers before him.

"Magretta's late again with her rewrites. She's getting worse, I think."

Jay was pulled back from a daydream of yachts, Caribbean beaches, and ski chalets in Val Claret. He sat up, shoving the stack of papers to one side.

"Give her a few more weeks," he said. "It doesn't matter anymore, does it?"

IV.

A few blocks to the west, Ninette Thomson was worried. Kimberlee Kalder, her megastar client, as she supposed they would say in Hollywood, was sending out all the well-known signs of a writer in flight to a new agent. Increasingly ludicrous demands—an espresso machine, for God's sake—temper tantrums, insistence on impossible terms from her British and American publishers for her next book, overturning all the carefully negotiated—and extremely generous for an unknown author—terms of the contract Ninette had painstakingly organized for her. Demanding Ninette take the new book when it was ready to a larger publisher, despite a contract option that stipulated she could *not* do precisely that.

Honestly, thought Ninette. It was worse than dealing with the commitment-phobic, hormone-blinded male. You always could tell when they had one foot out the door, headed for another woman's bedroom, if you knew the signs. Which Ninette, fifty-four and the survivor of countless "summer" romances, felt certain she did.

She stood, stretching the tension from her shoulders. She had to get home and pack for this castle fandango. Good of Easterbrook to include her, really, although she knew Kimberlee Kalder was the only reason. She, Ninette, certainly wouldn't have been invited for the sake of a Winston Chatley or a Portia De'Ath. She turned away from the large, modern desk that stood in front of a ten-foot, floor-to-ceiling window in her office. More and more, Ninette had started working from home—less temptation to frequent the wine bars that way—but she remained reluctant to give up the fantastic view and, more importantly, the prestigious address of her London office. Sometimes the only indicator of a good agent that a writer had to go by was the address. But the expense! The expense would have driven her down and out long ago if that wonderful manuscript of Kimberlee Kalder's hadn't shown up in her slush pile nearly two years ago.

Wonderful, she reminded herself, meaning saleable, meaning marketable, meaning the only things that mattered in today's publishing climate. Every day Ninette turned down manuscripts that were wonderful—wonderfully written, insightful, sad, funny, groundbreaking, heartbreaking, whatever. And not one of them met the blockbuster, plot-driven standards that were becoming the byword of the industry: less character, more plot.

Fewer and fewer publishers were willing to take a chance on an unknown writer. But Ninette, after years in the business, could sense a bestselling winner, and Ninette did persuade Easterbrook to take that chance on Kimberlee.

The last truly fine writer she'd taken on, knowing for certain she'd never make a fortune but not caring, had been Portia De'Ath, who was now selling at a decent little clip. Winston Chatley fell into the same category...

But it was Kimberlee, damn it all, who was paying the bills.

Now the silly, greedy little twit thought she could do better. Imagined a different agent, a different publisher, would bring in even more than the ridiculously large amount the first book had brought her already.

Kimberlee Kalder suddenly thought she didn't need her, Ninette Thomson.

Well, we'll just see about that now, won't we?

ABOUT THE AUTHOR

G. M. Malliet has worked as a journalist and copywriter for national and international news publications and public broadcasters. She attended Oxford University and holds a graduate degree from the University of Cambridge—the setting for the St. Just mysteries.

Death of a Cozy Writer, her first mystery, won the Malice Domestic Grant. She has also won the Romance Writers of America's 2006 Stiletto Award (thriller category).